"You can believe everything you've ever heard about me," Cain pronounced.

"If there was liquor missing, I probably stole it. If there was a fight, I probably started it. The only thing I didn't do was get anybody pregnant. But I wasn't too careful about that, either. I didn't give a damn about anybody but myself."

He looked at Ellie defiantly. He didn't want her thinking he was something he wasn't. But he could see he wasn't getting through to her when she replied, "The past doesn't matter, Cain. All that matters is now."

"You're wrong!" he snapped. If she had a brain in her head, she'd listen to the warnings of her family and friends and stay away from him. All in all, it was better not to care about her.

But no matter how he tried, he couldn't stop himself....

D1454861

Dear Reader,

Welcome to the Silhouette **Special Edition** experience! With your search for consistently satisfying reading in mind, every month the authors and editors of Silhouette **Special Edition** aim to offer you a stimulating blend of deep emotions and high romance.

The name Silhouette **Special Edition** and the distinctive arch on the cover represent a commitment—a commitment to bring you six sensitive, substantial novels each month. In the pages of a Silhouette **Special Edition**, compelling true-to-life characters face riveting emotional issues—and come out winners. Both celebrated authors and newcomers to the series strive for depth and dimension, vividness and warmth, in writing these stories of living and loving in today's world.

The result, we hope, is romance you can believe in. Deeply emotional, richly romantic, infinitely rewarding—that's the Silhouette **Special Edition** experience. Come share it with us—six times a month!

From all the authors and editors of Silhouette **Special Edition**,

Best wishes,

Leslie Kazanjian
Senior Editor

CHRISTINE FLYNN
Renegade

Silhouette Special Edition

Published by Silhouette Books New York

America's Publisher of Contemporary Romance

SILHOUETTE BOOKS
300 East 42nd St., New York, N.Y. 10017

Copyright © 1989 by Christine Flynn

ISBN: 0-373-09566-X

First Silhouette Books printing December 1989

Printed in the U.S.A.

Books by Christine Flynn

Silhouette Romance

Stolen Promise #435
Courtney's Conspiracy #623

Silhouette Special Edition

Remember the Dreams #254
Silence the Shadows #465
Renegade #566

Silhouette Desire

When Snow Meets Fire #254
The Myth and the Magic #296
A Place to Belong #352
Meet Me at Midnight #377

CHRISTINE FLYNN,

formerly of Oregon, currently resides in the Southwest with her husband, teenage daughter and two very spoiled dogs.

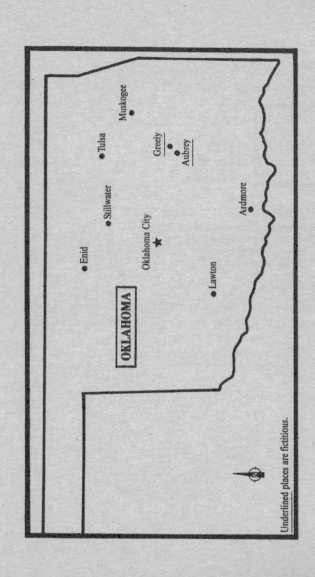

OKLAHOMA

Enid •

• Stillwater

Oklahoma City ★

Tulsa •

Muskogee •

Greely
•
• Aubrey

Ardmore •

• Lawton

Underlined places are fictitious.

Prologue

Cain Whitlow folded his arms over the steering wheel of his rusted blue Chevy, winced at the pain in his bruised knuckles and took one last look at the small, shabby house he'd lived in for years. Most of his possessions, along with a road map of the Southern states that he'd marked with a big arrow pointing west, were packed in the car. Once he pulled out of the driveway, he'd have no reason to come back.

He glanced at the floor shift, not at all certain why he wasn't putting the car into gear. He wanted to get out of Aubrey. He *had* to. Even his mother, who stood on the sagging front porch looking resigned, relieved and worried, knew that. It had actually been her suggestion that he leave, after she told him that as much as she hated to see him go, he'd never be able to make anything of himself if he stayed.

This last fight had undoubtedly convinced her of that, he decided. The sheriff had been out again, this time with the warning that after one more incident he'd have "the kid" turned over to the juvenile authorities. He probably would have liked to do it right then, but he couldn't get either of the two guys Cain had beaten up to admit who'd started the fight, and Cain, as usual, wasn't talking. He never said anything more to the sheriff than he absolutely had to. Old Hal Bennett heard only what he wanted to hear, anyway. Hal was just like his brother, the high school principal, in that respect. When Cain's mom had tried to talk Stu Bennett into letting Cain back into school, she'd said it was like talking to a tree.

Cain's mother knew the score. She'd come up against the good citizens of Aubrey often enough to know there were no opportunities for her son here. In the blunt, unvarnished way she had of talking, she'd even said that the Whitlows weren't the kind other people made opportunities for. Cain was so accustomed to the weary quality of her voice that he'd barely noticed her underlying bitterness when she said that—just as he hadn't paid much attention to the resignation that drained the spirit from the smile she wore for the men at the tavern where she worked. He knew only that she was having as tough a time as he was, and that a lot of the things he did hurt her even more.

It wasn't as if he *wanted* the reputation he'd earned. It just seemed that no matter how hard he tried, he couldn't do much of anything right—except tear down and rebuild automobile engines. He was good at that. Probably better than most, but there wasn't anyone around who'd admit it. He'd been tinkering with cars ever since he was thirteen and found an abandoned Chevy out by the Indian reservation. He'd actually gotten the thing to run again. It was the car he was sitting in now.

His mechanical abilities carried no redeeming value. Just last week, he'd asked the local gas station owner for a job.

The man had said he didn't need any help. Even as he'd spoken, a sign saying Mechanic Wanted hung in his window. The superiority in his voice and abject distrust in his expression had been much more honest than his actual words. He wouldn't hire Cain because everyone in town knew he was no good, and he didn't want a young hood making off with his tools.

Cain hadn't bothered to tell him that he'd never taken anything worth more than a couple of bucks, or that he'd never done anything to anyone who hadn't done something to him first. He'd been too busy dealing with the quiet rage of inequity so familiar to him that he didn't even realize it was there. He'd merely held the man's glance for a few long, hard seconds, then walked away without saying a word.

A motion on the porch drew him from his thoughts, and he jammed the car into reverse before looking back again. His mother, her long black braid hanging over her shoulder, was waving goodbye. He couldn't remember the last time she had done that. They'd really had so little to do with each other for being mother and son; mostly, he supposed, because their paths rarely crossed. It wasn't her fault. He knew how rough she had it trying to keep a roof over their heads on her wages and tips. He'd really wanted to help out. But obviously, there was little he could do to contribute.

Hating his powerlessness, and fighting an unaccustomed angry sting against the back of his eyelids, he stepped on the gas and screeched out into the street. A quick change of gears and he was lurching forward, certain that Hanna next door would be peering out her window and raising her cane at his squealing tires. He didn't care about Hanna. He felt better when he drove fast. The car responded to *him*, did what *he* wanted it to do. It was almost as if the only time he felt in control of his life was when he was speeding. Then, quite literally, his life was in his own hands.

He didn't look back. Not once as he headed out of town, past the grain silos and the patchwork landscape of oats and corn and barley, did he give a moment's thought to what lay behind him. The population of Aubrey, Oklahoma—1,293 people—had just been reduced by one. He was never going back. Never. He was on his own now. In a lot of ways, he'd been on his own for a very long time—and he was only seventeen.

Chapter One

It's been over a month since you've written him. If he was interested in settling up his mother's affairs, don't you think you'd have heard from him by now?''

A faint frown touched Ellie Bennett's pixieish features as she sorted though the morning mail. She hadn't said a word, yet her Aunt Jo had known exactly what she was looking for among the bills and advertisements addressed to Jo's Flower and Gift Shop.

It was rather discouraging to be so easily read. Still, Ellie's smile was easy, accepting. Jo, her Uncle Hal's wife, was unfailingly logical, and logic was an attribute Ellie, according to her family, tended to lack. More than likely, the diminutive woman with the graying brown curls was right.

"Maybe I should write him again."

"If you think it'll do any good, go ahead." Jo, making neat stacks of the invoices and payments her niece had opened for her, gave a resigned shake of her head. "But believe me, Ellie, you're the only person in Aubrey who wants him back here.''

Ellie started to say that it wasn't that she *wanted* him here, but since Jo looked preoccupied, she went back to work on the arrangement of pink carnations Paul Larson had ordered for his wife's birthday.

A couple of seconds later, she directed her thoughts to a sprig of baby's breath. "Maybe he just hasn't had the time yet." Why would a person ignore the passing of his own mother? she couldn't help but wonder. Or leave her home and possessions sitting unattended for so long? "Or maybe he didn't get my letter."

It was apparent that Jo was only half listening to her niece. The shop's customers tended to pay on their accounts toward the middle of the month. Between the day's mail and the payments Ellie had saved from last week, Jo was pleasantly occupied—or would have been, if the arthritis in her hands hadn't made writing so difficult for her. She always did the books and banking herself, insisting that Ellie was already doing enough for her by looking after the rest of the small business.

Despite her determination, it was difficult for Ellie to watch her aunt's efforts with a pencil. Jo was only fifty-four and had always been one of the most self-sufficient and energetic people Ellie had known. Her spark and the certain irreverence that only Jo Bennett could get away with were what made Ellie so fond of her. Jo was also the only member of the family, other then Ellie's Uncle Jay, who hadn't viewed Ellie's divorce from Brent Hanson last year as a major mistake.

Having relegated everything to its proper pile, Jo finally responded. "I suppose there are any number of reasons why he hasn't written or called. Could be that he isn't even among us anymore. For all anyone knows, he may have finally driven that old hot rod of his into a wall, or gotten into a fight that he didn't win." She reached for her calculator. "It's been twelve or thirteen years since he left here. Anything could have happened in that time."

Ellie turned the vase around, critically eyeing her creation. "I'm pretty sure he's still alive. I think his mom would have mentioned it to me if he wasn't."

To avoid the faint displeasure shadowing her aunt's expression, Ellie reached for the fern she'd knocked from the table. Jo might have sided with Ellie when she decided to leave her husband, but no one in the family had approved of her association with Amanda Whitlow. Not that she and Cain's mother had been especially close. Ellie merely rented the apartment over Amanda's garage and, being the basically friendly sort, Ellie had gotten to know Amanda as well as the taciturn woman would let her. She couldn't recall much about Amanda's son, though.

A rebel. A misfit. A hellion. Those were the labels she'd heard people apply to Cain Whitlow over the years. Ellie had only been twelve when he left Aubrey, and much more interested in her ballerina books and her friend Mitzy's new kittens than in what she'd caught of the adults' conversations back then. Still, she did remember his fast car and had heard about his drinking. Most especially, she remembered hearing about the fights that her Uncle Hal, the sheriff, would be called to break up. He had sat in the family study many an evening and told her dad about them while her father agreed that the boy was, most certainly, a problem. But all she really knew of Cain was what she'd overheard others say.

To be honest, Ellie had to admit that what she'd heard had left an impression.

Her warm brown eyes grew pensive. Drawing the length of her long auburn hair away from her face, she secured it with the barrette she pulled from the pocket of her green apron. "I really don't care if he shows up in person or not. A phone call would do just fine."

"I don't believe that's a courtesy you can expect from Cain Whitlow. From what I remember of him, he'd as soon tell you to go to hell as say thank-you."

"I don't want him to thank me." Granted, she had taken care of the funeral arrangements for his mother, but she'd done that for Amanda, not for him. There *was* a definite lack of courtesy involved here, though. How much effort did it take to pick up a telephone?

Annoyed, she jammed another carnation into the green Styrofoam taped into the vase. The stem broke. Giving her aunt a sheepish smile, she reached for another. "I just want him to tell me what he's going to do with Amanda's house so I'll know how much longer I can stay in the apartment. I hate the thought of moving, but I feel strange living there without paying someone rent. And the idea of the house just sitting vacant..." Ellie cut herself off. It was sad to see it looking so empty. Amanda had loved her little house.

"I don't suppose you'd consider moving back home?"

"Home" was Ellie's parents' comfortable ranch-style house in the new section of town where she had grown up. The new section was actually more than twenty years old, but in a town that seemed to be fifteen years behind the rest of the world, one didn't quibble over a decade or two. "I like it right where I am. You know that."

Ellie steeled herself, waiting for her aunt to say how inappropriate it was for her to be living above a garage. Specifically, Amanda Whitlow's garage. Amanda had been regarded as a woman of, among other things, questionable repute, and Ellie's relatives had not seen her as an appropriate landlady for a member of the Bennett family. To her relief, Jo said nothing. Ellie ruefully surmised it was because the main reason for the objections no longer existed.

"It is quite convenient being so close to the shop," Jo said, mentioning one of Ellie's own arguments for renting the place. "But with no one in the Whitlow house and the Robertses across the street on vacation, I worry about you being alone over there."

Jo was really worried, Ellie knew, about the break-ins that had occurred off and on during the past several weeks. Aubrey normally didn't have that kind of trouble. It was a quiet and fairly isolated little community, seldom intruded upon from the outside. With some of the farmers cutting back on their expenses, though, the migrant laborers who moved north from Texas in late summer weren't finding work, and one or two of them had taken on a less acceptable way of supplementing their income. The Haggerty place over by Cross Creek had been robbed just last week, and Rue Tyler's storage shed had been cleaned out only days before that. Ellie had once even thought that the thieves had hit Amanda's house, but it turned out to be a false alarm.

"I've got Hanna," Ellie said, relatively certain that no one would be interested in her tiny apartment. She had little for anyone to take, anyway.

At the mention of Ellie's next-door neighbor, Jo gave a snort. "She'd be a lot of help. What could she do? Trip the robber with her cane?"

"Don't underestimate her. There isn't much that gets by Hanna. She sits in her window all day just waiting for something to happen. The first sign of trouble, she'd be on the phone to Uncle Hal."

"What if the thief got to her first?"

A droll smile touched Ellie's mouth. "She'd talk him to death. You know how she is when there's anyone around to listen."

"Do I ever." Jo chuckled. "Some things never change."

As the conversation shifted again and the subject of Cain Whitlow was forgotten, Ellie settled into the comfortable, familiar pattern of her day. There was a certain pleasure in the routine, a security in knowing what people expected from you and what you expected from others in return. Everything in Aubrey seemed to happen in its own predictable way; nothing very remarkable ever took place to distinguish one day from another, or one week from the next. It was an easy existence—and a rather dull one.

Ellie tried not to consider that last thought. It never did any good to dwell on something that wouldn't change. As the day wore on, however, she couldn't help recalling her aunt's remark and wondering why the trite old phrase kept nagging at her.

Some things never change. In the far corner of her mind, an errant thought presented itself. It might be kind of nice, if just for once, something did.

It was all still the same.

The repetition of that thought had become a numbing litany for Cain in the past half hour. It had first occurred to him when he cut in from the highway and saw Aubrey's silos silhouetted against the long unbroken line of the horizon. It occurred to him again when he'd pulled up to the house he'd left so long ago and seen the lace curtains still hanging in the windows. The driveway was still littered with pods from the old cottonwood growing next to it, and the back screen door still squeaked when it was pulled open.

Feeling his stomach tighten, Cain let himself in with the key he'd never bothered to remove from his chain, and dropped his leather duffel bag on the linoleum kitchen floor. The room felt stuffy and close—and far too familiar for comfort. Less than a minute later, he'd shoved a six-pack of beer into the refrigerator and headed out the front door. The screen slammed behind him as he stepped out onto the porch.

He moved to the rail, refusing to acknowledge the slight tremor in his hand when he flicked a chip of peeling paint from the weathered wood. The sound of supper dishes being washed could be heard through a neighbor's open windows. From down the street, the muffled shouts of children playing underscored the occasional bark of a dog. The summer heat had always pulled people out of their homes so they could catch the evening's breeze, and over on the next block, barbecue smoke rose from someone's backyard.

It was all just as it had been when he left.

The breath he drew was controlled and deep, yet it didn't alleviate the tension he felt building inside him. Even the smell of the air, heavy with the pungent scent of loamy earth and freshly cut hay, brought reminders of a time he'd thought he had forgotten, or at least buried so deeply that he no longer had to deal with the memories. Yet now, standing next to the chair his mother had once occupied on just such evenings, hearing the same sounds he remembered from his youth, Cain could almost feel the time slipping away. And the awful insecurity he'd lived with for so long was trying to take hold again. Thirteen years had passed since he last stood in this spot. Thirteen long, hard years that, at that moment, seemed not to have happened at all. It was not a pleasant sensation.

Not sure how to deal with the feelings—or with the old resentments wanting to be remembered—he chose to simply ignore them. If there was one area in which Cain excelled, it was ignoring what he didn't want to think about.

Reminding himself that his return was only temporary—and finding more relief than he'd have expected in the reassurance—he propped his booted foot up on the front porch rail and tipped his head back to quench his thirst with a beer. He'd known it wouldn't be easy coming back after so long.

People from around here had long memories. He'd had proof of that less than half an hour ago when he'd stopped to pick up the six-pack of beer at the Cross Creek grocery. At least Old Man Weatherly hadn't told him to get the hell out of his store as he once would have done. Granted, the wizened old coot had eyed him with definite skepticism when Cain had made his purchase. But he hadn't automatically reached for the phone to call the sheriff, either. All he'd done was let Cain know that he was quite aware of who he was by muttering, "You're that Whitlow kid, aren't you?" Then he'd kept an eye on Cain until he walked out the door.

Wondering if Weatherly would ever forget about the two bottles of wine he had once stolen, Cain absently unbuttoned his shirt. Moments later the old country store and its ancient owner were forgotten, as thirst demanded another long swallow of cold liquid. Cain was hot. And bone-dry. He'd forgotten how dusty the roads where in late summer and how the heat that made them that way could suck the moisture out of a person.

He'd also forgotten how defensive he could get.

The beat of footsteps on the sidewalk had grown steadily louder for the past several seconds. The rhythmic sound didn't register, though, until it stopped. When it did, Cain became aware of the vague prickling sensation that comes with being watched. Lowering the bottle from his mouth, he slowly turned his head.

Running parallel to the opposite end of the box-shaped white house was the narrow driveway. Cain had parked his black Lamborghini there, but the squat, racy car was half-hidden by the low-hanging branches of the cottonwood tree. The woman just beyond the car's rear fender didn't seem to have noticed the vehicle at all. Having come to a halt, she was staring up at Cain as if she didn't know whether to hurry on past or turn and run.

Her predicament was actually the second thing Cain noted. First he'd noticed her hair. Smooth, except for the strands lifted by the breeze, it fell below her shoulders. Its deep mahogany color revealed streaks of reddish gold in the fading sunlight. A white clip held one side away from her face.

She looked young to him—and either shy or startled, though he couldn't tell which. She carried a sack of groceries and out of the top stuck a bunch of bright yellow daisies.

Cain saw her eyes over the flowers. Her chin tipped up. "What are you doing up there?"

He didn't know which threw him more, the challenge or the authority she managed to put into her gentle voice. "What's it to you?" he returned, wondering what gave her the right to question his actions.

"This is private property." The sack of groceries was squeezed a little tighter. "Now you tell me who you are and what you're doing drinking beer on Amanda's porch, or I'm calling the sheriff."

Had he been anywhere else at that moment, Cain would have appreciated her feisty protectiveness of another's property and found a way to make her smile at him rather than frown. It occurred to him, vaguely, that she was quite pretty—in the innocent sort of way that seldom appealed to him—and that with her full mouth and expressive eyes she'd have a rather nice smile. But his emotions, something he'd worked very hard over the years to control, were overriding such subtleties.

He felt his fingers clench around the beer bottle. His edginess had been increasing ever since he'd crossed the county line. Now, faced with the same suspicious hostility he'd always suffered in this town, that edge hardened. Defenses he'd thought well buried seeped to the surface.

"I'm drinking a beer because I'm thirsty," he replied, lowering his foot from the rail. It was this place, he knew. He was annoyed with her because of his inability to distance himself from his feelings about this town. He'd forgotten how much he'd actually hated it. "And the name's Whitlow. Any more questions?"

Oddly satisfied with the way her eyes widened, he stood with the bottle hanging at his side and his other hand on his hip. The deceptively casual stance seemed to draw her attention to the hard muscles of his chest visible between the sides of his open shirt. Skin tanned to the color of walnut contrasted starkly with the pale blue fabric, and a dark dusting of hair swirled downward over his flat belly. Cain couldn't help but notice that she seemed particularly intrigued with the way it disappeared beneath the waist of his well-worn jeans.

He caught her frank and fascinated stare. His own tended toward arrogance. "Who are you?"

Hesitation entered her voice. "Ellie Bennett" was her quiet reply. "I'm sorry. I didn't realize... I wrote you about your mother," she finally said. "You did get my letter, didn't you?"

It was a moment before Cain responded. That letter had sat in his post office box until last week when he returned from California. *This is so difficult,* it had begun, *but I know of no other way to let you know what has happened. Your mother died of a heart attack....*

"I got it," he said.

"I wasn't really sure if you had." Her voice grew quieter, softer, though he'd thought it amazingly soft already. "The only address I could find for you was a P.O. box in Orlando. It was in the front of Amanda's address book, but I didn't know how old it was. The address, I mean. Amanda had said you never stayed in one place for very long."

Cain had been about to thank her for the trouble she'd gone to. Instead, sensing criticism in her words, his expression hardened and his thanks fell silent.

The warm breeze picked up, rattling the leaves of the camellia bush beside her as she stood studying the cracks in the sidewalk. She seemed even warier of him than she had only moments ago. That unease showed in the skittish way she avoided his eyes. Cain had no idea what she was waiting for, but the longer she stood there, the more apparent it became that she had something else to say to him. Having nothing more pressing to do at the moment, he simply stared at her until she figured out what it was.

He didn't expect her to begin with a smile, tentative as it was. "I'm sorry I was so rude," she said. "But we've had some trouble around here this summer with people helping themselves to other people's things and I . . . well, I guess I thought you might be thinking about doing that." She pointed down the driveway. "I live up there. In the apartment over your mom's garage. But I already told you that in my letter. I owe you some rent," she continued, sounding a shade more nervous than she probably liked. "I'd have sent it with the letter, but I wasn't sure you'd get it. Let me put my groceries away and I'll bring it to you."

The blossoms bobbed against her chin as she shifted her sack. A shallow slash of skin, porcelain pale and innocently provocative, was now visible between the lapels of her loose sleeveless blouse. It was, however, the languorous brush of her skirt against her legs as she moved that Cain found so fascinating. As she turned away, the breeze nudged the fabric against her calves and outlined the long line of her thighs.

Finding himself more than a little intrigued, Cain was also aware of the effect her very feminine movements had on him. Everything about her seemed subtly seductive—the soft shades of golden fire in her gleaming auburn hair, the way her dark eyes had shied from his. Even her voice, hushed and gentle, had a sensual power to it.

She'd only taken a dozen steps when she stopped again. "Oh, about the fingerprint dust in Amanda's bedroom," she began, changing his contemplative frown to one of confusion. "I'm sorry about the mess. I'd have cleaned it up, but I didn't get a chance. You know the trouble I said we've been having? Well, I thought someone had broken in and the deputy had started taking fingerprints from the dresser before my Uncle Hal—he's the sheriff," she hurriedly explained, "decided it wasn't necessary. I'd have cleaned up, but my uncle was in a hurry so he had me lock up before I could do it. He said nobody had been in there, anyway."

Cain hadn't been in the bedroom. He'd spent less than two minutes in the house since his arrival and wasn't looking forward to going back inside. It just didn't feel right in there.

Whether Ellie had intended to or not, she had just raised several questions. Cain was certain, though, that she hadn't anticipated the one he asked. "Hal," he muttered. "Hal Bennett is your uncle?"

There was a certain caution in her nod. The brittleness in Cain's voice had no doubt put it there.

"He's still the sheriff around here?"

Ellie gave another tentative nod, obviously uncertain of the effect her confirmation would have on him. When a couple of seconds passed and he said nothing else, she hurried off.

She had said she'd be back, so Cain didn't bother to stop her. He had other questions, but he wasn't really thinking about the sheriff as he watched her go. Her remark about having thought someone had broken in was far more distracting than old resentments. He was wondering what had happened for her to think that a lawman's presence had been necessary in his mother's house. That was why, after checking out his mother's bedroom, he was waiting for Ellie when she approached the back door ten minutes later.

Chapter Two

Only thirty feet separated the steps leading from Ellie's apartment to the house's back porch. She'd gone less than halfway when she saw Cain's tall, shadowy frame fill the back screen door. The man, she had to admit, was a master at intimidation. From the moment he'd caught her watching him, she'd sensed his power to dominate. When he'd spoken his name, that power had been confirmed.

Given the chance, Ellie would gladly have changed the circumstances of their initial meeting. If she'd known who he was, she certainly wouldn't have challenged him. Never would she forget the way he'd looked at her in the moments before she'd spoken, or the chilling effect of his perusal once she had. One moment he'd regarded her with nothing more than the passive interest one reserves for an annoying fly. The next, his gray eyes had grown as cool as the wind on a winter morning. Accusing. Disdainful.

She straightened her shoulders, continuing her trek across the browning lawn. If he'd had the decency to call, he could have saved them both the discomfort of that little scene. She wouldn't mention that, though. As much as she hated to admit it, she rarely came out ahead when faced with someone stronger than herself—especially when caught unprepared as she'd been this evening.

She didn't feel that now was the time to ask his plans for the property, though that concern had been in the back of her mind for weeks. Maybe she would ask tomorrow, after he'd rested and, hopefully, his mood had improved. If he was as short-tempered as he was reputed to be, she wasn't about to irritate him with her presence any longer than was necessary. All she would do now was pay the rent she owed him.

By the time she reached the screen door, she had to admit that it was more than his reputation that made her wary. It was the slow and measured way he had of watching her. He seemed the kind of man who didn't give much; rather, one who waited and watched. Much as a panther stalks its prey.

"Here's the check," she said, stepping back so he could open the door and take it. She also held out a foil-covered plate. "I brought this in case there wasn't anything in the cupboards to eat. I didn't know if you'd made it to the market before it closed, and Rusty's Café isn't open on Monday nights anymore, so... here."

She shoved the plate toward him, not at all sure why he was scowling at it. "It's just cold fried chicken and potato salad left over from a picnic yesterday," she explained.

His frown deepened, not in displeasure, but in confusion.

"You don't like chicken?" she asked.

"No. I ... I mean, yeah. It's fine. Thanks." Cain looked at her, his glance uncomfortably direct. Why did you do this? he seemed to ask, but the question was gone from his eyes in the next instant. "Come on in for a minute."

"Oh, I didn't mean to stay," she began, trying not to sound as anxious as she was to decline the unexpected invitation. "I don't want to interrupt you."

"You're not interrupting."

"I'm sure you must be tired."

Impatience made his tone sharper than he'd intended. "I'm not tired. I just want you to come in for a few minutes so I can talk to you."

There was little that Cain found more aggravating than noncooperation, but he was also astute enough to realize that impatience wouldn't get him anywhere. The woman looked ready to bolt.

It was the frightened-doe look about her eyes that annoyed him the most. He couldn't help wondering if she'd be so leery if he were anyone else.

"I just want to talk to you," he repeated, his tone as unthreatening as he could make it. "I'd like to know why you'd thought someone had broken in. I looked around the bedroom and nothing seemed suspicious to me, except for the graphite on the dresser and windowsill, but you explained how that got there. And the arrangements you took care of for my mom ... I know I must owe somebody for that."

Reluctantly, Ellie abandoned thoughts of a quick departure. It was perfectly logical that he would have questions. And she was the only one who could provide him with answers. She'd even indicated in her letter that she'd help him in any way she could.

But she'd made that offer to a stranger who had no shape or dimension in her mind beyond an old reputation and a kinship with a friend. The man looming silent in the doorway while he waited for her response was definitely real. He was a living, breathing male, who was just a little bigger, a little more forceful and a lot more compelling than she'd have thought him to be—had she given the man himself much thought at all.

Faced with him now, her mind focused on little else. An aura of tension surrounded him—a kind of contained strength fighting to escape the restraints of civilized behavior. That tension felt almost tangible to her.

Moving past him as he stepped aside for her to cross the utility room with its old washer and shelves of canning jars, she wondered if she wasn't absorbing a little of that tension herself. She'd been in Amanda's house before. Several times. But she didn't remember it feeling quite this...close. No doubt that strange phenomenon had something to do with Cain.

The screen door creaked closed and Cain covered the width of the kitchen in four strides. Ellie claimed the small space in front of the sink for herself, watching him all the while.

There was a brooding intensity about his slate-gray eyes, a firm determination in the hard line of his mouth. Even his hair, the darkest shade of brown, contributed a touch of insolence in the way it fell across his forehead. His features were sharply defined and, in repose, one might consider them classically handsome. But she didn't think Cain ever let himself relax completely. Those compelling features were darkened by the lean, hungry look of a man who had fought hard for everything he had—and had no intention whatsoever of giving any of it up.

Never having learned how to fight, Ellie couldn't imagine how a person could become that hard. She also couldn't imagine why she was so intrigued by that quality.

"I don't remember the house being this small," she heard him say, and wondered what could possibly have prompted his thoughts to track so closely to hers.

He was at the refrigerator, opening its door to put the plate she'd brought him on one of its empty shelves. The refrigerator was tucked into the pantry and the overhead cabinets were so low that he had to bend his head to keep from bumping it.

"Could be you weren't quite so tall when you left." She remembered a picture she'd seen of Cain on Amanda's mantel. "Maybe it just seems smaller because you've grown."

There were actually several pictures in mismatched frames above the living room fireplace. The one Ellie thought of now was of a young Cain and an old Chevy with a large number painted on the side. The snapshot had been taken out at the county fairgrounds, Amanda had told her, at one of the stock car races Cain used to enter.

He'd been seventeen that year, and in the photograph he had appeared every bit as skinny as her brother at that age. Any resemblance to her older sibling stopped there, however. Dan had a broad smile that still came with ease. All she recalled of the smile in the photograph of Cain was its underlying defiance, the somnolent anger that had made his young face look hard even back then.

Ellie kept her glance trained on Cain's back as he hunched down to remove something from the bottom shelf. She wasn't thinking of that anger now, only of the adolescent slenderness that had filled out so remarkably. It was difficult to picture the man before her as a lanky teenager.

Cain had buttoned his shirt, a fact Ellie had noted with some relief when he'd pushed open the screen. The way it had hung open before had made his sexuality seem raw and taunting. Now, seeing the muscles beneath the blue chambray flex as he straightened, she decided that her relief had been premature. Buttoning his shirt hadn't diminished his blatant appeal in the least.

When he turned, he had a bottle in each hand. Ellie didn't notice. Her attention was on the muscular length of his thighs, rippling with power as he moved toward her. The focus of her glance shifted to the snug fit of denim on his hips, upward still past his flat and undoubtedly rock-hard stomach to the impressive width of his shoulders.

It wasn't as if Ellie had never seen a well-honed body before. Farming and oil drilling were about the only sources of employment in the county, and any man who put his back into his job had a body of iron. Yet there was something about Cain so different from the others—a kind of leashed energy in his movements, perhaps. Whatever it was, it was certainly...intimidating, she reminded herself when she met his eyes.

He was watching her, quite closely. The knowledge that he'd been completely aware of her bold perusal made her flush clear to her toes.

Totally baffled by her behavior, Ellie sought refuge in an inventory of the scuff marks on the floor. His expression had been a curious blend of indulgence and awareness, as if he knew how compelling she found him and was vaguely amused by her reaction.

If she hadn't been so disturbed by that reaction herself, she might have found his attitude most annoying.

"Maybe I have," he returned in response to the comment she'd made nearly a minute ago. "When I left here, I didn't think I'd ever see six feet." He held out one of the bottles. "Want this?"

She started to decline, until she saw that he was offering her a cola, not a beer as he'd taken for himself. Frowning slightly, she accepted it with a quiet "Thank you." How had

he known she didn't care for beer? she wondered, only to
have his observation cancel the insight with which she'd
been about to credit him.

"Didn't think you were old enough for this." He raised
his own bottle toward her. "Wouldn't want to contribute to
the delinquency of a minor. Uncle Hal probably wouldn't
be too pleased about that."

There was sarcasm in his tone, veiled like the cursory look
he tossed her way just before he headed out of the room, but
definitely there. Ellie knew that her uncle thought little of
the Whitlows, but she didn't have time to do much more
than surmise that the feeling must be mutual before Cain
disappeared into the living room.

She'd been about to tell him that she was hardly a minor.
At twenty-four, she was certainly old enough to be offered
a beer, and she hated it when people were condescending.
She might have told him that, too, if she'd had the nerve. As
it was, all of her nerve was presently being used to pretend
she wasn't the least bit affected by his opinion of her, her
uncle or anything else she could think of. Judging it best to
hurry up and answer whatever questions he had in mind so
she could get out of there, she started after him.

Cain heard Ellie round the corner just as he flipped on the
overhead light. The faint shadows fled from the corners,
revealing a room that looked much as it always had. The old
green sofa still had the crocheted protectors on its curved
arms and magazines were stacked on the end table beside it.
Lace curtains covered the windows. In front of the window
by the door stood a small round table with an arrangement
of bright plastic tulips. His mother had always liked bright
colors, especially yellow—like the color of the daisies Ellie
had carried in her sack.

He entered the short hallway and stopped at the doorway
of his mother's room when he flipped on the overhead light.

"I'm surprised the electricity is still on. I'd have thought the utility company would have shut it off when the bill didn't get paid."

"I paid it."

He turned to face her, his surprise tempering the ever-present toughness in his expression. "You did?"

"I had to. My power is connected to the house. If there's no electricity here, there's none in the apartment. I hope you don't mind," she added, fearing he might think her presumptuous.

His quickly muttered "Of course not" was dismissive, his thoughts clearly on more immediate matters. "What I want to know is why you thought someone had broken in here."

It wasn't easy being the focus of his attention. His glance had a tendency to stray over her body as she spoke, lingering just a little too long for comfort in certain places. The feel of his glance was decidedly unnerving. She didn't know if he did it to bait her, or if he scrutinized everyone as carefully.

To lessen his gaze's unsettling effect, she moved across the room to the window, concentrating on what she said rather than on the man listening to her words.

"I'd opened these." She reached for the edge of the yellow curtain. "And when I saw them closed later, I thought someone had been in here. I was *certain* someone had been when I saw one of the dresser drawers half-open. But Uncle Hal said I'd probably just gotten confused when your mom..."

She dropped the curtain, feeling the same doubt now as she had when her uncle had assured her that nothing was amiss. "This isn't making much sense, is it?"

Slowly Cain shook his head.

"I didn't think it was."

"Maybe it would help if you started at the beginning."

"I didn't know if you wanted to hear that part right now." A few perfume bottles in a mirrored tray sat on Amanda's dresser. Ellie's glance skimmed past them to the black powder smudging the pale knotty pine. That was where Mike, her uncle's deputy, had been checking for fingerprints. "The beginning would be when your mom had her heart attack."

Cain's stance was deceptively casual as he watched her over the yellow flower-print bedspread on the neatly made double bed. But even from across the room, Ellie saw the flicker of hesitation in his expression.

"Just tell me about the window," he said so abruptly that she was certain she'd only imagined the fleeting pain in his eyes.

At his terse instruction, she pushed her hands into the pockets of her cotton skirt and tipped her chin up. Both her mother and her Aunt Jo were forever telling her how naive she was. Apparently, they were right. Why else would she have thought it necessary to spare him details when he seemed so unaffected by his loss?

"I'd opened the curtains to let in more light after the ambulance left with your mother. There hadn't been time to pack a bag, and I'd wanted to get her nightgown and robe to take to the hospital. I remember thinking it would be easier to see with the curtains open. They'd taken her to Greely General and I was planning on driving over after work the next day. I know I was kind of rattled because I was worried about her, but I'd thought for sure that I'd opened the curtains.

"Anyway," she continued, pacing because movement helped to calm her, "when I got to the hospital, I was told that Amanda had passed away during the night and the nurse wanted to know who to call to take care of the arrangements. Since I had no idea how to reach you, I told her

I'd do it. That's why I came back here, to get the dress and things the people at the funeral home had asked for. The first thing I noticed when I came in the room was that the curtains were closed.''

"How'd you get in?"

"I have a key. Amanda gave it to me so I could feed her fish on nights she decided to stay over in Greely."

Cain's expression never changed. "Her fish?"

"Uh-huh. Tropical ones. She said they had a tank at the tavern where she worked. It was getting kind of crowded, so she started bringing the babies home."

Amanda's fish were now being cared for by the first-graders at Aubrey's elementary school. Had Cain asked where the fish were, Ellie would have told him. All he wanted to know was if anyone else had a key.

At the shake of her head, he prodded her on with a flat "Then what?"

Thinking him callously single-minded, she was determined to keep her explanation as unembellished as possible. Clearly he wasn't interested in learning anything else about Amanda. Other than seeming a little surprised about her keeping fish, he hadn't asked a single question about his mother.

"As I said, the first thing I noticed was the curtains. The second thing was the dresser drawers. The top one was open a little and some lace was poking out the side. I thought maybe I'd caught something in the drawer when I'd pulled her nightgown out of it the day before, so I opened the drawer to straighten it. It was a mess. As if someone had gone through it. I checked the other drawers and they were all messed up, too. Your mom was always so neat." She was certain he didn't want to hear about Amanda's personal habits, but it was necessary because the disorder had been so puzzling. "Everything was always in its place. That's why I decided I'd better get out of here and call the sheriff."

She went on to tell Cain that her call had resulted in her uncle's anticlimactic conclusion that nothing was so extraordinary, after all. To ease her mind, Uncle Hal had let her come in after him and they'd checked the house thoroughly. Nothing else had appeared out of order. There hadn't been any sign of a forced entry, so he had told his deputy to forget about trying to lift prints from the dresser since there wouldn't be any that didn't belong there. That had been that. Nothing but a false alarm.

Ellie thought her uncle had been most understanding, though. She'd thought he might be annoyed with her for wasting his and his deputy's time. At first he'd accused her of overreacting to all the talk about break-ins. Then he had suggested that it was simply the stress of having found Amanda so ill and then taking on the responsibility of her funeral that had made Ellie only *think* she'd opened the curtains. Perhaps she *had* opened them, then later closed them herself. As for Amanda's messy dresser drawers, he thought it entirely possible that the woman had merely become lax in her housekeeping skills. Habits, he'd pointed out, do change.

Ellie had found that statement odd coming from her uncle, especially since he was of the school that believed ingrained habits never changed. His type of thinking held such dictums as an honest person never lies, and once a criminal always a criminal. It was a truly inflexible philosophy, but the citizens in Aubrey liked it well enough to reelect him every few years. She hadn't questioned the deviation from his usual thinking, though. No one argued with Hal Bennett.

She said nothing of that to Cain, of course. All she reiterated was what her uncle had pointed out; that she had been upset and maybe things hadn't happened quite the way she remembered. In police work, he'd said, such errors in recalling an event happened all the time and were more common than most people might think.

Cain stood with his arms crossed as he considered both Ellie and what she had just told him. He wasn't concerned so much with Hal Bennett's conclusion as he was with the way his niece had so readily accepted those rationalizations. She'd sounded so certain of what she had and hadn't done.

Since nothing appeared to have been taken, he was wondering whether or not to dismiss the matter when Ellie moved past him to turn off the lamp by the bed. She stopped beside the nightstand, then hesitated, a pensive quality softening her expression.

A book lay facedown on the small table. Ellie reached toward it, trailing her fingers over the binding before picking it up. It was only half-read. A while ago, when she and Cain had walked through the living room, she had seen some unfinished needlework on the arm of Amanda's favorite chair. The one across from the television. Nearly everything in the house was as Amanda had left it.

She put the book back down, raising her eyes to where Cain leaned against the doorjamb. He'd followed her hand, his eyes trained on the unfinished novel.

Ellie felt something constrict in her chest. This can't possibly be easy for him, she thought. No man could be so devoid of feeling that his mother's death wouldn't affect him. If she, God forbid, were faced with the task of packing up *her* mother's possessions under such circumstances, she would be devastated. And she would have a father and brother and an aunt and uncles to help her through it. Cain had no one.

"For whatever it's worth," she said quietly, "I'm really sorry about your mom."

Cain hadn't expected the words, or the slug of pain they brought with them. He hadn't told anyone in Orlando why he was suddenly taking the vacation Carlo Bessari had been after him to take for the past three years. No one else knew of his loss. No one had spoken those words of sympathy. Only Ellie. Ellie with her lovely brown eyes and deliciously soft voice. He was at once grateful and angered. Angered because he didn't want to feel the pain when there was nothing he could do about it, and grateful because someone finally knew he did.

You don't want to think about this now, he told himself, and tried to steel himself against the innocence in her fragile features. His mumbled "Thanks" was as feeble as it sounded, but he didn't know what else to say.

She seemed to have expected his less than adequate response. "Look, I don't know what you plan to do with the house, but if you need..."

"I'm selling it."

"I see." Later, she told herself. Later she'd find out how his decision would affect her. Moving didn't seem like such a big deal when compared with the task Cain was facing. "You'll probably want to clear everything out then. Let me know when you plan to start. I'll help you pack, if you want."

She doubted very much that he'd do anything of the kind. Cain didn't strike her as a man who accepted help easily, and judging from the way his dark brows darted together, she figured he was preparing to decline her offer.

"Just think about it," she suggested and started past him.

"Why?" His fingers curved over her upper arm. A split second later, he pulled her around to face him, his expression as unyielding as his grip.

Startled, pretending not to be, she stifled her gasp of surprise. "Because I thought you might need the help."

"I mean why would you *want* to help. I don't get it."

There was such suspicion in his tone that Ellie almost forgot how hot his palm felt on her bare skin, or how unnerving it was to be so close to his aggression.

"I was thinking how I'd feel in your position," she told him with artless honesty. "I wouldn't want to face a job like this all alone. Offering to help just seemed like the right thing to do." How sad, she thought, that he should feel compelled to question such a simple gesture. That same look of distrust had been in his eyes when she'd handed him the plate of leftovers a while ago. "I thought of your mother as a friend and friends help each other out. Maybe I wasn't offering for you," she added, since he so clearly disliked the idea, "so much as I was for her."

That explanation appeased him enough to ease the pressure on her upper arm. Quite unconsciously, her hand moved to cover the spot as she took a step back.

Cain's skepticism was still firmly in place. "Which one of the Bennetts is your father?"

"I beg your pardon?"

"Come on. If the sheriff is your uncle, that leaves either the politician or the old school principal." Respectable, he thought, feeling his old hostilities strain against the holds he'd put on them. The Bennetts had all fairly reeked respectability. "Which one is your father?"

Ellie had no idea what had brought on this line of questioning or why it even mattered. The brooding quality of Cain's scowl didn't invite an inquiry, however, only an answer. "Uncle Jay is in the Senate. My father is Stuart, the high school principal." Whether Cain's expression invited it or not, she had to ask. "Why?"

"Terrific," Cain drawled, ignoring the query. What was old Stu's daughter doing renting an apartment from his mother?

"Why did you say that?"

"This must be a test."

Totally uncomprehending, Ellie simply stared up at him.

Cain, beginning to feel as if he'd slipped down Alice's rabbit hole, wasn't faring much better. Of all the people in Aubrey, the two people he wanted the least to do with were Stu and Hal Bennett. "I don't know your Uncle Jay. But let's just say that your father and I got along about as well as your Uncle Hal and I did, and that wasn't too well."

It was a gross understatement, but Cain wasn't up to explaining how he and Ellie's father had done battle over his first expulsion. Old Stuart had eventually relented and let Cain back into automotive shop, but not until Cain had spent twenty hours sweeping floors and mopping halls for ditching his other classes.

There were questions forming in Ellie's mind. Cain could practically see them in her expressive eyes. Wanting to change the subject before she could verbalize them, he cut her off just as she opened her mouth. "Either you've been disowned or things have changed a hell of a lot since I left."

"I haven't been disowned," she returned, finding the statement absurd. Her family hadn't always been pleased with her decisions, but disinheriting her had never been a question. "And I don't know that things have changed all that much around here."

"They must have. Who would ever have believed that a Bennett would consider a Whitlow a friend? It's a little like bending the laws of physics to say that fire won't ignite gasoline."

The sarcasm in his tone indicated just how implausible he found such a phenomenon. The Whitlow family—which had consisted solely of Cain and his mom after his dad walked out—had been held with the arm's-length regard reserved for the transient laborers who moved through the plains like locusts during harvest season. His father had been one of those laborers. Though the senior Whitlow had somehow managed to earn enough for a down payment on the little house, the family's social status was impervious to change. When the crops failed a couple of years later, and Cain's father left him and his mother just a few days short of Cain's seventh birthday, that status had dropped another notch. Once his mother took the job at the tavern outside of Greely, it had been downhill from there.

Considering that his mother had been all but shunned by the Bennetts and their ilk, he found Ellie's "friendship" with her a little hard to believe. Since he made no effort to hide it, Ellie clearly saw that doubt.

"I choose my own friends," she informed him, managing to make the softly spoken words sound like a form of defiance. "It just so happens that I liked your mother. I didn't know her all that well, but what I did know, I respected. Now, if you want help taking care of her things, my offer stands. There will be a lot to do here." And your pride won't be much help when it comes to packing everything up, she added to herself.

Had she been a little less of a lady—or a little braver—she might have spoken that last thought aloud. She wasn't about to challenge Cain, though. The man had a chip on his shoulder as wide as the Oklahoma panhandle and she wasn't about to try to knock it off herself.

As she stood there waiting for him to move from the doorway so she could pass, she knew she could relate to some of his antipathy. Down deep in a part of her that she'd never really explored, she almost envied his ability to express his anger. He'd obviously had problems with both her father and her uncle. Knowing the personalities involved, she could certainly see why. But oddly, despite the bitterness he hadn't been able to hide, she sensed that he'd once buried that anger and was now trying to overcome the feelings crawling out of his past.

Even as he dragged his hand through his hair and stepped aside so she could go, she could feel his tension turn inward.

Swearing silently, Cain released his breath. He was usually in better control of himself than this. Why should he care whom she was related to? He'd all but forgotten that those men existed, and they were certainly not a part of the life he'd made for himself. They didn't matter. The past didn't matter. As for Ellie, all she'd done was offer to help and he'd come on as if she was guilty of some unpardonable sin. This was quite an act for someone who'd certainly committed his share. Part of the reason for his attitude, he suspected, was that he'd found that women didn't give much unless they wanted something. Ellie's generosity had caught him off guard.

So had her practicality. He hadn't given any real thought to the task that lay ahead of him. As Ellie had pointed out, there would be much to do. In the back of his mind, he'd known that he had a lot to take care of, but he honestly hadn't entertained a single thought as to what all was entailed.

The house was small, but more than twenty years of living in the same place had allowed his mother to fill all the available corners. Aside from the furniture in the living areas and two bedrooms on the main floor, there was the basement. His old room was down there, though heaven only knew what occupied its space now—or what he should do with whatever it was.

The truth of the matter was that Cain didn't even know where to start. That in itself was an annoyance. It wasn't like him to experience indecision. At Bessari Motors, where he created the earthquake-inducing engines for the Bessari racing team, *he* was the person the mechanics came to for answers. Now, he didn't have a single one. And Ellie herself posed the biggest question of all.

She hadn't budged. Though there was plenty of room for her to pass since he'd stepped aside, she'd remained in the doorway.

He could have sworn that she'd hightail it out of there as soon as she could. That she was a little fearful of him was apparent. It was just as obvious that she was trying very hard not to be. He was intrigued by that struggle and vaguely respectful of it. But, as she stood there toying with the button closing the lapel between her breasts, he was more aware of how her subtle sensuality taunted him—and how difficult it would be to ignore it if she stayed around much longer. He was sure that neither her father nor her uncle would be too pleased to know that.

Not sure of what else to say, knowing he owed her this much, he finally mumbled, "I'm sorry."

She shrugged and gave him a smile that was far more understanding than Cain figured he deserved. "Don't worry about it. Just let me know if you need me. I work at the flower shop and don't close up until five o'clock, but I'm available most any time after that."

He started to tell her that he'd think about it and get back to her. He would have, too, if he hadn't also become aware of something else in the moments before her soothing smile faded.

He really should ask her to leave—for her sake as well as his. But it was easier to be in the house when she was in it, too. Something about her presence seemed to remove some of its shadows.

"Are you available now?"

Chapter Three

N_{ow?"}

The surprise in Ellie's voice was obscured somewhat by her reluctance. She'd thought for sure that if Cain did happen to accept her offer, he wouldn't want to begin until tomorrow at the earliest. By then, she'd have had time to figure out why she wasn't running as far from this man as possible. He was dangerous, and not just because everyone she knew thought him so.

He was dangerous because something about him increased the nagging restlessness she'd experienced lately. She had no idea why he should affect her in such a way, or why that effect should have taken hold so quickly. Maybe it was just that ever-present tension she sensed in him. Or maybe, more practically, she thought, it was just the heat. From the time she was sixteen years old, hot summer nights had always made her restless.

"You said yourself there's a lot to be done," he reminded her. "And I've only got a few days."

She had a way of looking at him that was at once bold and incredibly shy. "Do you think that will be long enough?"

"It's the best I can do. I left in the middle of a project."

Cain raked his hand through his hair, the gesture an outward expression of the strain he felt. He could take more time if he had to. Carlo wouldn't mind. But the sooner he finished up his business and got out of this town, the better off he'd be. He'd managed to fend off the old ghosts with a little rationality. He wasn't so sure that they wouldn't appear again. Aside from that, watching Ellie play with the button on her blouse was creating thoughts that could definitely get him into trouble.

The top she wore was way too big to tell how full her breasts were, and that in itself was oddly provocative. Her hips were slender, their shape more or less concealed by the fullness of her cotton skirt, but her waist was tiny, nearly small enough to be spanned by his hands. She was fine boned and fragile, the top of her head coming just to his shoulders. She would fit him perfectly, he was sure.

The room was already warm from the heat of the day. Evening had come, but at the moment, the air felt even warmer.

"Besides," he said, deliberately dragging his gaze from where it had settled on her mouth, "it'd give me something to do for the next few hours. I never can get to sleep before midnight." A resigned smile moved into his eyes. "Actually, it's more like one or two o'clock and even that's optimistic in this heat. How about it? Can you start now?"

Ellie would have bet her life that it wasn't easy for Cain to drop his guard. He was still careful to let her know by the caution in his expression that he didn't regard her as someone completely worthy of his confidence—if anyone truly was—but he certainly seemed more approachable than he had moments ago. He seemed to want her company. Despite the improvement in his attitude, however, Ellie had the feeling that he'd choke on the words before he'd admit as much.

"Did you bring any boxes?"

Slowly, Cain shook his head.

"Do you know where you want to start?"

Again he shook his head.

"Do you know what you want to do with any of this stuff?"

This time he shrugged.

"You really do need help, don't you?"

"I guess so." He smiled, a full-blown smile that made her feel very pleased with herself for causing it. It took the harshness from his features, and made her all too aware of how very susceptible she could be to him. "What do you suggest?"

That I leave right now, she said to herself. What she told him, though, was that, first, they should see if there were any boxes in the basement or the garage. "And we'll need newspapers," she added, starting toward the back door. "There's a stack out here."

It quickly became apparent that Ellie was more familiar with Cain's own home than he was. She knew where to find the tape and a felt pen to mark the boxes and how to unstick the knob on the portable fan to make it run on medium speed instead of high. When Cain asked how she knew how to fix the temperamental machine, she told him that she'd seen his mother do the same thing while they were making jam last June. One of the regulars at the tavern had given Amanda several flats of strawberries, Ellie explained as they carted their supplies into the small dining room. She and his mom had been awake half the night putting up the preserves. The heat from all the boiling kettles had made the kitchen even warmer than it was now, and that poor fan had been working overtime.

Despite his interest, Cain's tone was casual. "How long have you been living here? Above the garage, I mean."

Ellie sat on her heels in front of the china cabinet, tucking her skirt between her legs to keep it out of the way. Pulling over one of the boxes she'd found in the basement, she began wrapping dishes in newspaper. "A year last month. I found the ad for the apartment on the grocery store bulletin board the day I moved back from Tulsa."

Cain started clearing out the top shelves while she worked on the bottom ones. Because conversation made it easier to ignore his proximity, she went on to tell him how, because she didn't have a car, she'd needed someplace within walking distance of the flower shop. As small as Aubrey was, it was nonetheless a farming town. Except for the few places off Main Street where the community businesses were located, homes tended to be spread out, not clumped together as they were in the city. There weren't many places available close in and she couldn't afford to rent a big house—not that she wanted one. The tiny studio apartment suited her just fine.

"Couldn't you find a job in Tulsa?"

From the detached way Cain asked the question, it seemed to Ellie that he was only doing his bit to keep up the conversation. She appreciated the contribution. "I had one. I was a secretary at a dance conservatory." Her sigh was soft and wistful. "It was a great job." And the best part was that her own classes had been free.

The motions above her stopped. Tipping her head back, she saw Cain frowning down at her. His lack of comprehension was most obvious. So was his opinion of Aubrey when she heard the edge in his voice. "Then why did you move back *here*?"

"'Here' isn't such a bad place," she told him, feeling entitled to let him know her opinion, too. "But I came back because my aunt needed help with the shop." For several seconds, she stared down at the pattern of pink roses and green leaves on the cup she held. "I really didn't want to leave Tulsa, but Aunt Jo's arthritis was making it hard for her to work. And I really don't mind it here," Ellie explained, since regrets tended to diminish the things a person did have. "She never came out and asked if I'd move back, but Mom had been hinting around about it ever since my divorce. And every time I'd come home, I'd see how much harder it was getting for Aunt Jo to handle the shop...."

"Back up a minute." Holding a turkey-shaped soup tureen that Cain recalled his mother having bought at a garage sale years ago, he stared down at the top of Ellie's head. "You were married?"

She frowned up at him, less appreciative of his tone than of the interruption. "You sound as if you find it hard to believe someone would want to marry me."

"I think a man could want any number of things with you," he returned bluntly. He set the tureen back on the shelf. Lowering himself beside her, he let his glance roam shamelessly from her waist to her shoulders. "I just didn't think you'd have had time to go through a marriage already. How old are you?"

"Old enough to be offered a beer," she mumbled.

"Twenty-one?" he ventured, though he'd actually have put her a year or two younger than that. Her age really didn't matter. He was just curious.

"Twenty-four."

Ellie already knew that Cain was six years older than she or she'd have returned the pointed question. Feeling a totally unfamiliar streak of perversity, she almost did anyway. She was otherwise occupied, though, curious as to what conclusions he was drawing as his eyes narrowed on her face.

He seemed to be looking at her a little more closely than he had before, as if to find evidence of the years he'd missed. She supposed that, thanks to her mother's English ancestry and the good skin she'd inherited from her, she did look a little young, particularly when she didn't wear makeup. She knew from Amanda that Cain moved in much faster circles than she did, so to him, she supposed, she might even appear a little juvenile. Especially with her hair caught up in a barrette and wearing clothes that no longer fit as they should. She'd lost a little weight in the past year, mostly in places she could ill afford it. Everything she owned was a little loose—and terribly unsophisticated. Her ex-husband had often pointed out that deficiency.

Cain's first impressions of Ellie still remained. There was a freshness about her that appealed to him, a kind of unpracticed femininity that belied her years. He liked that he didn't have to look through a screen of paint to see the fine grain of her skin, and that her hair actually moved when she moved her head. Or maybe more logically, he thought, what he was seeing was simply a woman who wasn't as jaded as others he knew.

Actually, he was surprised to find himself as attracted as he was. He had really never paid much attention to what the guys at the plant called "wholesome" women, the kind the television showed feeding peanut butter to little kids. They were a foreign breed of females as far as he was concerned, and he'd had little contact with that variety as he moved within the male-dominated circles of racing. There, he tended to encounter groupies, or bored socialites who were looking for a fleeting diversion. That was okay. More worldly women appealed to him, those who knew the score and didn't get a relationship all tangled up with talk of a future. To Cain, the future never extended beyond the next morning.

"I still find it hard to believe that you're divorced," he said, because she seemed to lack the bitterness and cynicism of the divorced people he'd come across.

He was convinced of that lack when he heard her quiet "Me, too."

There was agreement in her words, and regret. It was the regret that touched him.

"Do you still care about him?"

Without hesitation, she shook her head. "No. I don't think I'd really cared for a long time. I'd just thought that marriage was supposed to be for forever. I didn't expect it to be perfect, but I thought that two people promised to love and to cherish and then they lived together until death did them part. I guess I was too young at the time to know that it didn't always work out that way."

She absently ran her finger over the handle of the cup. Her fingers were long and slender, her nails neat and unpolished. Delicate, Cain thought, liking the way the word fit her. "That happens sometimes, I guess."

Glancing away, he frowned at himself. What was he saying? He didn't know anything about marriage.

"It wasn't supposed to happen to me. I was supposed to have tried harder."

The self-blame underlying her disillusionment could be heard as clearly as the ticking of the grandfather clock over the whir of the fan. Cain, intimately familiar with that particular feeling, felt himself take a mental step away from her. His empathy for someone he scarcely knew startled him. It also made him terribly wary. Harsh emotions were familiar to him. He wasn't at all sure how to deal with the softer ones, those that involved caring and sympathy. More important, he wasn't even sure he *wanted* to deal with them. They seemed much more complicated.

He might have increased the distance he'd created in the literal sense if Ellie hadn't smiled at him just then. It was a gentle smile, considering the determination behind it, and its power was strong enough to make Cain want to stay right where he was. Something about her wouldn't let him pull any farther away from her. Maybe it was the bittersweet softness of that smile. Or maybe it was just that she was here helping him when she didn't have to be. Whatever it was, he knew he was growing more curious about her by the minute.

Because of that, he turned his attention back to the packing. "I can't believe how ugly this thing is," he muttered, picking up the turkey tureen again. "I think I'll just throw it away."

"Don't do that. Somebody might want it."

"Who'd want this?"

Ellie thoughtfully considered the brown and orange object with the bright red ceramic comb and yellow ceramic beak. "Well, your mom obviously did. Someone else might, too." Just because something wasn't to her taste—and, obviously, Cain's—didn't mean that it might not appeal to someone else. "If you don't want to keep it, put it in another box with whatever else you don't want and have a yard sale."

"I don't know what I'm doing with any of this yet." He stuffed the turkey into an empty box. Later, he'd figure out what to do with it. "But I do know I'm not having a yard sale."

He sounded agitated. A moment later, he replaced his agitation with resignation. His curiosity refused to be ignored.

"Was he from around here?"

Newspaper crackled as she wrapped another plate. The noise stopped at his question. "He?" she asked, then realized whom Cain meant. "Oh, Brent, you mean. Yes, he was. His family has a farm out by Cross Creek. The Hansons."

"Hanson," he repeated, but he wasn't trying to connect the name with a face. "If you were married, why do you go by the name *Bennett*?"

The shrug of her shoulders was deceptively casual. "Because that's who I am. If I'd kept his last name, people would tend to think of me as Brent's ex-wife instead of Stu and Claire's daughter, or just as who I am. Plain old Ellie Bennett." She blew a strand of hair out of her eyes and reached for another plate. "Did you know Brent?"

She was neither plain nor old, but Cain kept that thought to himself as he told her he didn't and emptied the rest of the shelf. The name meant nothing to him. That wasn't surprising, though. He hadn't been at all close to the kids he'd grown up with, and it sounded as if this Brent Hanson was nearer to Ellie's age than his own. Cain hadn't paid any attention to the younger kids at all.

"He was a big football star." Shaking her head, she rolled her eyes to the ceiling. "Everyone thought he was Mr. Wonderful. I guess I thought he was pretty wonderful, too," she added, remembering how ardently he'd pursued her. "He was so sweet to me before we were married and so...anxious."

The way she hesitated over that last word caused Cain's eyebrows to rise in speculation. "Anxious as in always trying to get you into bed?"

"Actually, it was the back seat of his dad's car. But he made me feel like I was the only woman in the world for him . . . until we got married."

Ellie had no idea why she was telling Cain this, other than the fact that he seemed willing to listen. Maybe there was some truth to the theory that it was easier to talk to a stranger than to someone you knew. With a stranger, you didn't have to worry about what they thought of you because you didn't know the person well enough yourself to care about his opinion. Or maybe she found Cain easy to confide in because she knew that, like her, he was a little less than perfect.

Whatever the reason, she found herself telling him things she'd never breathed to another living soul. Not even Jennifer Johnson, who had been privy to her most intimate secrets until her secrets had become too personal to share. Jennifer, like just about everyone else who knew Brent, had idolized him. He was the town's golden boy, the fair-haired son of a respected family, and everyone knew he was going places. His match with Ellie was considered perfect because of her family's status in the community, and for a while, she supposed it was. They'd moved to Tulsa where he attended college on an athletic scholarship. No longer subject to the scrutiny one lives with in a small town, he soon decided that Ellie wasn't quite good enough for him.

So it was Cain who heard about how Brent had met another woman in one of his classes shortly after school started, and how that woman had been replaced with another the following year. By the time the china closet was packed Ellie had admitted that her husband finally decided he'd been too limited in his experience to know what he really wanted when they got married and asked for a divorce. He'd changed his major from agriculture to law. Ellie's family had been thrilled with the prospect of her being a lawyer's wife, but Brent felt she was too unsophisticated for the role. There hadn't been a thing she could do to save her marriage at that point; nor had she wanted to.

Unfortunately, being a Bennett, she was expected to set an example in the community—and never admit to failure. As her Uncle Hal had pointed out, no other member of the family had bailed out of a marriage after only five years.

"Why did you stay with him that long if he was cheating on you?"

Cain's question was one she hadn't even considered until it had all been over. "Sometimes I think it was because I felt I didn't have any other option. I was expected to stay with him, so I did."

"Didn't you tell anyone what was going on?"

"Not really. My mom sensed that we were having trouble, but she said most people had problems the first few years and that it would get better eventually." She'd tried so hard to understand what Brent wanted so she could give it to him. She'd even tried changing herself, and when that hadn't worked, she'd tried changing him. That had been a mistake. "Some times were less bad than others, but it really never got better. When he finally got around to telling me he wanted out, I was actually relieved. I think that's what bothered everyone the most. I was supposed to be broken up about it and I wasn't."

Cain considered her for a moment. "Maybe they'd have understood if you'd told them what he'd done. At the very least you'd have made it less easy for him."

"Tried to get even, you mean?" Is that what you did when someone hurt you? she wondered, feeling oddly certain that he had. It was not in her nature to strike back, but she supposed that to some it might be their only defense. "If I'd told them about his running around, it would have hurt me more than him. Besides, it wasn't anyone's business but mine."

"You might get away with that attitude in the city, but in a place like this . . ."

He didn't have to finish the sentence for Ellie to know what he meant. Little was sacred in a town where everyone knew everyone else and where one of the major forms of recreation was finding out who'd done what to whom.

"Is it enough for you?" he heard himself ask. "Living back here now?"

Cain had no idea why he wanted to know that. Certainly what she did with her life was no concern of his, and she did seem to have particular areas of herself that were definitely not open to public view. Yet now, with him, she was open. Perhaps more open than she intended to be, and he felt compelled to take advantage of that before she decided that her answer was really none of his business.

It didn't occur to Ellie to guard her response. She'd already told Cain far more than was probably wise. "I miss the city a little," she admitted, minimizing her yearning for the color and excitement she'd discovered there. She loved Aubrey. She truly did. Yet ever since her return last year, she'd experienced a vague dissatisfaction with what she had, though she had basically everything she needed. It was terribly unfair of Cain to make her think of that now. "My family is here, and my friends. That's what's important."

He dismissed her conclusion. "Do you ever want anything else?"

She had. Once. "No."

It was immediately clear that she couldn't look someone in the eye and lie. The instant before she'd spoken, she'd looked away from him.

"What is it?" he asked.

Having been caught, she gave him a sheepish smile. What she had wanted had been given up so long ago that it didn't even matter anymore. The dream was gone. In its place was an indefinable yearning, a kind of longing that was totally without a shape or a name. The intense way Cain waited for her to answer made it clear that he wanted her to give it one.

Her tone was subdued, her expression almost wistful. "More."

The dark line of his eyebrows drew together.

"I can't really explain it," she said, wondering if he was going to get the exasperated look that had creased her father's face when she'd answered his question the same way. "I just want . . . more."

There was no impatience in Cain's expression, only a little reluctance before he quietly said, "I think I know what you mean."

Ellie met the conviction in his eyes. He understood. Somehow, he really knew how frustrating it was to want something that defied definition. And how powerless a person felt when there were people who thought you foolish for wanting in the first place.

At that moment, she didn't feel quite so alone—though before that moment she hadn't realized how often she felt that way—and she let her smile thank him for that. Somehow, it made it a little easier to know she wasn't the only one who questioned the status quo, even if it didn't change anything. "It's easier just to go along, isn't it? To do what others expect of you."

Years ago, Cain wouldn't have believed this conversation possible. Ellie's kind had been off-limits to him. By Aubrey standards, she probably still was. But Cain hadn't operated within those puritanical social parameters for a long time now, and the man he'd become wanted very much to remove the hint of defeat that dulled the vibrancy of this intriguing woman's smile. She'd failed the family standards, and in doing that, she'd set herself apart from them. He had the feeling that she might be rebelling a little in other ways, too. Or, perhaps she wanted to, but didn't know how. Ellie, Cain was certain, had been raised to conform.

He took a step closer. All he had to do was reach out and he could pull her to him. He didn't trust himself with the gesture, though. The thought of feeling her soft curves against him, of breathing in the clean scent of her gleaming auburn hair, already had him tightening with need. As off balance as he'd felt all day, he knew he'd be better off not touching her at all.

Besides, offering comfort was something he'd never done before. He wasn't even sure he knew how, or if she would want to accept his reassurance. It wasn't a risk he was willing to take.

"Doing something just because it's expected of you is a lousy reason," he told her, consciously changing his focus from her mouth. Soft. It looked so incredibly soft. "When you do that, you're acting under someone else's idea of what's best for you ... or of what you even are. You've got to be true to yourself, because in the long run, you're the one who has to live with you."

For a few scattered moments, Ellie could have sworn that Cain had been about to touch her. She would have accepted his touch quite gratefully at that moment, because at that moment it had seemed very right. But that time had passed as quickly as it had arisen and all she could do now was try to ignore the disappointment that lingered in its place.

"I think that's why I thought so much of your mother," she told him. Being true to one's self sometimes meant bucking convention and that took a kind of courage Ellie lacked. Amanda had had that courage, but it had borne a certain price. "She did what she thought was right."

Ellie had no way of knowing what thought she had just triggered. She knew only that Cain grew ominously quiet in the moments before he turned away from her. Whatever it was he was thinking about was not going to be shared.

He picked up the boxes they hadn't used, and after adding them to the stack by the wall, he collected the stray bits of newspaper from the floor and put them in the trash by the back door. A few seconds later, he recrossed the kitchen.

"It's after eleven," she heard him say as the sound of running tap water joined the tick of the clock. Through the doorway of the dining room, she could see him at the sink washing the newsprint off his hands. "I know you've got to work tomorrow, so I'd better let you go. Besides," he added, sounding only half-teasing when he shut off the water and grabbed a towel, "it wouldn't do your reputation much good if someone saw you leaving here much later than this. Thanks for the help."

He wanted her to leave. Now. He couldn't have made that any clearer if he'd tried.

Chapter Four

Jennifer Johnson had changed her mind four times in the past five minutes. And four times in the past five minutes, Ellie had fought to stifle a yawn as the woman she'd known practically since birth tried to decide what kind of floral arrangements to purchase for her parents' twenty-fifth wedding anniversary party. Ellie wasn't necessarily bored with Jennifer's indecision. She was just tired.

It had taken her longer than usual to get to sleep last night. She'd been too agitated to lie watching the moon play hide-and-seek with the clouds, so she'd stayed at the barre attached to her wall until well after one o'clock, when the strain and pull of well-disciplined muscles had finally left her exhausted—and thoughts of an enigmatic man with smoky-gray eyes had finally been forgotten.

"The tablecloths at the Grange Hall are all white, so it doesn't really matter what color the flowers are," Jennifer mumbled, flipping though a catalog of flower arrangements for ideas. "I just don't want pink. Pink is...dull. What do you think about red? Red roses," she went on, suddenly inspired by a picture of an elaborate centerpiece. "*That* would be gorgeous."

"It would also be expensive." Ellie pulled the book across the counter, absently wondering if Cain had still been asleep when she left for work this morning. There hadn't been a breath of movement in the house when she walked down the driveway to the sidewalk more than an hour ago. "You wanted a large arrangement for the buffet and baskets for the tables, plus corsages for your mom and the ladies pouring coffee."

"And Lucille," Jennifer remembered. "Can't forget my sister-in-law. She's in charge of the guest book."

"That's four corsages," Ellie said, changing the number on the order pad. "If you mean to stick to your budget, you might want to think about using red carnations for the tables and the roses for corsages."

She looked at the slightly pudgy brunette, who never made up her mind easily about anything, and saw her frowning down at a picture. For a moment, Ellie thought about acting on a standing invitation and inviting herself over to Jennifer's tomorrow night for dinner. Then she decided against it. All Jennifer ever talked about was what diet she was on this particular week, the current price of grain, fertilizer and irrigation equipment, and her two-year-old daughter. Jennifer had been on a diet since third grade so Ellie was accustomed to that, and she adored Jennifer's little girl. But not trying to lose weight herself, not being in the farming business and not having a child of her own didn't leave her and her old friend with much in common anymore.

The friendship wasn't at all what it once had been, and at times Ellie really missed not having someone around to confide it. Not, she reminded herself with a mental sigh, that she had any great confidences to share.

Knowing it would take a while for Jennifer to respond to her suggestion, Ellie looked beyond Jennifer's shoulder to the large display windows that faced Main Street. The silk floral displays there were low enough that they didn't obstruct the view. Between the arched blue letters spelling out Jo's Flower and Gift Shop on the glass, it was easy enough to see what was taking place on the street. There wasn't much activity out there, a normal circumstance for the time of day and week. A few people wandered by, hurrying through their errands before the heat of the day. For the most part, the faces were familiar. In a town this small, it was rare to see someone you didn't know or whose face you hadn't seen before.

It occurred to Ellie that it was a typically unremarkable Tuesday—in all respects but one. Ever since she'd come back to Aubrey she'd tended to concentrate only on the present, to live each moment as it came. It was easier that way. There were no disappointments when one didn't anticipate; no restless yearnings for "more." Yet ever since she met Cain, an odd sense of expectancy had robbed her of that serenity.

Even as the thought registered, anticipation charged her pulse. Dickerson's Market was directly across the street. Parked between a gray pickup truck Ellie didn't recognize and a blue one that she did was a squat, racy black coupé. There would be only one owner of that car.

Her thought was confirmed seconds later when Cain emerged from the market's wide door carrying several empty boxes.

"I'll just come back later," she heard Jennifer say. "The folks' anniversary is two months off yet, so I've got plenty of time." Picking up the sack containing the purchases she'd made at the dress shop next door, she redirected her frown to see what Ellie was staring at.

"I wonder who that is," was her blunt reaction to the stranger.

Feigning nonchalance, though she wasn't at all certain why pretending indifference was so necessary, Ellie said, "Amanda Whitlow's son." She turned her attention to repositioning the catalog on its standing rack. "He got here yesterday."

Jennifer remained turned to the window, her interest obviously piqued. "My, my. He's really an eyeful, isn't he?"

"He's all right, I guess."

"You always did have a gift for understatement." Craning her neck to get a better look at Cain, Jennifer didn't notice how quickly Ellie had looked away. She was more concerned with dragging up whatever she could recall having heard about him. "It's really a pity he had to turn out so rotten."

"We don't know that he has, Jennifer. He's been gone for a long time." There was an edge of challenge in Ellie's tone. The woman busily appraising Cain and his car was oblivious. "It could be that he isn't what everyone remembers."

"Could be he's worse."

"Oh, come on," Ellie prodded, convinced she was only playing devil's advocate. It was impossible to think that a man like Cain Whitlow would need her to defend him, yet she felt compelled to do just that. "All you and I really know is what we've heard other people say. You couldn't remember much more about him than I do, and all I remember is that he had a fast car."

"Looks like he still does." Moving over by the greeting card racks, Jennifer sought a better view as Cain stacked the boxes in the passenger seat of his car. Its doors didn't open out as they did on most vehicles, but forward and up. "I wonder how long he's going to be here."

"Not long. He just came back to sell his mother's house."

"You've talked to him? Oh, geez, that's right! You're renting from Amanda Whitlow. Or from him, now, I guess. Do you have to move?"

"I don't know yet."

Jennifer looked terribly conspiratorial all of a sudden. "I know you've never said much about her, but didn't you think it kind of strange that she never left her house except to go to work? No one ever saw her in town here. Well, hardly ever, anyway. But she must have had men friends. At least one, anyway." She paused for a few seconds, waiting to see if Ellie was going to catch the hint and contribute anything. When no information was forthcoming, she leaned idly against the end of the partyware rack. "My mother said Amanda had another child a few years after her husband walked out on her. No one knew who the father was, though."

Ellie had heard about that second child, too. Everyone had. Just as everyone knew that Amanda had given the baby up. Ellie was not, however, going to talk about Amanda, even if it was quite apparent that Jennifer would have loved it if she'd indulge her.

Amanda had been a proud woman, and to the people in town, Ellie supposed she had seemed rather aloof and cool. She'd certainly seemed that way to Ellie at first. But Ellie had the feeling that Cain's mother had developed that toughness as a form of protection. It stood to reason that a person would develop a thick hide when she was constantly forced to stand up for herself—especially after some of the decisions she'd been forced to make.

Ellie had come to know Amanda over the past year only by piecing together fragments of their conversations. But she knew that only two things had mattered to her after her husband walked out: her son and her home. She'd thought about taking in laundry, or trying to get a job at the five-and-dime, but she couldn't make enough money to keep the house that way. So she had gone to work in a tavern on the highway to Greely because it paid better. Women who took such jobs weren't spoken of too kindly in a town that carefully cultivated its conservative roots. But Amanda had held her head up and done what she'd felt she had to do to provide for herself and her son—even if it hadn't exactly ingratiated her with the rest of the community.

"Have you thought about blue?" she suddenly asked, fully expecting Jennifer's incomprehension. "I could spray daisies blue and arrange them with baby's breath."

The chime over the door interrupted Ellie's blatantly transparent change of subject. The United Parcel Service driver with his weekly delivery of flowers from the wholesaler stuck his head inside the door to offer his usual "How's it going, Ellie?" Then he shouldered his way through with two long boxes. "Got a couple more for you out in the truck. Think one of them is those vases you've been waiting for."

At the interruption, Jennifer sighed in defeat. She told Ellie she'd think about the carnations, but liked the idea of the roses better, then headed out the door with the promise that she'd get back to her soon. She knew Ellie was never much fun when it came to gossip, so there was no point in hanging around any longer.

Ellie thought it didn't bode well, though, that Jennifer took off in the direction of her sister-in-law's beauty shop over on the next block. Lucille was the biggest gossip in town.

Knowing that nothing could get more tangled than the Aubrey grapevine, Ellie pushed her pen into the pocket of the green apron she wore over her pink shirtwaist and resignedly told the driver that she'd help him bring in the rest of the delivery. Jennifer wasn't the first person to have wanted to talk about Cain this morning. No doubt half the town knew of his arrival already. Ellie had barely made it down the driveway on her way to work when Hanna had waved her over to ask whose car was parked under the cottonwood. Hanna's son had kept her out late last night at a bingo game, and she hadn't noticed Cain's car until this morning.

After the elderly woman had learned who owned the car, she'd spent ten minutes recounting the number of times in the old days Cain had awakened her with his screeching and squirreling around and the awful noise he'd make when he revved his car's engine while working on it in the driveway. Hanna would have been pleased to expand her story to twenty minutes if Ellie hadn't interrupted to tell her she was already late for work.

"Oh, I do go on, don't I?" Hanna had observed before sending Ellie off with a warning to "Be careful around that Whitlow boy."

Cain was hardly a boy. But now, as Ellie followed the driver to his big brown van parked at the curb, she thought it wouldn't hurt to heed the woman's advice. Ellie wasn't concerned that Cain, with his less than acceptable reputation, might harm her. She had to be careful about herself. Her glance slid cautiously toward his car. She'd seen him go back inside the market a while ago and he'd yet to come out.

"I know there's another one back here," she heard the driver mutter from inside the van. The sound of packages being shifted joined his instruction to "Just hang on a second."

Ellie started to tell him that she wasn't in any rush. But as she opened her mouth, she caught sight of Cain again and the words died away with her slowly released breath. He had a paper bag in one arm and gripped an empty box in his other hand. Where he was going to put them in that low-slung car, already full of boxes, she had no idea. Nor would she waste any energy trying to figure it out. He'd seen her and now that he had, some of the purpose seemed to fall from his stride.

The glimpse she'd caught of him earlier had been oddly unsettling. The sight of him now was jarring in a way she couldn't begin to explain. There was more to its impact than just the way his superbly formed physique filled out his black T-shirt and faded jeans. It had more to do with the bridled aggression he packed into his long-legged strides, and how his tension seemed to snake through the warm morning air. Even at that distance, she could clearly see his expression. Judging from the way he hesitated, he must have seen how still her own features had become.

He took another step toward his car, still watching her as he put his bag through the open window. Ellie thought he might smile, or at least nod to her. But there was no outward acknowledgment in his actions, and no familiarity to encourage a friendly wave or a greeting.

Had Ellie not reacted so oddly to him, she would already have called out a bright "Good morning," as she would have to anyone else she'd recognized. She was glad she hadn't now. There was nothing inviting in his expression as his glance shifted past her shoulder, returning briefly to her face before he looked away. He acted very much as if he hadn't seen her at all when, a moment later, he climbed into his car.

It was scarcely two seconds before Ellie realized she hadn't been the only one watching Cain. "I'd heard he was back," came the terse observation from behind her.

"Here it is!" The brown-uniformed driver appeared with the box just as Ellie turned to see Bernice Pruitt, the mercantile owner's wife, give her perfectly coiffed head a disgusted shake. Preferring to ignore the woman's comment, Ellie offered only a hurried "Hi, Bernice," before occupying herself with the task of signing for the packages and telling the deliveryman that she'd see him next week.

The van was already pulling from the curb when she started back into the shop with the two small boxes. Already one step ahead of her, the matronly woman graciously held open the door.

"Jennifer said he got here yesterday." Bernice shook her head again, her graying eyebrows pinched, much like the rest of her features. "It's downright shameful that he didn't show up once in fifteen years to see his mother, and now that she's dead, he's back to take all of her things."

Ellie shot the officious woman a quelling glance. Bernice's sympathy for Amanda was a little too sudden to be taken seriously. "It's been thirteen years," she corrected, telling herself she was only setting the record straight for Amanda's sake. Not for Cain's. Why should she defend him when he'd all but ignored her a few moments ago? And dismissed her so abruptly last night?

Just forget about it, she commanded herself, refusing to let him confuse her any more than she already was, and pulled the shipping invoices off the newly arrived boxes. With any luck, one of the packages contained the nursery vases she'd ordered.

"Thirteen, fifteen." Bernice was not going to be put off. "What's the difference?"

"Two years," Ellie replied, then nearly groaned out loud when she saw Lucille, still in the pink-flowered plastic apron she wore to do dye jobs, come rushing through the door.

In a town that thrived on gossip, Ellie was something of a misfit. She would talk to anyone about books or movies or flowers or whatever else they wanted to discuss, so long as the conversation didn't turn to judging the lives of people she knew. People had reasons for doing what they did, and often those reasons could be known only to themselves. Often, too, those reasons could never really be explained—or accepted by those content to sit in judgment. No one wanted to hear that kind of rationale, though.

Bernice and Lucille weren't the only ladies who left the flower shop that morning disappointed that they lacked an exclusive to share with their neighbors. But that didn't stop them from passing on that they'd talked to Ellie, who had spoken with Cain because he was now her landlord. Ellie could only surmise that being able to say they'd talked with her gave them a certain credibility over those who hadn't. It also seemed to give that elite group an exclusive option on advice.

"You don't want to associate with him any more than you absolutely have to," was the common and urgent theme.

In exchange for that well-intentioned interference, everyone got the same response. She could have said that the warnings were unnecessary, since he was making it abundantly clear that he didn't want to associate with her. But that would have required an explanation she didn't care to offer. Instead, she offered another equally honest and much simpler reply. "I've barely met the man. I'm not going to be rude to him."

When the next person stopped by to ask if it was true that Cain Whitlow was back, they got the same answer everyone else had. Ellie said that he was here to sell Amanda's house and, to be fair—since she couldn't ignore how he'd patiently listened to her ramble on last night—that the man was rather nicer than she'd heard he'd be.

That opinion met with more than one pair of raised eyebrows. Ellie figured it was also what brought her uncle into the shop just a few minutes before she was due to close. He'd heard what she'd told everyone else.

Hal Bennett was the archetypal county sheriff. At fifty-five, he had the experience to back his air of superiority and enough years ahead of him to ensure that no one thought him too old for his job. Tall and trim in his tan uniform, Mountie-style hat and the reflective sunglasses Ellie hated, he had a way of staring down at a person that could make him feel very small and insignificant. Hal Bennett was the law in and around Aubrey, and everyone knew it. What a lot of people didn't know was that there wasn't anything more important to him than family. Grandpa Bennett had died back when the three Bennett boys were still children, and Hal, being the oldest, had taken charge. It was a position he still maintained.

Dropping his hat on the back counter where Ellie was trimming the stems of the gladioli that had been delivered that morning, Hall took off his glasses and drew his fingers through his thick, iron-gray hair. Her father was three years younger and she had noted lately that his hair was already thinner than Hal's. Hal wouldn't have tolerated that sign of aging.

"Understand you've got a new landlord, Ellie." His manner was offhand, but Ellie knew him too well to think the statement casual. "What's he said to you?"

"Not much," she returned, maintaining the same quiescence she had all day. "I just met him last night. Do you want some pop? There're a couple of cans in the fridge in back."

"Save 'em for yourself. What do you think of him?"

In many ways she found Cain more intriguing than anyone she'd ever met, but her uncle would not be pleased with that answer. She wasn't too pleased with it herself. She chose to ignore the question.

"Why is everyone so concerned about Cain Whitlow? He's been the only topic of conversation all day." And for the most part, the only thought on her mind. "Doesn't anyone care about anything else?"

A small smile tipped up the corner of Hal's mustache. He seemed to have accepted her response as boredom with the subject, a position that suited Ellie just fine.

"Whitlow upset a lot of people when he was a kid. This whole town was relieved when he left, and now everybody's just a little worried that he might cause trouble again. We don't want his kind around here. If he just settles up his business and gets on his way, I'm sure everything will be just fine. In the meantime," he went on, polishing his sunglasses on his handkerchief, "he gives Lucille something to talk about. We were all getting a little tired of hearing about how Art barely survived his hernia operation."

Ellie had to smile at that. Art was Lucille's husband. Judging from the fact that the man had returned home the day after his surgery, there was little credibility to Lucille's assertion that his life had hung in the balance right up to the moment he was discharged.

"But a word of advice, honey," her uncle went on as Ellie turned her smile to the last of the brilliant orange gladioli. "Don't forget who he is. You've always had a soft spot for strays, and this Whitlow character is a little like that wandering tomcat you took in when you were a kid. You remember that old tomcat, don't you?"

Her nod indicated that she did.

"Do you remember how sweet he was when you fed him and how he'd curl up by your back door and wait for you to bring his milk?"

"Uh-huh."

"And how badly he scratched you when you picked him up to try and pet him?"

Three faint white lines on the inside of her arm were a permanent reminder of that encounter. She'd been eleven when that happened and hadn't seen that stray since. "I'm not going to get scratched, Uncle Hal."

"I just want to make sure. I know you, Ellie, and from what I've been hearing, you're all but standing up for Whitlow. I know you befriended his mother, and though none of us liked the idea, we did see where renting that place from her made some sense... to you, anyway," he qualified. "Her son's a whole 'nother matter. Your Aunt Jo and I talked and we'd feel a lot better if you'd come over to the house and stay with us while he's here. I know your mom and dad would feel the same way if they knew what was going on."

Ellie's father was at an annual educational administrators' convention in Austin. Because he always took her mother with him, and they always took the week following the convention as their vacation, they weren't due back until her Uncle Jay's birthday in two weeks. Ellie, knowing how her mother could worry about the smallest things, was suddenly very grateful for their absence.

"There's nothing going on, Uncle Hal. And as for staying with you, it simply isn't necessary." Dropping the last flower into a green plastic bucket of water, she set the container into the cooler beside the front counter. Now that that was done, she could lock up and go home. "I'm fine right where I am. Is Aunt Jo coming in tomorrow?"

Hal reached for his hat. "I have no idea." His glance was shrewd and assessing. He was not about to let her change the subject. "One more thing, Ellie. I'd be having your mother saying this to you if she was in town, but since she isn't, I'll have to do it myself. You've never met a man like this Whitlow character before. I know his type, and given that you're a real pretty little gal, who's been living alone for a while now... well, his kind knows how to spot a vulnerable female. Be careful around him.''

Her quiet ''I will'' brought a look of relief to his face. Ellie would be true to her word. Her family expected her to act with caution around the man, therefore she would. If there was some difference between their idea of what she should be cautious about and her own, well, that couldn't be helped.

''Oh, before I go,'' Hal said, preparing to do just that while she hung up her apron and locked the receipts for the day in the wall safe, ''one of the reasons I stopped by was to see what Whitlow's planning on doing with all the stuff in the house. You know, the furniture and clothes and all that. If he says anything to you about it, let me know, will you?''

Ellie didn't think her uncle's interest in Amanda's possessions particularly curious. Every Labor Day the lodge held an auction to benefit the disadvantaged children of the area—mostly the offspring of the migrant workers who lived on the outskirts of town. As he had been for the past several years, Hal was on the organizational committee that collected usable goods for the event. He obviously had the auction in mind. Ellie thought the cause was a good one, if Cain would be inclined to donate some things to charity.

With the thought of mentioning that to Cain, Ellie approached the back door of Amanda's house a little less than an hour later. It was apparent from the number of empty boxes Cain had collected and left stacked on the stoop that he planned on getting the packing project underway. He hadn't asked her to come back and help him with it, though. And she wasn't going to offer again.

She tapped on the screen-door frame. After the pointed way he'd ignored her this morning and how he'd all but pushed her out the door last night to be rid of her, she'd have to be slightly daft to think he wanted to see her. She'd make it quick.

The knock was so faint that the sound barely registered. Even then, Cain didn't acknowledge it. He was too lost in his examination of what he'd found to realize that the tapping was on his door.

He stood in the far corner of the basement, in the section that had once been curtained off as his room. The bed was still there, only now it was piled with boxes. Tacked to the pale blue walls were curling pictures of cars he'd torn from hot rod magazines; old cars, bulky and prehistoric compared to what was on the road now, but new when he'd put them up. The high windowsill, with the late-afternoon light spilling through its panes, still held the model cars he'd spent hours down here putting together. They were covered now with a layer of dust.

Though his old room was much as he remembered it, Cain hadn't slept here last night. He'd slept in the spare room upstairs, partly because it was a room fairly free of memories, but mostly because he hadn't had the energy or the inclination to clear off his old bed. He'd undertaken that task about an hour ago. Before that, he'd spent the greater part of the day fixing a banging pipe that had kept him awake most of the night. The whole house, he'd discovered after a careful walk through, was sadly in need of repair.

The house wasn't occupying his thoughts now, however. Just after he started going through the clutter on his bed, he'd come across a small leather box with a metal clasp on it. Intrigued, because he couldn't recall ever having seen it, though it looked easily as old as he was, he had pried off the small lock—then had spent the past several minutes going through all the letters his mother had saved. His letters. From the looks of it, she'd kept every card and scrap of paper he'd ever sent her.

There was a postcard from Houston, where he'd first found a job at a gas station. Another postmarked a few months later from Phoenix, where he'd worked as a grease monkey doing tune-ups. Finally, dated two years after that, a card from the Long Beach Raceway, where he'd sneaked into the pits and met Carlo Bessari, the gruff and grayed scion of grand prix racing.

The cards he'd sent those first few years after he left Aubrey said little other than where he was and whether or not he had a job. He'd always signed them simply *Cain*, because he never used the word *love*. The letters that came later were less cryptic. In those, he had said at least whether he liked what he was doing. Since they had all been written after he went to work for Bessari, they occasionally contained a newspaper clipping of the team's performance. With one of the later letters, he'd sent the article that had placed him in such demand with the cognoscenti of the racing world. Cain's refinements and technical innovations on Bessari's cars had made the Bessari team unbeatable. The job offers had come flooding in. Cain had turned them all down. He owed his success to the man who'd given him the chance to achieve it. The thought of working for anyone else was too disloyal for Cain to even consider.

A faint creak sounded from across the large open space. Cain scarcely noticed. His thoughts were distracted by the odd tightness building in his chest. That sensation wasn't caused by recalling the path his life had taken, but by the knowledge that his mother had liked his letters well enough to keep them. He had never known her to be particularly sentimental. She had been a woman who tried to forget about yesterday as soon as it was over and faced what lay ahead with resignation. It meant a lot to him to know that she'd allowed herself these reminders of times that she'd probably just as soon forgotten. And maybe, just maybe, she'd finally been a little bit proud of him.

He didn't know why that thought made his heart feel so heavy.

The creak of the screen door sounded again. "Cain? It's Ellie. Are you here?"

Ellie stood on the stoop, swatting at a fly as she peered across the back porch. Cain hadn't answered her knock, and now she waited to see if he'd respond to her call. After a few seconds of silence came his muffled, "In the basement."

His tone was cool and distant. Quashing the cowardly voice that told her to come back later, she headed down the narrow stairs located by the kitchen door. When she reached the bottom, the tentative smile she'd managed faded completely.

Cain *had* to know she was there—she stood less than six feet away from him—but he hadn't so much as looked at her. His head was bent over a letter he'd pulled from a yellowed envelope, and though all she could see was his profile, she could tell that whatever he was reading had all of his attention.

She saw his jaw tighten as he pulled something else from the envelope, then as he stared down at it, a look of unalterable sadness crept over his beautifully molded features. His wide shoulders seemed to slump under some intangible weight and he slowly set the letter and what looked to be some sort of a check beside a small leather box. That box sat on an old dresser. Atop its scarred surface were several more envelopes and two checks similar to the other.

Ellie started forward, then hesitated. "Cain? What it is?"

"She never cashed them."

"Never cashed what?"

He nodded toward the box, his bleak expression tearing at her. She'd never seen a man look so defeated.

"The money orders I sent. I wanted her to have that money. To spend it on something for herself." It seemed to him that she'd hoarded it away, as if the thought itself were gift enough. "I wanted to make things easier for her." He shrugged in bewilderment. "Why wouldn't she let me?"

His voice was naturally deep, with a low reverberating quality that made it dark and husky. Now there was a certain thickness to it, as if his throat were tight. The breath he released was a little shaky, too.

It was apparent that Cain wanted very much to understand why his mother hadn't spent the money he'd sent her. Knowing Amanda as she had, Ellie suspected that she might have kept the little stash as her nest egg.

"Perhaps she was saving it for a time when she really needed it," she suggested gently.

"She didn't have to do that. I would have sent more."

"Don't you think it helped her peace of mind to know that she had a little money tucked away? I'm sure it must have represented some security for her."

The muscles in his neck tightened as he swallowed. When he spoke again, his voice was little more than a raw whisper. "I would have taken care of her."

At a loss as to what else to say, wondering if she should intrude any further, Ellie took a tentative step toward him.

If she had ever seen anyone who looked as if he needed the comfort of a human touch, it was Cain at that moment. Yet she was certain that he would never admit that he needed to be held. His pride wouldn't allow him to concede to such a weakness. She'd seen that same inflexible pride at work yesterday when they'd stood in his mother's room and she'd explained to him about the curtains. She'd thought him cold and unfeeling then. But now, watching him close in on himself as he crossed his arms, she wondered if he wasn't simply protecting himself from things he didn't want to feel—or didn't know how to cope with.

"It's all right to be sad, Cain. She was your mother. You're allowed to miss her." Slowly, so as to be sure he wouldn't pull back from her, she reached out her hand and curled her fingers over his forearm. Having been without physical comfort for so long herself, she understood the need for a pair of arms to hold you. But she wasn't thinking of herself right now, nor of how he might interpret her touch. She saw only a man who was grieving, and who didn't deserve to do it alone. "It's even all right to cry."

There was such compassion in her voice, such understanding in her eyes, that Cain couldn't begin to refuse what she was offering. Before he could even question himself, he was responding to that unrestrained generosity of hers. He pulled her against him, wrapping her in his arms. Her own arms wound around his neck, encouraging him to make his hold as tight as he needed it to be.

It's even all right to cry. Cain would have argued that last point with her, if he'd been able to trust his voice. He didn't trust anything about himself at the moment, least of all what he was doing. He'd never dealt well with hurt. It had always seemed easier to run from the source of pain or fight it rather than to face it. Even now, he wanted to deny his grief over the loss of the woman he'd disappointed so often. Ellie wasn't letting him run, though, and somehow, feeling her small soft body absorb his shuddering breaths, he found that loss a little easier to acknowledge.

His face was buried in her neck, her hand cupped at the back of his head, soothing him as he breathed in the scent of spring clinging to her skin. She was comforting him as she would a small child, and Cain, needing that healing caress, allowed himself to cling to her—until he realized a few moments later his hold was too tight. He was hurting her.

At least that was what he thought when he heard the tiny moan muffled against his cheek. It was that sound that caused him to lift his head and loosen his arms. But what he saw in her eyes when he looked down at her and what he felt in his own body as she shifted away, had him pulling her right back again.

This time, she didn't tuck her head into his chest. He lifted his hand to her face, and when his mouth closed over hers, an entirely different sort of desperation took over.

Chapter Five

Desperation. Ellie had felt it when Cain first reached for her. Now, she tasted it in his hot, hungry kiss. He held her face between his hands, his lips tracing a fevered path from her cheek to her temples, then to her chin and throat before his mouth claimed hers again. The quick intrusion of his tongue had him pulling her sharply against him, his embrace filled with possession and need.

She strained toward him, too stunned by the swiftness of her response to question why she allowed her gasp of surprise to soften to a moan of longing. Or why she encouraged the bold stroke of his hand down her side and over her hips.

She had only meant to offer sympathy. That was why she had reached for him in his grief. But the feel of him holding her so close, of the strength and solidity of his body seeking the comfort of hers, had sparked an awareness she'd known she couldn't conceal if she stayed in his arms any longer. She'd thought about pulling away from him before he could see how he'd affected her. That hadn't worked. He'd loosened his hold, but he'd looked down at her with such need that she hadn't been able to think at all.

She'd come alive under his touch, responding with an intensity she hadn't known she possessed. She gave and he took, and that only made her want to give more. It made perfect sense to her and no sense at all. Maybe it was because the more she gave the more he seemed to want, and no one had ever needed her quite that way. Or maybe it was because her entire body felt electrified and the only way to seek ground was through him.

As frightened as she was compelled by the sensations Cain elicited, she was scarcely prepared to cope with her own reactions, let alone his abrupt withdrawal. His fingers bit into her shoulders. A moment later, he'd pushed her back, holding her at arm's length.

His eyes were closed as he drew a deep, calming breath and slowly released it. When he opened them, his hands falling away to find his pockets, she saw the stark desire in their gray depths—and the plea that denied that yearning.

"Ellie. I'm sorry." There was confusion in his eyes. And disbelief. "That shouldn't have happened."

Feeling shaken and unsure, Ellie hugged her arms over the simple pink dress she wore. The practical, self-protective side of her couldn't have agreed with him more. The part of her that had felt a little less lonely last night when they'd talked by the china closet, wouldn't allow her that defense. Part of him understood her, and that was too important to ignore. "It probably shouldn't have. But I'm not sorry that it did." Her voice fell to a near whisper. "I'm only sorry that you are."

She saw his chest expand with his slowly indrawn breath and caught the flash of hunger in his darkened gaze. Her own breath stilled when she saw his glance fasten on her mouth, still swollen from his kisses.

He could reach for her again and she would come to him. The realization filled Cain with relief. Not because it appeased his ego, but because he hadn't scared her off. He wasn't going to take advantage of her admission, though. She was just as dangerous to him as he was to her. Maybe even more so.

She gave him a small smile. When he didn't return it, she hugged herself a little tighter. He had the feeling she was still pulling herself back together and that the task might take a few moments.

He could appreciate that effort. As he held her, he'd thought of little other than how easy it would be to forget everything by burying himself in her softness. Feeling her yield to him had made his control come precariously close to snapping—until a sliver of rationality had slipped between the sensations and finally taken hold.

Cain hadn't always been rational or logical or any of the things a reasonable person needed to be. Now, having learned how tough it was to live with the consequences of acting first and thinking later, he wasn't about to slip back into old, self-defeating habits. He had a life away from here that was ordered, predictable and free of complications. If it was a life that others might find lacking, that was their problem. With the exception of a few of the people he worked with, there was no one whose opinion really mattered to him. Even to those few, he didn't consider himself especially close. He liked it that way and there was no room in his life for any changes—or any intruders. When he left here, he would forget, once and for all, everything he'd ever known about this place. A relationship with this woman would just be another reminder.

A relationship with him wouldn't do her any good, either.

It was obvious enough by the reception he'd received at both the market and the hardware store this morning that his reputation hadn't healed much over the years. Knowing how talk thrived, he supposed it could have become even worse as his sins were embellished. Some of the people he'd run into had stared at him for a minute. When they'd recognized him they'd lowered their eyes and hurried away. Others had given him a wary smile, as if they wanted to be sure to stay on his good side. Those who bothered to speak had asked only how long he planned on staying.

His voice was edged with the acceptance of earned inequities. "You don't want to get involved with me, Ellie."

At the certainty in his words, Ellie's head snapped up. No less than half a dozen people had echoed that same sentiment today. Every time she'd heard it, she'd bristled on the inside while maintaining her well-taught composure on the outside. Hearing it from Cain only compounded the irritation that had festered all afternoon. The gleam in his eyes that dared her to defy him made it worse. She felt as if she'd just been backed to the wall, and that was not a position she was comfortable with.

"That decision is mine to make. Whether you or anyone else around here believes it or not, I'm perfectly capable of deciding who my friends will be."

He recalled that she'd said something similar to that before—about his mother. "You don't want me for a friend," he informed her flatly.

Impatience urged her on. Why was it that people failed to understand what she said? "I didn't say I did. What I said was that the decision was mine to make. Not yours and not anyone else's." Her chin tipped up, challenge vying with pique. "But since you brought it up, why wouldn't I?"

She expected to hear variations of the same theme she'd already heard; about how Bennetts didn't associate with people from "the wrong side of the tracks." Or, if he was inclined to be more creative, about how her uncle and her father would probably come unglued if they knew she was standing in his bedroom wishing he wasn't sorry he'd kissed her. She did not expect the response he threw back at her.

"Because I don't know how to be one."

"That's a crock."

They were even. The quick astonishment in Cain's expression indicated that he hadn't expected her reply, either. It amazed Ellie too, since she wasn't accustomed to waving red flags.

"You want to clarify that?"

She immediately backed down. "Not especially."

She was thinking of last night and how he'd listened to her. That was what a friend did. Listened without judging. Now, though, he was being just like everyone else. Only more so. It seemed that he was bound and determined to make her fight back.

"Do it anyway. I'd like to have some idea of what it is we're arguing about."

"We're not arguing about anything." The statement was ludicrous, considering the challenge darting between them. But in truth, her argument wasn't so much with him as with everyone else. He just happened to be the one who'd finally pushed her past her limit. "It's bad enough that the people who know me feel so compelled to try to run my life. But you...you've barely been around for twenty-four hours and you presume to inform me about what I want. I'm so sick of—" Realizing what she was about to say, she cut herself off with a muttered, "Oh, forget it."

Cain didn't seem at all inclined to do that. "So sick of what?" he demanded.

He asked for it. "Of everyone telling me that I don't want to get involved with you."

"So yell at them about that. Not me."

The suggestion was laughable. One did not yell at one's friends. One most especially did not yell at family. Not in the Bennett family, anyway. Differences were discussed politely, then Ellie pretty much did as she was told. "It wouldn't matter if I did. They wouldn't listen."

"So what are you going to do? Use me to get back at them?"

"I'm not trying to get back at anyone."

"Then why in the hell are you here?"

Goaded by his demand, she glared up at his implacable expression. Her words were clipped, her expression defiant. "I came to tell you that there's a charity auction you might want to think about donating some of this stuff to. Personally, I don't care what you do with it."

She turned on her heel, amazed at the emotions this infuriating man caused her to feel. She'd gone from composure to anger in mere minutes. In between she'd felt concern, confusion, desire and heaven only knew what else.

"Where are you going?"

"Home."

She could feel his scowl following her as her foot hit the bottom step.

"I thought you said you'd help me pack."

Nothing he could have said would have surprised her more. With her back to him, though, he couldn't see that surprise as she pounded up the steps. "I'm going to fix something to eat first. If you're hungry, it'll be ready in half an hour."

The screen door slammed behind her. Marching across the yard, taking deep breaths to calm herself, Ellie could scarcely believe that she'd implied that he was welcome to dinner.

Neither could Cain. But then he couldn't believe how bad he felt about having upset her. He didn't think that Ellie riled easily, or that she was particularly accustomed to venting steam. But she'd definitely been angry. The fire in her eyes had attested to that. Just as the fire in her kiss had spoken of her deeper passions.

Cain gave his head a shake and started up the stairs. Right now, he wasn't going to think about how she'd responded to him. If he was smart, he'd forget he even knew how sweet she tasted. He wasn't going to think about anything at all except making her understand that, while he could use some help with the packing, it wasn't necessary for her to keep feeding him.

He was so focused on that thought that he forgot all about the small blue velvet bag he'd noticed lying in the box of his old letters.

As it had with Ellie, the screen door groaned open then banged shut.

She heard that distinctive sound as she plopped a pot down on the short gray Formica counter by her two-burner stove and wished he'd given her the half an hour she'd more or less asked for. The clunk of his boots was deliberately heavy as he climbed the stairs to her door, the sound quite determined.

So was his expression when she opened the door.

"It's not ready yet," she said before he could open his mouth. She'd cut him off because she wasn't going to argue anymore, and it looked very much as if that was what he wanted to do. She rarely lost her temper, and she had no intention of doing so again. It took too long to settle down.

She turned away, leaving the door open.

"I want to talk to you," he called after her.

She said nothing, her slender shoulders remaining rigid as she pulled a bag of rolls from a white-painted cupboard. A moment later, she none too gently set a can of green beans next to the bag and began rummaging around in a drawer.

Cain stepped inside, closing the door as he watched her across the open space of the small studio apartment. She wore the look of a woman who was torn between abandoning her irritation or giving in to it. "I didn't mean to upset you."

"I'm not upset."

She was a terrible liar. "I'm sorry anyway. Okay?"

It occurred to Cain that he'd just apologized twice in less than ten minutes. Apologies weren't something that came easily to him. As he acknowledged that thought, he had to admit another. It suddenly mattered very much that his apology was accepted. He wasn't, however, going to push the point. Not in the mood she was in.

Cain ventured farther inside, glancing about the sparsely furnished room to familiarize himself with her territory. A daybed covered with a blue throw and pillows sat a few inches from a large window on the far side of open space. To the left of it hung a very healthy-looking fern. Other than a portable television and a stereo on some low shelves, there was little else in the room—except for a table and chairs that looked as if they'd come from an ice cream parlor. They sat by the window next to the door.

What caught Cain's attention was the way the table and chairs reflected back at him. Part of the wall he faced was covered with foot-wide squares of mirror. It was also bisected by a long rail that served no purpose whatever that Cain could see, except possibly as a place to hang towels.

He turned to where Ellie stood in the tiny kitchenette. She'd yet to acknowledge what he'd said, so a different approach seemed to be in order.

That approach was dictated by the aroma of something rich and spicy beckoning him closer. The tantalizing smell went straight to his stomach. Despite his intention to tell her that she was not responsible for his nutritional welfare, the prospect of canned stew for supper suddenly lost its appeal.

"What are we having?" he heard himself ask.

She set the lid of the Crock-Pot on the counter and speared the small roast she'd put on that morning before she'd left for work. "Barbecue beef." The roast, dripping thick red sauce, was deposited on a plate. "And beans and rolls."

"Do you always cook like this?"

"Only on Tuesdays. If you want to help, you can get the plates. They're up there." She nodded to the cupboard above the sink. "We'll need three."

He was about to ask what was so special about Tuesdays when he heard himself say, "Three?"

"One is for Hanna. Her son has a meeting in Greely on Tuesday nights, so I take her her dinner."

"Who else do you feed around here?"

"Just the birds."

A considering frown etched his brow as he opened the cupboard. She fed the old lady next door and the birds. Last night, after she'd shown up at his back door with a plate, she'd said something about feeding his mom's fish. He didn't have to ask to know that she probably fed strays, too.

"Here are the dishes. Now what?"

She told him he could get the butter and jam from the refrigerator, while she heated up the beans. After she'd fixed a plate for Hanna, she ran the elderly neighbor's dinner over to her. Ellie thought about having Cain go to Hanna's so she could have a couple of badly needed minutes alone, but decided it would be simpler to take the meal herself. She could spend a few moments with Hanna now, and wouldn't have to explain why Cain had delivered the older woman's dinner.

The errand only took minutes. Hanna's favorite game show was on, so she hadn't been at all inclined to visit. Ellie wouldn't have been good company even if she had. She felt touchy and tense, and no matter how hard she tried, she couldn't let go of her agitation. She wasn't sure of the specific reason for that failure—until she and Cain had dished up their own plates and carried them to the small table.

She'd barely sat down when she began to toy first with the napkin in her lap and then with her silverware. Despite her claim to the contrary, she wasn't the least bit hungry.

After a full minute of seeing her push her food around, Cain laid down his fork and leaned back in his chair. It seemed to take her a moment to realize that she was being patiently watched over the bowl of yellow daisies centered on the table. When she did, she looked even edgier than she had the moment before.

"Would it help if I told you it won't happen again?"

"What won't?" she returned, trying for nonchalance.

She was staring at her green beans. He dipped his head lower, trying to see her eyes. "That I won't touch you."

She was afraid that was what he meant. There was a very simple reason why she was still upset. She didn't know how else to handle what Cain had made her feel. *Any* of it: the longing, the irritation. It was terribly unfair that he seemed to know that, too. "I don't know if it would or not."

Cain had to hand it to her. Ellie was nothing if not disarmingly honest with him. He couldn't help but wonder just how honest she was with herself.

"I won't say it then. I'm not sure it's a promise I could make, and believe it or not, if I choose to give it, I do keep my word."

Ellie met his glance, holding it even though she wanted to look away when she saw the coolness there. She didn't know which was more disconcerting—his admission that he might find it difficult to avoid touching her, or the way he seemed to assume that she thought he wouldn't keep a promise. It seemed easier to deal with the latter. "It never occurred to me that you wouldn't do as you said."

"Good. Then you'll know you can believe me if I say I'll keep my hands to myself. Now, about this auction you mentioned," he went on as if he were clear on the abandoned subject even if she wasn't. *If* he told her he'd keep his hands to himself, was what he'd said. Not that he would. "What kind of a charity is it?"

Caught off guard, as she thought he'd intended her to be when she noticed his faint smile, Ellie quickly regrouped. "It's for children. Mostly for the children of migrant workers. What they can't use directly is sold and the money used for food and medical care."

Cain considered this for a moment. "If it's for little kids, I suppose that would be okay. Do you think they'd be interested in taking everything?"

"Everything?"

"Uh-huh." With a nod of confirmation, he sliced into his meat. "Pretty much all of it, anyway." He would keep a few of the small items such as the old box of letters. Not because they'd been his, but because they had meant something to his mom. "You're welcome to whatever you want...since you were her friend. But the rest..."

His shrug saved him from repeating himself and allowed him to take another bite of the roast Ellie had yet to taste. She had no idea what had happened in the past few moments, but there was a certain acceptance on Cain's part that hadn't been there before. A guarded acceptance, to be sure, but Ellie found herself exceedingly grateful for the change

With it came a certain casualness. The kind that allowed for the easier conversation they'd shared last night.

It was that lack of pretense that allowed him to tell her that he'd thought about keeping the old grandfather clock in the living room, but that his apartment in Florida was too small to accommodate anything else. That prompted her to ask just where, exactly, it was that he lived.

The name of the little town outside Orlando was unfamiliar to Ellie, but she couldn't help noting how Cain warmed to the subject when she asked if that was where he worked, too. He actually worked in a lot of places, he told her. But the company's plant and the proving grounds outside of Orlando were his headquarters.

"What are proving grounds?" she asked, and quickly learned that it was simply the area where they test-drove their cars—and that made her ask what the cars where like.

Before she knew it, she was being given a crash course in Formula One racers. The single-seat car was similar to those that raced in the Indianapolis 500, she learned, only lighter, and with the changes required by the Fédération Internationale de l'Automobile—or the FIA, which governed the sport—this year's engines would be different from last year's, which were different from the year before. Each car had to have its own individual chassis design, too, and his team was constantly innovating to make their designs better. All that was what helped keep him employed.

It was easy enough for Ellie to see how completely Cain's work absorbed him as he spoke. The drivers were the stars, but Cain lived, literally, for the nuts and bolts of the business. Changes were constantly made and refined; the push to go just a little bit faster than the last time an ever present goal. He loved the competitiveness of it, she could tell, even though she had absolutely no idea what there was about improved gear ratios and torque and electronic combustion systems that could demand such intensity. To her, cars were things you put gas in to get from point A to point B. Since she didn't have one, she really hadn't given them much thought.

What she did find fascinating was *him* and his taking for granted opportunities most people were never offered. In any given year he would find himself in no less than half a dozen countries. Grand prix racing was to Europe what football and baseball combined were to the average American sports fan. And only one of the races was held in the States each year. Yet, Cain didn't seem to find that circumstance particularly remarkable. He brushed off the trips to Monaco, Portugal, Argentina and South Africa and all the other places on the grand prix racing circuit as if they were merely forays into the next county.

"I've always moved around," he told her after she sliced him another portion of the roast he'd been eyeing. "Those cities are just where I have to be to make sure my engines win races. They all look pretty much the same after a while."

If he thought that, he couldn't possibly have been looking, she thought. She'd read about these places and seen pictures, and there was a definite flavor to every single one of them. "But Monte Carlo," she said, her tone indicating her incomprehension at his dismissive attitude. "And Salzburg. And Paris! Didn't you see the Eiffel Tower or go to the Louvre? Or what about Notre-Dame?" she hurried on, thinking of the sites the tour books named. In Tulsa, she'd spent hours combing through the brochures picked up from the travel agency located next door to the dance studio. And every book she'd ever read about famous dancers had mentioned the great European theaters where they performed.

Cain frowned as he tried to remember what little he'd actually noticed. The frown deepened as he wished he'd noticed more so he could tell her about it. She seemed so hungry for whatever firsthand information he could give her, yet there was so little he could say that he felt would interest her. His life was pretty much confined to machine shops and drafting rooms and test facilities. Occasionally, on the Riviera, he'd do a little gambling. In Spain, if it was the right time of year, he'd go to a bullfight.

He didn't think that was what she wanted to hear about. If the posters on her walls were any indication, her tastes were more refined than his. There was a travel poster of a Parisian street in spring above the table where they sat. Over the daybed, a troupe of ballerinas danced toward the open window. The poster over *his* sofa was of a sleek red Ferrari with a lithesome blonde draped over its hood.

"I saw the Eiffel Tower. But only," he had to admit, "because we had to drive around it on the way from the airport. I didn't make it to too many places that didn't have a course. Except Bordeaux," he added, remembering. "A race sponsor had a chalet there, and he invited us for a party after our team won. It was pretty impressive."

"The party or the chalet?" she asked, not caring how unworldly her eagerness might sound.

A deep chuckle preceded a definite "Both. There were eight of us guys in a house with fifty-some odd rooms and something like two servants apiece. The count must have invited the whole countryside to his party. I have no idea how many people were there. Hundreds," he guessed. "But I didn't stick around long enough to meet many of them."

She clearly found such a lapse puzzling. She was also too interested in hearing about the jet-set crowd who catered to his elite racing world to waste any time figuring it out for herself. Propping her elbows up on the table, she rested her chin on her clasped hands. "Why not?"

"I was beat. I always am after a race," he added with a shrug. "I'd had all of nine hours sleep in three days and the only thing that interested me was a bed and twelve hours of uninterrupted unconsciousness. But that's beside the point. I wanted to tell you about the vineyard behind the chalet.''

He did, in great detail. Especially about the winemaking process, which he'd found interesting, though he didn't really care for wine all that much. As he watched Ellie listen, he became aware of something he'd never experienced in a woman's company. When she asked him a question, she seemed genuinely interested in his answer—and in his opinion. He liked that. What he didn't like was the way he had to keep reminding himself that all he wanted from her was her help with the house.

By the time the dishes had been cleaned up and Cain asked if she was ready to get to work, Ellie had decided to forget about the inauspicious beginning to the evening. That didn't mean she wasn't still confused by his attitude. Every so often she'd catch him watching her with a certain heat in his eyes. But for all practical purposes, he was treating her much as she suspected he treated the men he worked with.

She wasn't given any time to decide if she should be offended or pleased. When Cain set his mind to a task, he approached it with a single-mindedness that bordered on exhausting. Ellie discovered that questionably commendable trait shortly after he deposited her and half a dozen boxes in the middle of his mother's bedroom. He felt that she, being female, was in a better position than he to decide what was good enough to be given away and what should be trashed, so he left her in charge of closets and drawers while he took down the worn curtains and dismantled the bed.

That task didn't take long. Neither did the chore of taping up the now-filled boxes. The bathroom, next on his list, took merely twenty minutes of sorting and tossing. It was the kitchen and pantry that took time. After those were done, and while Ellie was emptying the hall linen closet, he told her he wanted to do the living room next.

"Wait a minute." Pushing back the wisps of hair that had long since abandoned her barrette, Ellie frowned up from where she sat cross-legged on the hall floor. She was packing sheets and towels from the lower shelves. Cain stood over her, pulling blankets from the upper ones. "Is it written somewhere that everything has to be done tonight? You said the realtor you called this morning isn't coming for two more days. We've been at this for hours."

"Do you want to take a break?"

She shot him the drollest glance she could manage. "Have you looked at your watch lately?"

The question prompted the action. For a moment it looked as if he couldn't quite believe that it was almost 1:00 a.m. Chagrin touched his expression. "I guess it is getting a little late. Instead of a break, you should probably go home."

"Gee, Simon. You're so generous."

Her reference to Simon Legree had him hunching down beside her.

She wished he hadn't gotten so close. All evening they'd been bumping into each other as they reached for the same item, or passed each other in the narrower spaces. But all those times, the contact was accidental and therefore easier to ignore. It was not so simple ignoring the feel of his hand on her shoulder as he steadied himself.

"If you were getting tired, you should have said something."

"I did," she pointed out, unwittingly relieved when his balance allowed him to pull his hand away.

"I meant before now." His smile grew indulgent. "A night's sleep might help make us a little more efficient. We're getting ahead of ourselves." He took the two towels she held and put them back on the shelf in front of her. "I'll need those," he explained. "They'll come in handy after I shower. I don't suppose we left any soap in the bathroom?"

There was an almost lazy quality to the way he let his glance roam over her face, as if he had all the time in the world to commit every shading and nuance to memory. There were times when he'd look at her that way while they were talking and she would wonder if he was even aware of what he was doing—or if he knew how very vulnerable his perusal made her feel. She thought he might. It was almost as if he felt that by probing deeply enough, he could read her most intimate ponderings.

That thought was rather disquieting and she sincerely hoped that it was not the case. His comments and questions had elicited a detailed image of him dripping wet from the shower, which was not a very practical thing to think about when each breath she drew brought with it the scent of the subtly spicy after-shave he wore.

"There's a bar on the sink." She turned back to the shelf. "I'll go home when this closet is done."

"Leave it. I've kept you longer than I should have." Without thinking, he reached out to push a strand of hair from her cheek. Rather than jerk his hand back as he'd been inclined to do, he let himself enjoy the feel of her smooth skin. "Go home. It'll all be here tomorrow."

He stood abruptly, knowing that if he didn't move away from her, he'd wind up touching her again. He wasn't sure either one of them really wanted that. A strange sort of truce had gone into effect and he wasn't willing to test it to see how strong it was. He knew only that she'd as much as said that she wanted to be his friend, and here in this town he could certainly use one. He didn't want to mess that up.

That was why a few minutes later, after assuring her that he was going to call it quits for the night, too, he stood at the back door and watched her hurry up the steps to her apartment. It wasn't necessary for him to do that, but something he didn't bother to question wanted to make sure she was safely inside before he turned away.

Having no idea where that last thought had come from, Cain headed downstairs to turn off the basement lights. They'd been on ever since he'd followed Ellie up hours ago. He didn't turn them off right away, though. Reaching the bottom steps, he caught sight of the box of letters—and that reminded him of the little bag he'd seen nestled in one of its corners.

A few moments later, holding the blue velvet bag in his hand, he loosened the gold string at its neck, turned it upside down and let its contents fall into his palm.

For nearly a minute after he tossed the bag aside, he stood turning the object over and over. It was a pin of some sort. An inch high oval of the palest gray-blue. In its center, carved of some sort of ivory-looking stone, was the profile of a woman. The piece was edged with a fine filigree of gold.

Cain moved closer to the light. The cameo was truly exquisite, and if he were to guess, fairly expensive. It was also something he'd never seen his mother wear. Yet, there was something familiar about it. Startlingly so. That familiarity nagged at him until, finally, he realize what it was.

The profile. Feature for feature whoever had carved the delicate piece had captured Ellie perfectly.

Chapter Six

Ellie sat on her bed, absently toying with the edge of a sheer white curtain as she stared down at the light burning in Amanda's basement window. A moment later the light went off, followed by others as Cain worked his way upstairs and through the small house. When all was as dark as the moonlight would allow, she stood and pulled down the shade.

She should go to sleep. As late as it was, she'd have to set her alarm to be sure she made it to work on time. Yet she didn't feel the least bit tired.

That wholly unfamiliar feeling of anticipation teased her nerves, making her restive and anxious and absolutely certain that any attempt to sleep would be nothing but an exercise in frustration. Already frustrated, she saw no point in fueling the feeling.

She'd been fine until Cain had touched her cheek. It was such a little thing, but that caress had been so gentle, his smile so tender. Those were not qualities she would have associated with Cain, but having glimpsed what the man was capable of, she'd felt oddly cheated when he refused to give more. His eyes, his touch, had told her he wanted very much to kiss her. Yet he'd pushed her away as he had last night, and as he had when he reached for her in his grief.

Having no desire to stand listening to the crickets serenade one another, Ellie gave a disgusted sigh, marched into the tiny dressing room that led to her even smaller bath and stripped off her clothes. Instead of a nightgown, she pulled on her leotard. The music would help. And the dance. She could lose herself in them. Right now, she wanted more than anything else simply not to think.

Ellie didn't bother with the rigid discipline of the formal warm-up she'd taught herself. After pulling on her dance slippers, she leaned over until she felt her muscles stretch and give and waited for the music she'd put on to begin seeping inside her. The gentle strains of violins melded with the plaintive cry of a flute, and she cleared her mind to let the music begin its transformation. When the music touched her, she could become an ephemeral Giselle or a silly Petrouchka. She could be a sprite, or a sorceress, or wind or a willow. It didn't matter, as long as for a while she didn't have to be Ellie. Because, right now, by being Ellie, she'd have to admit that she'd never been quite so frightened in all of her life. Not of Cain. She didn't think he would hurt her, not intentionally. She was afraid of what he had unleashed inside her.

Ellie had always lived by the rules. For most of her life she had followed familial and social dicta without question. As she grew older she'd kept the rules out of habit and an inherent desire to keep the peace. After all, to be accepted, a certain code of conduct had to be followed—or at least not deviated from too drastically. Thinking about it now, she wondered if she hadn't sacrificed her own inner peace to maintain that outward compliance. Cain didn't seem to worry about appearances as she did, and in a way, she envied him that ability.

He didn't seem to be bound by the same rules as other men. Though he'd succeeded in a society that measured a man by his accomplishments, Cain didn't quite fit within society's constraints. She knew that he never had fit in in Aubrey. Just as she knew that Aubrey could never accept him now. His vagabond existence would be regarded as reckless; the people he associated with, too removed from a traditional life-style to be considered "upstanding" citizens. Yet Ellie had never believed that everything could be categorized as good or bad, or black or white. And she simply couldn't feel the same abhorrence everyone else in her acquaintance did toward someone who didn't subscribe to their idea of fundamental values.

Cain's failure to conform wasn't a problem for her, and neither was his less than lily-white reputation. A boy had committed those transgressions and he was a man now. A man whose brooding arrogance was contradicted by a deep and unyielding strength of purpose. A man whose emotions ran so deep that even he might not know what he was capable of feeling. Beyond all that was what had drawn her from the moment they'd met—the element of danger about him that appealed to the timid part of her soul; a sort of daring that she found incredibly sensual. She wanted to feel that kind of excitement herself, to experience again the heady recklessness she'd felt in his arms.

She waited restlessly for the melody to take hold. Her thoughts were disturbing, but not nearly as disturbing as the realization that she didn't want to fight them.

The music took longer than usual to reach her. It was well after two in the morning before she slipped between her sheets. She had no idea at what time she finally fell asleep. She knew only that, when the knocking on her door awoke her the next morning, she was nowhere near ready to get up.

The pounding seemed to go on for forever, fading in and out of her consciousness along with bits and snatches of other sounds: the voices of children, the barking of a dog. Then the annoying noises stopped and for one groggy moment she felt grateful for the silence. Now she could drift back to sleep.

Within an instant, her eyes flew open and darted to the clock. The sounds suddenly made sense. The dog making all the racket was Sukey, little Cindy Baker's collie. And he was barking at the kids on the way to school, which meant Ellie should be leaving for work right now. She was due to open the shop in fifteen minutes. But the knocking...

Scrambling out of bed, she stumbled across the room and flipped back the latch.

Cain had just reached the bottom step. At the sound of the door opening, he glanced around. For a moment, he said nothing, his surprise at her appearance evident as he took in the length of her shapely legs exposed beneath her short white sleep shirt, and the beguiling sleepiness softening her features.

He allowed himself one last leisurely sweep of her body. "I thought you'd already left."

Combing her fingers through her hair, imagining how wild it must look, Ellie moved backward as he slowly started up the steps again. There was something vaguely predatory about the way he moved. She'd noticed that about him before. Somehow, though, with his eyes smiling approval of her skimpy attire, she felt a little more vulnerable to that quality at the moment—and to him.

His dark hair was still damp from his shower. She could tell from the tiny nick in the cleft of his chin that he'd just shaved. He smelled of soap and spice, and his smile was at once disarming and incredibly sexy. Any nerve in her body that hadn't been awake before definitely was now.

"I overslept."

"So I see." He'd reached the top step and stopped. It was with visible effort that he kept his attention on her face. "I won't keep you. I just want to ask if you'd give whoever's in charge of that lodge auction a call and find out how they want to handle this stuff. I can rent a truck and take it to them, or they can come and get it."

"No problem. I'll call this morning."

"There's one other thing. The realtor is coming out today instead of tomorrow." His glance shifted over her shoulder, sweeping the interior of her room. "Your apartment goes with the rest of the property. Would you mind if I let him in to take a look at it?"

It hadn't occurred to Ellie just how protective she was of her little space until she thought of a total stranger intruding upon it. Granted, it was rented space. But it was really all she had. "Will you be coming in with him?"

The question made him hesitate, or perhaps it was the unease in the inquiry that brought his quick reserve. "Not if you don't want me to."

"Oh, I do. If you let him in, I want you to be with him." She gave an awkward shrug. "It's just that I'd feel kind of funny having someone I don't know in my home without me or someone I trusted being here."

The coolness that had so abruptly entered Cain's expression vanished as quickly as it had appeared, yet his thoughts were impossible to discern as he considered her explanation. "I'll be with him," he assured her. "You'd better hurry up and get dressed or you'll be late for work," he added, as if she wasn't already aware of the fact. Grinning at the humorless look she shot him, he bounded down the steps—and ran right into Ellie's Aunt Jo.

Jo did not look pleased with the encounter. Dressed as she was, Ellie had to admit the situation probably didn't look too good to the casual observer. She saw her aunt's glance bounce from her to the man balanced on the bottom step. Conclusions were being drawn. And those conclusions could be quite erroneous if the scene were taken at face value. Ellie looked very much as if she'd just gotten out of bed—which she had. Cain, with his hair still damp, appeared as if he'd just come from the shower—which he had. There had also been a decidedly teasing quality in both Cain's comment about her being late and in Ellie's answering glare, which, if one were to stretch the point, could imply a certain familiarity with each other. Just how far the determination of that familiarity went depended on the mind of the observer.

To some, Ellie admitted to herself with some chagrin, it could appear that they had just spent the night together—which they certainly hadn't. But she had to concede that it might certainly look that way.

"Good morning, Ellie," Jo said, her tone remarkably bland. "Cain," she added, acknowledging him with the nod of her head. "I don't suppose you remember me. I'm Josephine Bennett. The sheriff's wife. And Ellie's aunt," she added, pointedly noting the relationships. "It's a bit early to be visiting, isn't it?"

Ellie was sure Cain would have preferred to walk off and say nothing. He was not a man who liked having to explain himself, and an explanation was clearly what her aunt wanted. Yet he, too, had apparently noted how compromising the situation looked for her.

"I was just asking Ellie to get some information for me. About an auction," he added, his tone pleasant though not amenable to challenge. "I don't believe that would be called a visit necessarily, especially since I was only at her door for a couple of minutes. She's running a little late this morning."

"So it would appear." She held Cain's glance for a few seconds, assessing his coolly confident defense, then looked up at Ellie, who hadn't so much as breathed since she'd seen her. "I was going to walk over to the shop with you, but since you're not ready, I'll go on over and open up. We'll talk there."

Without a word, Ellie turned to go inside. There was little doubt as to what her aunt would want to talk about.

"Oh, I know nothing's going on, Ellie," Jo said, dismissing her niece's explanation before Ellie could even get started. "I know you better than that. What you need to understand is that just being seen with him can hurt you. What if it had been someone else who'd shown up when I did? What if it had been Lucille? I can only imagine what kind of rumors would be flying by now."

"Would you have believed them?"

"Don't be ridiculous. Of course not. As I said, I know you."

"So does everyone else in town." Refusing to react as her aunt thought she should, Ellie continued to calmly clean the glass of the refrigerated flower case. "I don't think anyone around here would believe that I'd have an affair with someone I'd known for less than three days." Nor would I care if they did, she thought.

Stunned by her own defiance, Ellie made a quick mental retraction. That wasn't true. She did care. And she cared very much for her aunt for being so concerned. "Besides," she continued, hoping to alleviate some of that concern, "Cain isn't interested in me. All he's interested in is selling his mother's house." Ellie heard a hint of disappointment in her voice, but either Jo didn't catch it, or she was astute enough to say nothing.

"Well, let's hope he does it soon."

"He's got a realtor coming out today," Ellie told her, then found herself wondering off and on for the rest of the afternoon if Cain would be leaving once the property was listed.

She got her answer almost as soon as she reached Amanda's house.

Cain was waiting for her when she returned home that evening. Sitting on the top step of the front porch, his booted feet planted on the step below and a can of cola dangling between his knees, he watched her come up the sidewalk.

"The realtor said I'd have a better chance of selling the place if I fixed it up," he said when she stopped in front of him. "I figure it'll take me about a week."

He had no idea why she smiled; he only knew he was glad she did. After the encounter with her aunt this morning, he hadn't been too sure what to expect when he saw her again. As emphatic as she seemed to be about picking her own friends, though, he should have known to expect the response he got now.

"Need help?"

Setting the can of cola behind the post on the porch, he stood up, reached into the pocket of his jeans and pulled out his keys. "That's what I was waiting for." He nodded toward his car. "Want to go to Greely and help me pick up some paint?"

It could take either forty minutes or a little over an hour to get to Greely, depending on which road you took. Cain took the back road, the one that went through the hills and skirted Cherokee Lake. Ellie didn't ask why he took that route, assuming that he'd have told her if he'd wanted, but she was glad that he had. She preferred the winding two-lane road to the arrow-straight highway. The road climbed a little as they left the flatlands. The trees spilling down the foothills of the Ozark plateau gave a cooler feel to the scenery. After the browns and golds of the grain fields and dusty cattle ranges, the lusher greens were a welcome change.

"Is that all he had to say then?" she asked, wondering what else the realtor had mentioned. "That the market is slow and that the house needs fresh paint?"

"And new appliances," Cain added, his attention on the curving road. "The hot water heater is shot, and he thought throwing in a new stove might help sell the place. He did have a question about your apartment, though. He wanted to know if you taught dance lessons."

"Why would he ask that?"

"Because of the mirrored wall and the rod attached to it. At least, that's what he pointed to when he asked the question." He let his glance slide toward her for a moment. "Do you?"

"No," she returned, her attention on a ragged row of oil derricks off in the distance. "I'm hardly good enough to teach. You need training for that."

If she'd had the training, she might even have been an exceptional dancer—or so the professional instructors at the conservatory where she used to work had told her. She had a wonderful, natural ability. Unfortunately, her technical skills were far from perfect, and she'd never be able to do anything *en pointe*. Dancing on toe required skills and development she simply didn't possess. That was understandable, considering that until she was nineteen she'd never had a formal lesson in her life. She'd taught herself everything she knew from the books and cassettes she'd borrowed from the county's mobile library while she was growing up.

"You *do* dance then," he said, his glance sliding over her slender curves as if that explained something to him.

"Only for myself."

Several seconds passed as Cain considered how she'd turned away from him. The more he learned about this woman, the more certain he was that she was holding back. Not from him, necessarily. But from herself.

"That's not the way you wanted it, was it?"

"We don't always get what we want, do we?" She smiled, trying to keep her tone light. "Just about every nine-year-old girl who sees *The Nutcracker* wants to be a ballerina. I was no different."

And like most nine-year-olds who profess a burning desire to study ballet, Ellie's obsession was passed off as of no real import by her parents. By the time she was thirteen and learned that dance lessons were necessary if she wanted to perform, she was waved off with the explanation that she was too old to begin any real training now. Real dancers began their careers at five or six. Some, even earlier. Besides, dancers were from Chicago and New York and Los Angeles, not from Aubrey, Oklahoma.

Not wanting to dwell on that long-abandoned dream, she turned her attention back to Cain. What she'd wanted back then didn't matter anymore. It hadn't mattered for a long time. She gave him a tiny frown. He had an uncanny knack of digging deeper than she was comfortable with, but he appeared satisfied with her explanation and more interested now in the passing scenery than in her.

She felt vaguely annoyed with him for making her remember how it had hurt to have her interests dismissed as inconsequential. Her frown intensified. He didn't notice, which she decided was probably just as well.

Ellie noticed that he seemed perfectly comfortable behind the wheel of his car, relaxed as he was in the contoured black leather seat. Concentration etched his brow as he focused on the twists and turns of the pavement. Their pace was hardly sedate, but he wasn't exactly burning up the road, either. With all the power waiting to be unleashed beneath the hood, Ellie was a little surprised at his moderate speed.

"How fast will this go?"

The lift of his eyebrow was slightly sardonic. "Why?"

"I'm just curious."

His eyes narrowed, his tone smoothly quiet and testing. "Do you want to go faster?"

His right hand moved to the console between them, his fingers folding around the knob of the shift. He was challenging her, waiting for her to decide. For one reckless moment, Ellie almost said yes. The thought of flying around the curves and bends with Cain controlling the powerful surge of the engine was strangely exciting, and Ellie couldn't begin to explain why. She knew only that a strange kind of tension had suddenly begun building inside her and that Cain was fueling it.

"We're going fast enough," she finally said.

"I can handle the car."

"I'm sure you can," she returned, not necessarily thinking about the vehicle. "You used to be notorious for speeding."

The muscle in his jaw jerked and he pulled away from the shift. "I imagine I used to be notorious for a lot of things."

Ellie would have given anything at that moment for the ability to retract her words. Cain had already pulled back from her, withdrawing into himself as she'd seen him do before. She was sure that he'd have dismissed her entirely had they been anywhere else. But that was impossible to do in the confines of the car.

She'd stepped on to the edges of his past and he clearly wasn't comfortable with that. Had he been anyone else, Ellie would have immediately retreated, loath to increase the discomfort. But this was Cain, and suddenly it was terribly important to her that she get beyond his defensiveness.

"Do you shut everybody out?" she asked quietly. "Or is it just me?"

He refused to acknowledge her question.

She tried again. "You don't play fair. You know that?" The accusation was justified in Ellie's mind. "You can poke around in my life, but I'm not supposed to touch yours."

"Don't," he muttered, his hands tightening on the wheel.

Recognizing a brick wall when she saw one, she turned her irritation to the window. It was a full minute before either one of them spoke.

Cain was the first to break the strained silence. "Maybe I just don't want you to think any worse of me than you already do."

Amazed to discover what he'd been thinking, her annoyance vanished. "I don't think badly of—"

He cut her off, not wanting a chance to reconsider what he'd decided to say. "You can believe just about everything you've ever heard about me, Ellie. If there was a fight, I probably started it. If there was liquor missing, I probably stole it. The only thing I didn't do was get anybody pregnant. Not that I know of anyway. But I've got to admit I wasn't too careful about that, either. I didn't give a damn about anybody but myself." He looked over at her, his expression defiant. "I don't much give a damn about anybody now," he added, wanting her to understand that before he glanced away. "And I did drive fast. I still do."

His shoulders were rigid, his profile a study in stone as he stared straight ahead and waited for her to shrink away from him. He had the feeling that she hadn't fully appreciated the extent of his transgressions. In some perverse way, he needed to make sure she did. He didn't want her thinking he was something he wasn't, or that he could be any different than what he was. With Cain, what you saw was what you got. If the woman had a brain in her head she'd listen to the warnings of her family and friends and stay away from him.

He wasn't thinking only of Ellie; he was protecting himself. If he pushed her away now, he wouldn't have a chance to get closer—and she wouldn't have a chance to pull away from him first. It was better not to care about her. Simpler. Safer.

His logic and his intellect agreed wholeheartedly with that conclusion. But some other part of him, some part that kept wanting to surface no matter how valiantly he tried to keep it down, was beginning to care about her anyway.

From the corner of his eye, he saw her pleating the fabric of her white pants. He wasn't at all sure what she would say, what her verdict would be, or why, considering he would never see her after next week, her opinion even mattered.

"I'd kind of wondered about how much of what I'd heard was true."

Tucking her hair behind her ear, she turned toward him. "If you were trying to scare me off, it didn't work. I'm not afraid of you, Cain."

He could scarcely believe the gentle smile she gave him, or how it diffused the tension he'd been battling. She wouldn't judge him. That was a powerful reassurance to have. It also made it more difficult to keep his barriers in place.

"It might be better for both of us if you were."

She turned away from the conviction in his expression. There was something going on between them that she didn't quite understand—and that he clearly didn't want. Yet every time he'd push her away, he'd draw her back again. It was getting frustrating.

"I wish I'd known you before," she said, because maybe then she'd have understood him better. "There had to be reasons for what you did."

Drawn by the pensive softness of her voice, soothed by her basic acceptance of him, Cain couldn't help but respond. She assumed there had been some kind of rationale to his behavior, which was more than anyone else had ever done. Others had simply figured he was no good. He'd been told that so often, he'd even believed it himself.

There had to be reasons for what you did. Her words held a reprieve for him, and he felt grateful to her for that. He'd never considered that there might actually be something behind all of his earlier rebelliousness—until now.

"Maybe at one time there was," he said, and prompted by her encouraging silence, he found himself unearthing long-buried pieces of his past.

She wouldn't judge him, so he could say things to her that he'd never said to anyone else. Miles vanished beneath the wheels, as he remembered how much of what he had done as a teenager had been simply angry reaction. To what, though, he wasn't quite sure. It seemed that when he was younger, his rationale seemed clearer, his motivations more immediate. The kids used to call his mom names, so he'd hurt them back by giving them bloody noses. That was how the fighting had gotten started, and the pattern had been established. As he grew older, he'd found that he didn't have to have a reason to get into a fight. The fights just sort of found him. "My fists solved problems for me that I couldn't solve otherwise," he told her. "It didn't take much to set me off."

"Is that how you first met my uncle?"

"I'd met the sheriff before that started. He picked me up for truancy out on the highway."

That had been the first time he left home, he told her. When he was ten. "I was hitchhiking to Tulsa to see if I could find my father and bring him back. He'd been gone for years then, so even if I'd made it, I wouldn't have found him." With a self-deprecating smile, he mocked his own innocence. He'd been so naive. His mother had been pregnant with another man's child, and Cain, wanting to help because his mother had been so sick, had thought that bringing his father back was the answer. "You couldn't have told me that at the time, though."

Cain's pride had been as strong as his determination. He hadn't told anyone why he was going to Tulsa, because he wasn't supposed to know that his mother was going to have a baby. He'd overheard her on the telephone, telling the child's father—a man whose name she never mentioned— that she would have the child without him. Cain's loyalty to his mother wasn't the only reason for his silence. It hurt far too much to admit that his own father didn't care enough about him and his mom to come back on his own.

Hal Bennett, however, had been equally as determined to get Cain to tell him why he'd run away, and Cain's silence on that point had made him appear surly and uncooperative. It had done no good to tell the sheriff that he hadn't really been running away; that he'd have been back at school in a few days. The sheriff, however, having already labeled him a delinquent and a troublemaker, hadn't believed him.

Cain didn't mention the unfairness of those initial dealings with Ellie's Uncle Hal, or with her father, when he told her that the incident had also gotten him suspended for truancy. He recounted only the broader details, and those with the same detachment he reserved for more incidental childhood recollections—such as the memory of picking blackberries down by the creek. He still had no use for Hal Bennett and others like him who formed knee-jerk judgments, but Cain knew that Ellie cared about her uncle, so he wouldn't say anything against him. He was all too familiar with how it hurt when someone spoke ill of someone you cared about.

"That was all a long time ago." Hoping to convince her as he'd convinced himself, he added, "None of it matters to me anymore."

Ellie didn't think Cain was aware of the lack of persuasion in his tone. There was a lot of hurt and a lot of untapped feelings buried under that protective shell of his. He was letting her see beneath the surface, and what she glimpsed made her certain that much of his past *did* still matter to him. She was also fairly sure that the parts that mattered most were those he hadn't shared.

"A lot of it *does* matter, Cain. You wouldn't be who you are if it hadn't been for those experiences. I think maybe they've made you a little stronger than most."

She could have called him cynical or unfeeling or cold. Women had called him those things before, along with a few less flattering adjectives on a couple of occasions. That Ellie thought him strong made him smile. "You're very good for a man's ego, you know that?"

His grin came as something of a surprise. She'd found that he tended to be rather stingy with real smiles. "That's what friends are for," she said, liking the way his eyes crinkled at the corners. "And by the way, you do know how to be one."

She leaned forward and narrowed her eyes as she perused the complex array of buttons and switches and digital displays on the dashboard. "Which one is the air conditioning?" she asked, fully aware of how intently he was watching her.

"This one."

"Mind if I turn it off and roll down the windows?"

"Go ahead."

When she pressed the indicated switches, the flow of cool air stopped and the windows slid down to let in the warm and rushing wind. Ellie gave her head a toss to get her hair out of her eyes and ran her hands along the edges of the buttery-soft leather seat. "This really is a great car," she said with a sigh. "Maybe we *could* go just a little bit faster.

Cain downshifted, and flashed Ellie a grin that did something very strange to her breathing. "A lady after my own heart," she heard him say over the rush of the wind, and it didn't occur to her to deny it.

He pressed down on the accelerator. Suddenly pinned to the back of her seat, Ellie gasped in startled delight.

They arrived in Greely shortly after six. Greely was much bigger than Aubrey, though by big city standards it lacked certain amenities. It did have a mall, though, and a great pizza parlor, which was where Cain headed at Ellie's request. "Feed me first, then I'll help you pick out the paint."

Mumbling something about being grateful for cheap labor, he pulled into the lot. He'd cut the engine and was removing his keys when he saw her frowning at the clasp of her seat belt.

"That thing sticks sometimes," he said, slipping out of his own to reach across the console. "Here. Let me do it."

The clasp was on her right side, which meant that Cain had to lean across her to get at it. No sooner did he have the clasp in his hand than he regretted his actions.

His face was inches from hers. She was so close that he could see the tiny flecks of gold in her warm, brown eyes. She smelled of something soft and powdery, and the scent of fresh air clung to the air spilling over her shoulders. He thought about pulling back, about letting her do the task herself. He also thought about tasting the soft part of her mouth.

He was far too aware of her. All the time he'd been driving, he'd been conscious of the way the wind whipped her hair around her face, of her breathless laugh when they rounded a corner and the road plunged down like a roller coaster. She'd felt the exhilaration that came with speed and she'd let herself go with the feeling. He'd caught a glimpse of a woman who could be uninhibited and free. Seeing that side of her nature had reminded him of how passionately she'd responded in his arms.

He shouldn't be thinking about that. It wasn't wise, especially when he knew she was thinking of it, too. Her thoughts were betrayed by the shuddering breath she drew, and the quick awareness entering her eyes.

He has to feel it, she thought. There was no way he couldn't. The attraction was always there. Taunting. Teasing. But he was much better than she at pretending it didn't matter. Or maybe for him, she thought when she felt him pull back a little, it really wasn't of any consequence. It was entirely possible that she was just being her unsophisticated, naive self. What was special to her might not be of any significance to someone who'd experienced so much more than she had.

"We seem to have a talent for getting into compromising positions, don't we?" he said, angling his head so he could see if the tab had gotten caught in the latch, which was usually the problem. "First, your aunt shows up this morning and now this."

The belt was free a moment later. Ellie, trying very hard to act as nonchalant as he was, reached for her purse. It was irritating to discover that her fingers were shaking as she pulled out her hairbrush. "That didn't look very good, did it?" she asked, referring to the earlier incident.

Cain's eyes were dark, but his expression was teasing as he remembered how she had looked in that thin nightshirt she'd worn. "Probably not to your aunt," he agreed. "But parts of it looked very good to me."

Chapter Seven

Had it been up to Ellie, she and Cain would have lingered over their pizza instead of rushing through the meal. They also might have slowed down to do a little window-shopping when they threaded their way through the mall to a major department store, where Cain had Ellie pick out the appliances, because he said he knew nothing about such things. Ellie was drawn by her surroundings and wanted to take time to enjoy them, but Cain tended to be rather myopic. His focus was solely on obtaining the items necessary to complete the job he had to do.

His single-mindedness when presented with a specific goal was a trait Ellie had seen in him before. As they looked over paint chips, and Cain muttered about how dumb it was to have so many shades of white, Ellie wondered if he hadn't deliberately honed his ability to block out distractions. For someone who as a teenager wouldn't have been given a nickle's worth of a chance to make something of himself, Cain had accomplished a great deal. He certainly hadn't said as much, but she knew from what he'd told her of his responsibilities at Bessari that he was respected. He hadn't earned either that respect or his position by being unsure of his goals, and she felt certain he'd had to prove himself often enough before he achieved them. She had to admire him for that, even if she did find his immediate preoccupation a little exhausting.

After leaving the home improvement department, where they'd purchased the paint and painting supplies, they combed the hardware section for new hinges for the screen doors and replacement screens for the windows. Cain arranged to have most of the paint, the new stove and the hot water heater delivered, and they took the other purchases with them. They loaded up the car with the help of a freckle-faced stock boy, who went positively bug-eyed at the sight of the sleek black Lamborghini in the back of the parking lot.

In a tone just short of reverent, the enraptured youth whispered a quiet "Man!" as they stopped beside the vehicle. He set down the four gallons of eggshell latex paint Cain had determined he should take with him and gingerly touched the strakes atop the sloped rear flank. "This is some hunk of machinery. Is it yours?"

Cain was apparently accustomed to the homage being paid his car. Seeming a little preoccupied, he mumbled a distracted "Mmm," and touched a sequence of numbers on the security pad by the handle to unlock the door. A moment later, swinging the door up like a large black metal wing, he shoved a bag of brushes and drop cloths into the small space behind the driver's seat.

The boy handed him a can of paint, which Cain stowed as well. "What'll she do?"

Ellie heard the question as she raised the passenger door and glanced across the low roof. She was just wondering what a car could possibly "do," when she saw Cain smile.

"Legally she'll do fifty-five. On a track, I've buried the needle."

"You race her?"

"Naw. I just wanted to see what she had in her. We clocked her at 170, but then she got the shakes. You want to see the power plant?"

The kid, looking as if he were being offered free tickets to a rock concert, held out another can of paint. "You mean it?"

"Why not. Let's get the rest of this loaded and we'll see what makes her go."

Ellie watched in fascination as Cain grinned at the boy. He was still smiling a minute later, when they leaned over the car's engine, which was behind the passenger compartment.

She couldn't see him from where she remained by the passenger door, but she could hear every word being said. Not that she understood much. As far as she was concerned, they might as well have been talking in Swahili. Their conversation was revealing, though, in another, more significant way. Cain was easily—willingly—accommodating the boy's interest. He was patient with questions, encouraging any the boy wanted to ask. Back in Aubrey, from what she'd heard, he was avoiding conversation with just about everyone. Everyone, that was, but her.

"Hey, Ellie," she heard him call as he stepped back into view. "Start it up for me. Will you?"

He tossed her the keys before she could answer. A moment later, he gave her a shrug, the gesture seeming to say, *What can I do? The kid wants to see it.* But Ellie could tell by the animation in Cain's expression that he wasn't really opposed to obliging the young man.

She slid into the smooth leather seat and put the car in neutral. All evening, even in his hurry, Cain had seemed oddly relaxed, more at ease with himself than she'd ever seen him. The ever present edginess had all but vanished; his tendency toward defensiveness had been remarkably curbed. Now his reserved attitude was conspicuously absent. It was as if the bristles had begun wearing away when they left Aubrey, and now, away from there, he could finally be himself.

The transformation was most intriguing.

The car sprang to life with a refined roar. Getting a thumbs-up from Cain, she set the brake, after discovering that it was not in the same place as on her mother's more modest Chevrolet, and climbed out. As she did, two things occurred to her: first, that Cain was now so absorbed with his car that he'd forgotten all about her; second, that it was really stupid to wonder why she was letting that bother her when there were other things she could be doing. It wasn't that often that she got into Greely. Since she was here now, she might as well take advantage of this little delay.

Her Uncle Jay's fiftieth birthday was a week from Sunday and she'd yet to find him a suitable present. She and Cain had passed a men's clothing store in the mall. She'd look there while the enraptured youth, now admiring the sharp down-slope of the front fenders, finished drooling over Cain's "radical wheels."

It was only minutes after she told Cain where she'd be that she felt him behind her. She was standing at a display of wallets and belts, grimacing at the prices, when she heard his quiet "What are you looking for?"

Turning so quickly that her hair swung across her face, she gave a breathless little laugh. His nearness had startled her. "I didn't expect you so soon." She drew a handful of hair behind her ear and cocked her head to one side. "Does that happen a lot?"

It was apparent enough that Cain knew she was referring to the boy's interest in his Lamborghini. He didn't even hesitate before he shrugged. "Once in a while. It's not a common car."

And you're not a common man, she couldn't help but think. "Is that why you drive it? Because it's different?"

"Maybe." He grinned. "I don't really know. I never gave it much thought. I just like driving it."

Without thinking, he reached over to tuck back a strand of hair she'd missed. Caught off guard by his impulsiveness, a little surprised by it, he shoved his hands into his back pockets and took a step away.

Ellie noticed that his stance drew his shirt tighter over his chest, spreading the unbuttoned part of its placket to expose a V of dark hair on his chest. Up close or out of reach, he was dangerously appealing.

Realizing she was staring, hoping he hadn't noticed, she gamely raised her glance. When she did, he lifted one eyebrow.

"You didn't answer me. What are you looking for in here?"

He truly had the most incredible eyes. Hard, yet gentle somehow. She was sure he'd hate it if he knew how easy it was for her to see that gentleness. He was always so quick to cover it.

"I'm looking for something for a very special man."

The heavy arch of his eyebrow rose fractionally.

"My Uncle Jay," she said, turning back to a glass-enclosed case by a display of cashmere sweaters. Once, just once, she wished she had the nerve to cross that invisible line he kept drawing between them. Playing by his rules was getting a little nerve-racking, especially when she wasn't sure she understood the game. "I saw a smoking jacket in the window when we came by here before, but that doesn't seem quite right, after all. What do you think of those?"

He glanced down at the cuff links she indicated, one set gold the other silver. "They're okay, I guess. If he needs cuff links."

His opinion was not exactly helpful. "He doesn't *need* much of anything. That's what makes it so difficult to buy for him. I want something he'll really like."

"He's the senator, isn't he?"

She nodded.

"What's he like?"

A little like you, she found herself thinking, then wondered at the incongruity of the thought. It was impossible to picture her very proper uncle in a pair of snug jeans and a chambray shirt that never quite got buttoned all the way. Just as it was equally difficult to picture Cain in a three-piece, pin-striped suit. Cain was too untamed to be stuffed into such conservative garb. Yet he and her uncle did share a few qualities. They were both a little difficult to figure out, and they both had a nose-thumbing disregard for conventional behavior.

Jason Collier Bennett was his own man. He did things his way and didn't apologize for stepping on toes. He had earned that right by devoting himself entirely to his constituents and sacrificing any personal life he might have had. Jay had never married; his only family was his brothers and their families. While he didn't get along especially well with Hal, a circumstance Ellie blamed on their strong personalities rather than any lack of brotherly affection, he was close to her father and had always seemed especially fond of Ellie. Ellie, in turn, adored him. He treated her like an adult when she was a child. He was also the only member of the family who didn't feel the necessity to counsel her on the course of her life. Only once had he given her advice and that had been when she graduated from high school.

"You just always do what *you* know is right," he'd told her. "And don't compromise yourself. Once you do that, you're putting other people's values ahead of your own and pretty soon you'll have nothing left to believe in."

At eighteen, she hadn't realized how elemental his advice was. At the time all she'd thought was that he sounded awfully fierce about the philosophy. What she remembered right now was that Cain had said something quite similar just the other day.

"He's rather like you," she decided to say aloud, since after she'd thought about it, the comparison didn't seem so inconsistent after all.

A dubious frown crossed his face. For a moment, Ellie thought he didn't care for the idea of being likened to a Bennett. Then she realized he was only curious. The first day they met, when he'd been so insistent on determining which Bennett was her father, he'd said that he didn't know this particular uncle. That wasn't surprising. After Jay's election as a county representative years ago, he'd moved to Greely. With his rise up the political ladder, he'd gone on to Oklahoma City and Washington, D.C. He really hadn't spent much time in Aubrey.

"Would you mind expanding on that?" Cain asked.

His tone was deliberately neutral, his expression the same as he waited for Ellie's response. In turn, Ellie tried not to smile. A commendable effort, but a useless one.

"Oh, you're both a bit on the independent side. And arrogant, and opinionated. Maybe even a little bullheaded," she added, her smile becoming impish when his glance turned droll. "There are a few differences between you, though," she went on blandly. "He prefers large, comfortable cars to racy ones. And he likes wine," she added, when she remembered that Cain didn't particularly care for the stuff.

There were other distinctions, too. Uncle Jay was more polished than Cain, his sophistication a by-product of his years courting and being courted by Washington's political elite. Cain was worldly, but in a different way, one that was more basic and easier for her to relate to. It was the very roughness of his edges that created his mystique.

"That's what you should get him, then."

Somewhat preoccupied with the way his eyes held hers, Ellie found her train of thought had been derailed. He was smiling at her, a lazy kind of smile that did strange things to the muscles in her stomach.

"A large comfortable car?" she asked when she realized he was waiting for her to say something.

"I was thinking more along the lines of a bottle of wine."

"May I help you?"

A rather tall and decidedly attractive saleswoman, the same one who'd ignored Ellie's entrance into the small and expensive store, had appeared at Cain's elbow. She raised a perfectly plucked eyebrow in Ellie's direction. Then her glance, suddenly enhanced with a warm smile, bounced immediately toward Cain.

"The store is closing now," she said to him in a soft drawl. "But if there's something I can show you, I'd be happy to help."

The invitation in the woman's voice was real enough. It was in her eyes, too. And to her, Ellie was as significant as the rack of belts behind her.

Cain, aware of the woman's interest, if not her very female appeal, mumbled a distracted "No thanks," without giving her much more than a glance. He was too busy watching Ellie.

She'd turned away, pretending great interest in the buckle of an ornately scrolled brown belt. She didn't want to look at Cain for fear she'd see the woman's interest being returned; not that she cared one way or the other what Cain did, or whom he found attractive, she told herself. She just hated the way she felt at the moment, and didn't want him to see that. He tended to see far too much where she was concerned as it was.

There was no mistaking the look the woman had just given Ellie. She had just been dismissed as inconsequential. She'd been subjected to that cool dismissal before—by one of Brent's girlfriends. But while the saleswoman had cast her off as no threat, Ellie's equally quick assessment of her had been just the opposite. Stylish, curvaceous and confident, the woman was everything Ellie knew she herself wasn't.

A quick frown of inadequacy skittered over her delicate features. Abandoning her survey of the belt buckle, she crossed her arms over her simple green blouse. With her arms wrapped so tightly, she could nearly feel her ribs, which made her aware of yet another shortcoming. Where the raven-haired woman beside her had seductive, voluptuous curves, Ellie had little dips and bumps.

"Ellie?" she heard Cain say as if he were repeating himself. "Did you want to look at those cuff links?"

She shook her head, the brush of her hair over her shoulders making her think that all she needed was a headband and she'd look like Alice in Wonderland. That thought didn't help at all. The saleswoman's hair was very short, cut up high on the sides and back and fluffed up on top the way Ellie had seen it done in magazines. On the woman the style looked fantastic. If Ellie had tried to wear hers that way, she'd have looked like a boy.

"No," she finally said in response to his question. "I'll get the wine, as you suggested."

Though she was smiling—if the strained curve of her mouth could be called a smile—she wouldn't meet his eyes. Cain, oblivious to the saleswoman's shrug, found Ellie's behavior rather telling as he ushered her out of the store.

Dusk was giving way to darkness, and there were very few cars left in the parking lot. Cain's car looked a little lonely sitting all by itself between two pools of dull light cast by security lamps. They headed toward it, Cain watching Ellie and Ellie watching the toes of her sandals as they crossed the rows of yellow lines on the blacktop.

They'd been in the car for nearly a full minute before Ellie realized that Cain had yet to start the engine. In the pale blue light of evening, she saw him watching her, his expression patient. He was obviously in no hurry to go.

"Are we waiting for something?" she asked.

From the way he shifted to face her, his back fitting comfortably against the door as he angled himself in the seat, it appeared that they were. His mumbled "Uh-huh" confirmed it. "We're waiting for you to tell me what happened back there."

"Back where?"

"Oh, come on, Ellie. In the store. That woman asked if she could help and you practically crawled inside that belt rack. Do you know her?"

"I'd never seen her before."

"Then what happened?"

Her glance slid from the dashboard to the floor. "Nothing happened."

"Ellie."

She said nothing, her reticence growing in direct proportion to Cain's exasperation. It was as clear to him as the twilight sky that he wasn't going to get anywhere by pushing her. Cain, though, didn't give up when he wanted something. Ever. And when he wanted something, he was about as subtle in his pursuit as a tank. "You were intimidated by her."

It had been a blind shot, but it hit the mark. Ellie's eyes flew to him, wide and filled with denial. She couldn't look at him and lie, however, and her glance returned reluctantly to the floor.

Frowning, he ran his fingers over the smooth leather covering of the steering wheel. "Aggressive women can be intimidating, Ellie. Sometimes, even to aggressive men. But you," he told her bluntly, "are intimidated far too easily."

Refusing to consider his evaluation as valid, she muttered a tight "No, I'm not."

Cain started to counter, then thought better of it. There were other examples of her diffidence that he could give her. He could point out how she'd accepted her uncle's explanation about the break-in into his mother's house in spite of what she'd seen with her own eyes. And how, just this morning, she'd hurried into her apartment to dress the instant her aunt instructed her to do so. He wouldn't say anything else, though. Her hang-ups were none of his concern—and it was precisely because he *was* concerned that he needed to create some distance between them.

"Suit yourself," he dismissed with the cool indifference that protected him so well. "If being walked on feels good to you, that's your business."

Her quiet intake of breath told him his words had stung. That was exactly what he'd intended them to do, but he hardly felt proud of accomplishing his goal.

He reached for his keys. He could see that Ellie made little attempts to be her own person; even if she couldn't. But despite those attempts, her family had her wrapped around their collective little fingers. Ellie had the confidence of a mouse around aggressive or assertive types. "A defenseless little mouse," he muttered, switching on the ignition.

"What did you say?"

With a scowl, he shook his head and reached for the gearshift. "More than I should have. Just forget it."

"No." Her hand darted out, covering his to keep him from putting the car into gear. Quickly, she pulled back, feeling terribly self-conscious at the gesture. "You called me a little mouse." She ignored the "defenseless" part. "My Uncle Jay used to call me that."

For a moment the only sound to be heard was the surge of the engine as Cain revved it impatiently. Finally, not looking as if he really wanted to, he asked, "Why?"

"Because I never used to say much, I guess." There were times when Ellie could have sworn that the old adage about children being seen and not heard had originated in her parents' home. A child did not speak unless spoken to, and only by being quiet was she allowed to remain in the company of the adults. Her silence had made her parents rather proud of their well-behaved offspring, and making her parents proud of her was something Ellie had always tried to do. "I used to think it was nice, the nickname, I mean."

But that was when she'd thought it a term of affection. For her uncle it had been. Now, hearing it from Cain, she was instantly aware of all the name's connotations. None of them were flattering.

She fervently wished she'd kept her mouth shut a moment ago.

Over the creak of soft leather as she twisted to look away, she heard Cain's muttered "Oh, Ellie."

Staring out at the deserted parking lot, she felt her insides clench. She hated it when people said, "Oh, Ellie," to her in that patiently exasperated way. Uncle Hal and her mother were always doing it. "Oh, Ellie," they'd say, as if she didn't have a brain in her head. "You don't know what you're talking about." Or, "Oh, Ellie, you can't possibly think that's so." The last person in the world she needed to hear it from was Cain—especially right now.

"Don't you think we should go?" she asked, feeling very foolish for having relayed something he couldn't possibly have cared about.

Cain's better judgment certainly told him they should go. But Ellie looked so vulnerable trying to act as if she wasn't hurt. How often had he covered up so no one would know how bad he felt? He'd pretty much mastered the tactic, but Ellie...Ellie was lousy at it.

His sigh was heavy, the only expression he could find for his inability to maintain the distance he'd sought to put between them.

It was the sound of that sigh that made Ellie stiffen. He was annoyed with her. She was sure of it. At least she was until she felt his hand moving the hair back from the side of her face.

"I said I'd try not to touch you again. But you make it very difficult. Impossible, I think."

It was the feel of his callused fingers gently brushing her skin as much as his words that made Ellie stop pretending. That was, after all, what she'd been doing all evening— pretending it didn't matter that he could never really care about her. Yet always, in the back of her mind, was the quiet hope that he would touch her again. She knew it wasn't a particularly wise thing to want, but something about Cain didn't allow for conventional wisdom. With him, she could only think in the present. Possibly because, with him, she knew there was no future.

Her thinking made little sense to her. She didn't care. For once, she didn't want something just because it made sense.

Her eyes held his as he ran the back of his knuckles down her cheek. "You shouldn't look at me that way, Ellie."

"What way is that?" she all but whispered.

A beautifully tortured expression tightened the rugged angles of his face. "Like you're not going to stop me."

She turned toward his caress, her simple acceptance of his touch more significant to him than anything she could have said. Knowing he'd pay for it later, he let his hand fall to her shoulder and drew her toward him.

Ellie felt the gentle pressure of his fingers on her upper arms. A leather-covered console separated the seats and he guided her over it, sliding his own seat back to settle her on his lap. The switch of positions took mere seconds. With his hand cupping the side of her neck, he let his thumb caress her throat, his eyes darkening at the expectation filling hers.

"You are," he told her, "far too tempting."

His mouth brushed hers gently, a mere feathering of skin over skin. Once. Twice. "Stop me," he murmured.

Encouraged by her whispered "No," he gave up the restraint to still the sweet trembling of her lips.

Ellie's arms wound around his neck, her heart hammering as anticipation gave way to longing. This was what she'd wanted, what she'd ached for. Cain holding her, touching her, filling her with that exhilarating recklessness she'd felt before in his arms. His scent, his taste blocked out the old doubts and inadequacies. There was no room for them among the brighter, headier sensations he caused her to feel. She opened to him, greedy for the sense of vibrancy he offered.

The instant she responded, he pushed her head back into the crook of his arm, his mouth working over hers in answering need. His demand took its force from gentleness, and she had no defense against that. Not that she wanted one. For now, all she wanted was the heady oblivion his kisses created. Because in that oblivion, he allowed her to feel a kind of passion she'd never known existed.

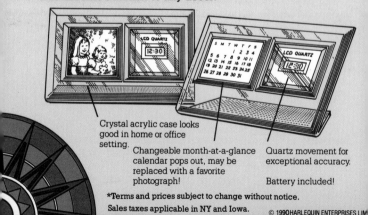

WE EVEN PROVIDE FREE POSTAGE!

It costs you *nothing* to send for your free books — we've paid the postage on the attached reply card. And we'll pick up the postage on your shipment of free books and gifts, and also on any subsequent shipments of books, should you choose to become a subscriber. Unlike many book clubs, we charge *nothing* for postage and handling!

Take it slow, Cain thought, marveling at the swift urgency sweeping through him. Take it slow, he warned himself again, wondering how he was supposed to do that when she felt so wonderfully compliant. There was no hesitation, no holding back. Her response was untutored, natural and wholly capable of driving him right over the edge.

Brushfire. The word leaped into Cain's mind as his tongue slipped over hers and his hand closed over her breast. She stiffened for a moment, then relaxed with a little moan that sent liquid heat pounding through his body. He felt as if he were the bone-dry grass that covered the plains in the summer and that a match had just been set to him. Quick, insuppressible, that fire could rage. But he would control himself. He wanted to savor her. Enjoy her. Know her tenderness as well as her passion. Her skin was damp from the still heat of the night, growing damper as he kissed the corners of her eyes, her temples, her throat. The bud of her breast grew rigid in his hand and he was so hard that he hurt.

He could take her right here.

His fingers slipped to the buttons on her blouse. A moment later he found the front clasp of her bra. It gave with the merest flick, his hand immediately closing over the softness he was seeking. Ellie's fingers covered his, whether to hinder or assist, he wasn't sure. It didn't matter. Somewhere in the back of his mind, a voice of warning had sounded. It was the echo of his own thoughts.

Take her? Here? What was he thinking?

The answer to that particular question, he determined through a mind-muddling haze of desire, was that he *wasn't* thinking. He'd been without a woman for so long that the heat inside him had apparently melted a vital part of his brain. Had the woman been anyone but Ellie, his next move would have been to a motel. For a number of reasons, his move now was away from her.

He moved his lips to her temple and drew a deep breath, while pulling the front of her blouse closed. He hated to let her go, but what he wanted and what he needed to do weren't at all the same. It was better if she thought he put no meaning to their physical attraction, if he treated it only as the biological reaction that it was. If that truth wounded her a little, that couldn't be helped. It was better than having her think there was more to their relationship than there could be.

"Ellie," he said, easing her forward, "I'm not going to be here that long. Another week. Two at the most."

His words confused her, as did the sudden gruffness in his husky voice. "I know that."

"Then let's not mess it up, huh?"

She truly did not understand him, or what had happened in the past few moments to make him withdraw from her. Not at all certain that her voice wouldn't betray the trembling she still felt in her body, she chose silence over the questions poised on her lips and shakily redid the clasp and buttons he'd unfastened.

"Look," he began, feeling it necessary to provide the explanation she couldn't yet ask for, "I know you don't like it when someone tells you what you do or don't want. But in this case, I know I'm right. Sex isn't what you want. With me, that's all it would be."

Confused and anxious, maybe even a little embarrassed, she slid back into her own seat and sat with her hand covering the pulse at the base of her throat. She supposed she should be grateful to him for being so honest with her. Or possibly, humiliated that he would so boldly assume her willingness to sleep with him—though, based on her response to him, he wasn't totally out of line with that assumption. She was neither. Her only thought when she saw the shuttered look in his eyes before he looked away to head the car out of the parking lot, was that Cain Whitlow was still fighting. Only now, the battle he was fighting was within himself.

It had been nearly eleven o'clock when they arrived back in Aubrey and Cain had watched Ellie hurry up the steps to her apartment. And it had been well after midnight the last time he looked at the luminous dial of the clock on the floor beside his bed in the basement. He had no idea what time it was now. He'd been asleep for a while, though. He must have been because the moon was now shining through his open window, its descent into dawn not too far away.

It was too warm, the air too still for comfort even with the narrow windows above him open. The heat had made what sleep he'd managed restless and fitful, but it was heat of a different kind that had made him awaken.

The drive home had been tense, his and Ellie's conversation minimal at best. Because of her silence, Cain had been left with nothing but his thoughts for company.

Cain rarely dreamed and when he did, he tended to forget those detached sequences of subliminal imagination once he awoke. Now, he could neither forget nor ignore the images that that still burned in his mind. Ellie had been in his arms, soft and willing and wanting him as desperately as he wanted her. He'd tasted again the sweetness of her mouth and felt the sensual yearning of her body as it molded itself to his. He'd ached with the pleasure of feeling her small breast strain against his hand, and gloried in the supple strength of her legs as they'd wrapped around him.

Consciously, Cain had refused to give in to his desire for her. At a deeper level that desire taunted him relentlessly.

That need was what had awakened Cain. What accompanied him back toward sleep was an aching sort of emptiness so real it actually hurt.

He was barely aware that his right fist had tightened. In it was the cameo—the one with the profile that reminded him so much of Ellie. He'd taken it out of its velvet bag around midnight and had been looking at it before he'd first fallen asleep.

Since he had nothing better to do with it, he'd decided to give it to her tomorrow.

Chapter Eight

By the middle of the next afternoon, Cain wasn't thinking about either Ellie or the cameo. All of his energy was focused on the repairs needing to be done. Work, especially the physically demanding kind, was a great escape, which was why he began his overhaul of his mother's home by clearing it out.

With a detachment bordering on numbness, he emptied the house of its contents, storing everything, with the exception of his bed and the kitchen table and chairs, in the garage. Beforehand he'd hauled out all the junk in the garage. He'd take it to the dump as soon as he could figure out how to get it there.

The next morning he tackled the outside, preparing it for paint by tying back the shrubs, removing screens and beginning the tedious task of removing the chipped and peeling layers of old paint. When the sun set, he moved inside to the easier task of painting interior walls. He was only good for about half a room that night.

The following morning, he placed a call to Carlo Bessari. He didn't call to explain the reason for the time off he'd requested, though the subject of his mother's death finally did come up. But he'd been in Aubrey for nearly a week and needed to tell his boss that he'd be gone for a little longer than he'd first planned.

"No problem," he heard his boss say from his villa in Palermo. His Italian accent was heavy. Born in Milan nearly sixty years ago, Carlo was the last son of a very old, very wealthy family. His involvement with high performance cars had begun as a hobby. Now, thirty years later, he involved himself in little else. "You can take what time you need. Two weeks. Three. These things . . . well, these things, they happen."

Pushing aside his coffee cup, Cain rose from his chair at the kitchen table and stepped over a can of paint. He wasn't comfortable with his boss's expression of sympathy—and for Carlo, that was what his last words had been.

Cain translated that discomfort into his pacing during the call. But the cord of the phone attached to the wall under the cabinet was too short to go any appreciable distance. He was more accustomed to cordless telephones.

"I just thought you should know why I won't be at the plant when you get there on Monday. I still plan on making the association meeting in Monte Carlo on the first, but in the meantime, I'll have Rick take over for me on the tests we're running on the new fuel cells. I'll talk to him about what I want done there."

Having reached the sink, which contained the paintbrushes he'd rinsed out last night along with a roller and a paint tray, he retraced his steps to the stove. "I should be out of here in about ten days. Sooner if I can manage it." He cast a skeptical eye about the room. Instead of revarnishing the cabinets, he'd decided to just paint over them. The pristine coat of white enamel on those above the drainboard made those below it look even worse. "This place needs a lot of work."

His weariness must have been evident in his tone. "So hire painters or carpenters of whatever it is you need," Carlo suggested in his usual, insistent way.

"I can't do that."

A deep, seldom heard chuckle joined the faint sound of static. "With what I pay you? Of course you can."

"It's not a matter of money."

"There is no labor there?"

That wasn't it, either. "I just want to do it myself."

After a moment, a knowing "Ah" came over the line. "It is duty then."

"I suppose," Cain returned, not having really thought about what it was that had been driving him the past couple of days. He'd just never doubted that the repairs were something *he* should do.

"Duty," Carlo repeated. "That, I understand. Certain things we cannot put in the hands of a stranger. Some people, they can give away their responsibilities. But you, Cain. You have integrity. I always know that about you. You need more time, you call."

Assuring him that he would, Cain broke the connection and placed another call to the test facility outside of Orlando, to speak with the young mechanic he had hired just last month. Rick was on the line within the minute. But before Cain got down to business, he asked this newest assistant, who he'd heard was something of an expert in the area of wines, to track down a particular vintage for him—the one Ellie had mentioned yesterday when she'd stopped to talk to him on her way in from the flower shop.

With a deference that would have amused Cain had he been in a different frame of mind, the young man assured him that the matter would be taken care of, and after a quick "I appreciate it," Cain turned the conversation to work.

It was with some reluctance that, nearly an hour later, he broke the contact with the life he'd created for himself to face the part he'd yet to escape.

Soon, he reminded himself. Soon.

According to the arrangements Ellie had made, her Uncle Hal himself would pick up the furniture in the garage, along with the boxes she had helped pack. He had agreed, reluctantly, though Ellie didn't mention that, that Cain could use his truck to make a trip to the dump.

Since their return from Greely, Ellie had walked a cautious circle around Cain, not knowing quite what to make of his attitude toward her. He was friendly enough, she supposed, but she couldn't help noticing how careful he was to maintain a certain indifference toward her.

The past couple of evenings he'd been working outside when she came home from work. She had asked how the repairs were going, and after he told her what he'd done that day, she'd tell him to be sure to let her know if there was anything she could do to help. She'd known from the way his jaw clenched before he said a word that he'd decline her offer. He'd been very careful, however, to say "Thanks, anyway."

They were being very polite and very civil and Ellie could feel the gap widening between them.

At the moment, standing next door on Hanna's back stoop while she waited for her elderly neighbor to answer her knock, she wasn't pondering Cain's behavior. She was thinking about how distracting it was when he ran around half-dressed.

From her position by Hanna's vine-covered back porch, she could clearly see him perched at the top of a ladder, scraping paint from under the eaves of his mother's single-story house. His jeans rode low on his hips and his shirt had been abandoned to the heat, allowing a tantalizing view of his beautifully bronzed and muscled back. Sweat gleamed on his skin, his muscles flexing and relaxing with his movements.

Though it was barely ten in the morning, it was already nearly eighty degrees, and Cain was working on the shaded side of the house to escape the intensity of the sun. Beyond him, the lawn sprinkler turned in lazy circles, cooling the birds flapping beneath the spray. It would soon become too hot for even the birds, and they would seek the shelter of a shade tree. Cain, Ellie knew, would continue working, even when the sun burned directly overhead. And when it grew too dark to see, he would move inside and work in there. He'd followed the same pattern for the past three days. Last night, it had been nearly midnight when Ellie saw his lights go out.

"I thought I heard somebody out here." Hanna, using the tip of her cane, pushed open her screen door. The knot of her fine white hair at the top of her head had slipped a bit off-center. She reached to straighten it. "Come on in, child. You on your way into town?"

Ellie couldn't help but smile at the woman's phrasing. "Town" was two blocks away, yet Hanna spoke as if it were miles. "That's why I stopped by. To see if you need anything. I can be back in an hour or so, if you do."

It was a habit of Ellie's to make the offer a couple of times a week. Hanna's son saw to most of her needs, but he'd recently taken up with a young widow over by Cross Creek and had become a little lax with his visits. Hanna, Ellie was sure, encouraged his absence. At seventy-two, she was still holding out for a grandchild. Having been a late bloomer herself, she refused to give up hope that her dear Leonard might someday marry.

"Not working today, huh?"

"Aunt Jo's at the shop this morning."

"She's feeling pretty good now, is she?"

Knowing that the lively old woman was hinting for an update on Jo's health, Ellie took the time to tell her how much better her aunt seemed to be this week. The inquiry wasn't just idle interest. Hanna was most sympathetic to attacks of arthritis. But she did tend to go on and on about whatever article she'd last read about its treatment and invariably made Ellie promise to tell her aunt all about it, too.

"So," Ellie said, after delivering that promise, "do you need anything?"

"As a matter of fact, I do." Instead of giving Ellie a grocery list, which she sometimes did, or asking her to run by the drugstore, she muttered, "Come on in here for a minute," and slowly led the way into her crowded living room.

Hanna liked flowers. More accurately, the woman was obsessed with them. They were in the pink rose-print of her sofa and chairs, on the green-and white lily-print wallpaper, and in the still life pictures hanging just about everywhere. Even her dress was covered with tiny lavender violets. Since Ellie worked in the flower shop, Hanna figured she must share her love, and invariably she brought Ellie in to show her a new picture Leonard had painted for her or a new pattern, floral of course, she was working into her crochet.

The room was actually far too busy for Ellie's taste, but she always told Hanna that her son's creations, usually paintings of vases full of indefinable blooms, looked wonderful.

Thinking she was about to be treated to another of Leonard's works, Ellie dutifully waited in the oppressively stale air, while Hanna turned down the television, which had been blaring with Saturday morning cartoons, and ambled over to the window.

"This thing won't work."

"Your air conditioner?"

"Mmm." Poking at the buttons, Hanna let out a disgusted sigh. "Leonard just bought the thing new for me last month, and I can't get so much as a whiff of cool air from it now. Comes with a guarantee, but by the time I get it shipped to one of those authorized repair centers and get it back, I won't be needing it."

Ellie's expertise with such things was limited to the operation of an on and off switch. Not knowing what *she* could do about it, she nonetheless reached over and pushed the buttons herself. There was a soft whirring sound, but no air came out.

It's no wonder the room is so stuffy, she thought, then realized it would only get worse as the day wore on.

"Have you called Murray?" Ellie asked, mentioning the local handyman.

Hanna's topknot bounced with her nod. "Yep. But his wife says he's out at the Nelson place helping Ed with his broken-down balers. Doesn't expect him back till late tonight. Then first thing in the morning, he's got to run out to Dalton to finish a job he started there. That snooty Bernice Pruitt's got him next. He can't get here before midweek."

Quashing a smile at Hanna's description of the mercantile owner's officious wife, Ellie tried to come up with an alternative to Murray. "What about your son?"

"What about him?"

"Can't he fix it?"

"Len? Not so's it won't be broken worse than it is. That boy doesn't know nothing about anything mechanical. He's always been more the literary type."

Leonard, who'd finally moved to a place of his own last year at the age of thirty-six, was far from "literary," despite the fact that he taught seventh and eighth grade. Ellie believed a more appropriate term was *nerd*, but she wasn't about to say so.

Hanna considered her dilemma for another few seconds before a look of profound reluctance skittered over her wrinkled face. That she had some reservation about whatever had occurred to her was quite evident in her hesitation.

Finally, looking as if she had no other choice, she turned her pale blue eyes to Ellie. The look there was oddly cool. "You don't suppose that Whitlow boy over there could fix it, do you? I never did cotton much to him, but as I remember it, he was always tinkering with mechanical things."

A dull thudding started in Ellie's chest, its cause lying somewhere between the way Hanna had spoken of Cain, and her own anticipation at having a reason to talk to him. She thought it best not to dwell on either. "I could ask him."

"I'd be beholden to you," the elderly woman returned and slowly lowered herself into her rose-print easy chair. A moment later, she turned up the television by its remote control unit, apparently wanting to divert herself before she could question the wisdom of having the brash young man inside her home.

Once out the door, Ellie crossed Hanna's back lawn and headed for the fence. Holding the material of her yellow cotton sundress so it wouldn't catch on a nail, she climbed over the low, split rails separating Hanna's yard from Amanda's. She walked straight to the ladder, shielding her eyes against the glare of the sun as she looked up at Cain. In the warm still air, a shower of curled paint chips came drifting down.

"Have you got a minute?" she asked, moving forward when the dusting of chips settled.

Angling sideways, the scraper dangling in his hand, Cain wiped his forehead with the back of his arm. "Depends."

His tone didn't sound particularly inviting. It sounded even less so when she heard his muttered "Damn it," just before the old towel he'd draped over the top rung landed on the ground with a soft plop.

She reached for the rag. "Now's a bad time. I can tell."

"What was your first clue?"

He was smiling. It wasn't much of a smile. But it was enough to let her know that she wasn't the cause of his irritation. The one she sent back held a touch of sympathy. The strength-sapping heat, combined with the long hours he'd been putting in, was bound to test the humor of the most even-tempered soul. All things considered, she couldn't find fault with his mood.

Watching him descend, she tried to keep her attention on something other than his naked torso. Not an easy feat when she so easily remembered how solid his body had felt against hers.

"You don't have to do this all alone, you know," she told him, but wasn't about to repeat her offers of assistance. He'd only refuse again. "I'm sure you could hire someone to help you. Phyllis Cavanaugh has two boys in high school, and I know they've been looking for odd jobs this summer. Her husband, Luke, was laid off after he hurt his back working construction, so I'm sure they could use the money."

Cain skipped the last two rungs, his booted feet making a distinct thud when he came down on the scraggly lawn in front of her. He pulled a red handkerchief from his back pocket and wiped it across his face. When he withdrew it, the look he gave her indicated that he'd heard such advice before. "I doubt that Luke Cavanaugh would want his kids working for me. He and I weren't exactly what you'd call the best of friends. The last time I saw him, he and I got into a little bartering session." At her obvious incomprehension, he promptly expanded. "We traded black eyes."

"That was a long time ago," she said quietly.

"Yeah. Well, I'm not interested in seeing if he's changed his opinion of me, and I'm sure he feels pretty much the same way. I just want to get this house finished so I can get out of here."

There was a note of warning in Cain's voice, like the menacing buzz of the honeybees darting around the feathery red blossoms of a bottlebrush tree by the corner of the house. One did not deliberately provoke Cain without the risk of getting stung.

Refusing to feel wounded by Cain's wish to be gone from this place, she concentrated only on his pigheaded refusal to accept help. That stubborn pride of his was a constant source of exasperation to her. She was about to point out that her suggestion would only have facilitated his goal, when he beat her to it.

"It would go faster if I had someone to do the trim, though. Especially inside. Think I could talk you into doing it? There's a case of 1974 Heitz Wine Cellars Cabernet Sauvignon in it for you."

Just yesterday, Ellie had learned from her aunt that the wine Cain had just mentioned was Uncle Jay's favorite. She'd also learned, upon calling a liquor store in Greely, that if it could even be located, it was outrageously expensive. Last night after she asked Cain about his day, she'd passed on that information to him.

As he stood looking as if her answer didn't matter to him one way or the other, Ellie realized that the one thing she could count on was Cain's being truly unpredictable. Just when she was sure that he was determined to paint every square inch of this house by himself, he decided to have her help him with it. As an incentive, he'd even traced down a rare vintage of wine. The man, she was sure, was determined to drive her batty.

"A case? I can barely afford a bottle."

"I got you a good deal," he said matter-of-factly. "Besides, you'd work it off."

Her delight at being able to give her uncle something so extravagant was painfully short-lived. Cain, she realized, had just put a price on what, until now, had been free.

"You don't have to give me the wine for helping you. I offered before to do that for nothing."

"Fine. If you don't want it, I'll send it back when it gets here."

"I didn't say I didn't want it. I do. One bottle anyway. That's all I can afford."

"And I told you, you don't have to pay for it."

"Yes," she muttered, feeding off of his insistence. "I do."

"Does that mean you aren't going to help me?"

"What it means is that I don't want you to *pay* me for helping you." Didn't he understand that friends helped each other without expecting something in return? Or was that the problem? Was he insisting on some form of payment for what she did for him because he didn't want to feel obligated?

It certainly appeared that way. It also appeared that he wasn't terribly pleased at having his offer refused. He gave her a long and level glance and abruptly turned away.

A garden hose lay curled at the faucet located by the bottlebrush tree. Picking up the end of the hose, Cain turned on the spigot and took a long drink of water. Before he turned it off again, he bent his head and let the liquid run over his neck.

Rivulets of water coursed down his chest as he stood up straight, snaking over the hard plane of his stomach to be absorbed by the waistband of his jeans. Ellie watched in fascination as the denim darkened with the moisture. Slowly, her glance worked its way back up to the tiny droplets that clung to the dark hair spreading fanlike over his chest.

Ellie's own throat was a little dry. She looked up, her gaze locking with his. Still holding her glance, he spread his hand over that broad expanse of exquisitely honed muscle. With a deft downward motion, he flicked off most of the water, then hooked his thumb behind the snap of his jeans.

Several seconds passed, silence charging the heavy air. He wouldn't look away and she couldn't. With each erratic heartbeat she felt the awareness between them become that much more tangible. She saw Cain focus on her mouth before his slumberous gaze drifted over the thin cotton covering her breasts. The breath he drew was slow and deliberate, as if his recollection of how she'd responded to his touch was as clear in his mind as it was in hers.

"You wanted something," he reminded her.

"Yes." The word was little more than a whisper. Clearing her throat, she tore her eyes from his, determined to block the memories his heavy-lidded expression elicited. "Hanna's air conditioner is broken. Do you think you could fix it?"

The lift of his eyebrow was slightly sardonic. "Does she know you're asking me?"

"It was her idea."

He kicked the hose aside. "I doubt that," he muttered, thinking of how often in the past couple of days he'd caught the woman watching him, only to turn away when he made eye contact. He couldn't even count the number of times in his youth he'd seen that old woman—and she'd been old even back then—threatening him with that damned cane of hers.

He looked toward the sky. The sun would be cresting soon and he'd lose his shade.

"It *was* her idea, Cain. She specifically asked if you would do it."

There was a note of insistence in Ellie's voice. It surprised her a little, but she did nothing to temper it. It was true that the people in town weren't being very fair to him. But he was being just as closed-minded in his own way. Neither side was willing to give the other a chance. Cain could prove he was the better person by making the first move.

"I've got enough to do here. And it's not getting any cooler. Radio says it could hit ninety-five again."

"Which is why Hanna needs her air conditioner fixed. You know how hard the heat can be on older people, Cain. Hanna's already had one stroke."

The muscle in his jaw jerked, his agitation evident as he drew his fingers through his hair. At the back, where it was damp, several dark strands curled toward his ears. "Does she know what's wrong with it?"

Ellie shook her head, her long ponytail swaying over her back. It appeared that Cain was about to capitulate, but with him, she never knew quite what to expect.

Cain wanted nothing to do with anyone in Aubrey that he didn't *have* to deal with. By avoiding contact, he avoided trouble, and though he had no intention of doing anything to cause a problem, he had the distinct feeling that trouble

could still find him here. Hanna was not a cause for concern, however, even if the old biddy did have the disposition of an unripe lemon. If helping her out was that
important to Ellie . . .

Ending the thought before he found himself putting any
significance to that particular circumstance, he muttered,
"I'll get my shirt."

He started toward the house. Ellie, wondering if he knew
how kind he was for giving in, headed for the stairs to her
apartment.

His puzzled "Where are you going?" stopped her just
short of her goal. Apparently, he'd expected her to return to
Hanna's with him.

"To change my clothes."

The quick once-over he gave her made it clear that he
found nothing at all wrong with the pale yellow sundress she
was wearing "Why?"

"I thought you wanted me to help with the trim."

The confusion registering on his face was priceless. He
was consistently keeping her off balance so Ellie felt it only
fair that he hadn't expected her response. Besides, he
couldn't be indifferent to her when he was trying to figure
her out.

With her foot on the bottom step, she turned to face him.
"That is what you wanted me to do, isn't it?"

Actually, having her help him was exactly what he
wanted. Ever since this morning, he'd been considering
Carlo's remark that there were some things a person
couldn't trust to a stranger. They could, as he was beginning to understand through Ellie, be shared with a friend.
And Ellie, though he'd known her for scarcely a week, was
as close to a friend as he was likely to get.

"If you wouldn't mind."

"I don't. But only if you let me buy the wine from you."

That idea appeared to hold no appeal for him. "How about this. I'll let you help, if you'll—"

"*Let* me help?" Smiling, because he was, she planted both hands on her hips. "You make it sound as if I should be dying for the opportunity."

"Aren't you?"

It was so good to have him looking at her with that wonderful, teasing grin. Turning so he couldn't see how very much it pleased her, she muttered, "Hardly" and scurried up steps. "I'll meet you at Hanna's in five minutes."

He was still grinning when he let the screen door slam behind him and disappeared into the house to wash up. The man had definitely looked smug, she thought, darting up the stairs wearing a ridiculous grin of her own.

When she saw him a few minutes later, all traces of his less serious side had vanished. It had been a while since she'd seen that tense set of his jaw combined with the brooding quality that made his eyes look so cold. When they went through Hanna's back door, his defensiveness was definitely back in place.

In a way, Ellie couldn't blame him.

Hanna could be a real pill at times, apparently believing that age excused a person from the manners expected of everyone else. As soon as Ellie brought Cain into her living room, the weathered old woman eyed him with skepticism, then offered him a reluctant "It's over there," rather than the more generous greeting one usually gives a neighbor one hasn't seen in more than a decade. It wasn't necessary for her to say it was good to see him again if she didn't feel it was. But Ellie, perplexed by the woman's rudeness, felt she could at least have offered him a reasonably civil hello. It was obvious that Hanna had no intention of doing any such thing, as she picked up her gardening book and settled back in her chair to watch Cain's every move. Ellie wouldn't have blamed him if he'd walked right out the door.

Hanna's lack of courtesy was most evident to Cain. He looked over at Ellie, his expression totally devoid of emotion, and turned away. The slow rise and fall of his shoulders told of the deep, calming breath he drew. He had told her he'd take a look at the air conditioner. Once he said he'd do something, he intended to keep his word.

Without saying a thing, he unplugged the window unit and, using the screwdriver he'd stuck in his back pocket, removed its front panel.

From where Ellie stood near him, she could clearly see Hanna's expression. The woman didn't trust Cain. He was doing her a favor, yet she was acting as if he might pocket her precious figurines if she didn't keep an eye on him. Maybe she even feared him a little, Ellie thought, though what threat he posed to Hanna was beyond Ellie's comprehension. She knew only that she'd never witnessed such overt incivility before. Knowing that it was her request that had subjected Cain to it made her feel terribly awkward—both for herself and for him.

It was with no small amount of relief that Ellie heard Cain's muttered "That should do it."

Forcing brightness into her voice, Ellie turned her frown from Hanna. Suddenly, she didn't have quite as much respect for the woman as she'd once had. "What was wrong?"

"The belt connecting the motor to the fan had slipped off. It should run fine now." The front panel was screwed in place and the unit plugged back in. Moments later, a blast of cool air ruffled the edges of the crocheted doily on the end table by Hanna's chair. "What do you want this set on, Mrs. Whitney?"

"Medium," came the terse reply.

Ellie was sure the woman would offer her thanks as Cain punched the appropriate button and pushed the screwdriver back into his pocket. Hanna did nothing of the sort. All she did was smooth the wrinkles in her flower-print dress and pick a piece of lint from the arm of her chair before turning her attention to her book.

"Thanks, Cain," Ellie said, hoping her own appreciation would make Hanna's oversight a little less glaring.

"It's okay. I'll see you back at the house."

"I'll be there in just a minute."

His nod was tight, much like the thin smile he gave her just before his long, powerful strides carried him from the room.

As soon as she heard the back door close, Ellie was beside Hanna's chair. She was hardly in the habit of challenging her elders, but she couldn't accept her neighbor's behavior without questioning it.

"Hanna," she began, her hands folded tightly, "may I ask you something?"

"Of course, dear." Her smile was so pleasant that Ellie could scarcely believe this was the same person who, only seconds ago, had been so totally lacking in common courtesy. "What is it?"

"Why were you so rude to Cain?"

Clearly taken aback by both the question and Ellie's uncharacteristic boldness, Hanna blinked. "Rude? Why, I treated him just like I always did."

A groan of disbelief caught in Ellie's throat. If that was the way he'd been treated, it was no wonder he'd been so reluctant to come over here. "You might have thanked him."

Hanna shrugged. "I look on it as payment. He owed me."

"For what?"

"For one thing, for all the times he woke me up at two in the morning with the god-awful noisy car he used to drive. Never a night went by that I got a decent night's sleep, worrying that he'd be so drunk he'd drive it right over my front porch. And my poor Leonard," she went on when it looked as if Ellie was about to interrupt, "that boy was so scared of him that he wouldn't even go outside if Cain was out there."

Ellie didn't bother to point out that Leonard would probably have been frightened by his own shadow. Hanna obviously felt quite justified in her feelings, and nothing Ellie could say right now could undo years of holding those convictions.

"It should be more comfortable in here in a few minutes," Ellie said, wanting to remind Hanna that whether she wanted to thank him for it or not, it was Cain who'd made that comfort possible. "I'll see you later."

"You still running into town?"

There was a frown behind the question. It was directed to the very worn and very short cutoff jeans Ellie had changed into. Tucked into them was a pink tank top that had definitely seen better days.

"I decided not to. Did you remember something you needed?"

Still frowning at Ellie's apparel, Hanna muttered absently, "No. I was just curious. You don't usually dress that way."

It was clear from her tone that Hanna didn't approve of the rather skimpy attire.

"I'm going to help Cain paint," Ellie explained, knowing full well that Hanna wouldn't approve of that, either.

Chapter Nine

From the top of the ladder, Cain saw Ellie jump the fence and march past the bird feeder hanging off the end of the garage. The stiffness of her shoulders spoke of indignation; her long, leggy strides, of quiet determination. She was all huff and ire, tempered possibly with embarrassment.

There was no doubt in his mind that she planned to say something about what had happened at Hanna's a few minutes ago. But he didn't want to discuss the incident at all. As far as he was concerned, it was over and done with. There was nothing to be said about it.

She was still a couple of feet away when he heard her call his name. To keep from seeing the concern he knew would be so unashamedly evident in her face, he kept his back to her. He knew there was no way Ellie would understand that what had happened at Hanna's really didn't matter. He'd learned a long time ago that it was easier not to care about how some people acted toward him—especially anyone from this backwater town.

Feeling that he had better things to do than waste his energy being upset, he turned his attention to the rusted nail he was prying out. He apparently applied more force than was necessary. The thing slipped out so easily that he almost sent the hammer flying. What went flying instead was a colorful curse.

Ellie heard his muttered expletives as she approached, which made her hesitate before calling his name again. Shielding her eyes against the bright sun, she squinted up at him. He barely glanced at her.

"You still going to help?" he asked.

The terse question threw her a little. "I said I would. But I want to apologize for—"

His interruption was immediate. "Good. The back bedroom is done except for the trim. Why don't you do that first, then start on the baseboards in the living room." The monotonous rasp of the scraper against wood underscored his request. "I want to finish this up, then I'll be in to roll the walls."

He hadn't so much as glanced at her as he spoke, his attention fully on his task. He was becoming obsessed with its completion. Ellie could see that determination in his every movement.

There seemed to be a little irritation behind his determination at the moment. Feeling fairly certain it had something to do with what he'd refused to let her talk about, she drew a deep breath of the hot, dusty air and slowly released it. She couldn't force him to accept her apology for her neighbor's rudeness. She supposed she could get to work, though.

There were hours of work left to be done on the outside of the house. He hadn't even started the prep work on the garage, which meant it would be hours before Cain went inside. Ellie had hoped they would be working together.

"Is there anything I can do out here?"

"Not really." His reach had extended as far as it could go. It was time to move the ladder again. "Unless you know how to patch a roof."

"How big a patch?" she inquired, thinking it couldn't be too difficult to hammer a few shingles in place.

He hadn't been serious, but she was—which finally made Cain look at her. "*Do* you know how to patch a roof?"

"I don't know. I've never tried."

He couldn't help smiling as he shook his head. "Just between you and me, it's not that difficult. But even I'm not crazy enough to crawl up on the roof in this heat. That's a job best done first thing in the morning."

Ellie could actually feel the tightness leaving her shoulders as Cain's tension began to subside. It was unnerving to be as attuned to him as she was, but she had recognized the deeply rooted anger he insisted on denying. She hadn't been fooled by the way he tried to cover it with activity. They weren't so very different in that respect. He hid his disappointments in work. She escaped in her dance.

She'd been looking toward the roof. Now, just beyond his left shoulder, she noticed a section of wood below the rain gutter where the grayed and dirty paint still peeled and curled. On either side of it, the wood had been scraped smooth. "What I should probably do is just stay out here and supervise. You missed some," she pointed out as he started down the ladder.

"Yeah, I know. I'll have to go back and get that later."

"Why not do it now?" she asked, thinking that doing it now made more sense than dragging the ladder back to that spot again.

"There's a birds' nest in the gutter. If I get too close, I might scare them."

Ellie's glance darted upward, delight registering on her face. "Are there babies in it?"

"Three," Cain replied, moving to stand beside her. With her head tipped back and her hair flowing over her shoulders as she searched for the spot where the nest might be, Cain found himself thinking again of the cameo still tucked away in his bedroom. Something about that pendant bothered him. But he wasn't thinking of that right now. He was thinking only of how closely Ellie resembled that same, gentle profile. The curve of her brow beneath the wisps of her bangs, the slight tilt of her nose, the delicate fullness of her lips. All were the same. Only the stone of the cameo was cold, and Ellie breathed warmth into everything she did.

"Do you want to see?"

Her grin was infectious. She reached for the ladder Cain had just descended.

"Careful," he instructed, steadying the ladder as she started up. "The fourth rung is split, so step over it." His glance followed her, the view making any further instruction impossible.

Ellie's cutoff blue jeans had worn whitened spots on the seat, a hole in the right back pocket and frayed legs. They were also decidedly short. From this angle, Cain had a totally unobstructed view of the curve of her bottom and legs that seemed to go on forever. The muscles of her thighs were tight, her calves gently shaped. There was strength in their suppleness, and her smooth skin, honeyed from the sun, looked incredibly, wonderfully soft.

A certain heaviness centered in his lower stomach. Those legs would feel like heaven wrapped around him.

"You'd better get down now," he heard himself say and felt enormously relieved when she didn't ask why. She stretched a little farther to take one last peek, then started back down, hesitating just above the fourth rung.

"Is it this one that's split?" she asked, unable to see where she was stepping.

"Yeah. Hang on a second." He reached up, spanning her waist with his hands. Her flesh felt firm beneath his grip, and the heaviness in his stomach compressed when she turned to put her hands on his shoulders.

"Here you go," he said, his voice unnaturally strained as he lifted her to the ground.

It was with deliberate effort that he kept his glance from skimming the soft swell of her breasts as, releasing her, she lifted her hand to push her hair back again. "Well, I guess I'd better get to work," she said with a shrug. "You're sure there's nothing I can do out here?"

"Positive," he returned, thinking it best to keep her as far away from him as possible. With a surge of lean muscle, he lifted the heavy ladder and repositioned it against the down-slope of the roof.

When he said nothing else, Ellie finally walked off, looking very much as if she'd rather have stayed.

Ellie had wanted to stay. She would also have liked to find out what had made Cain withdraw so abruptly. One minute she was looking at the baby birds he'd refused to disturb, and everything was fine. The next, he was helping her off the ladder and acting as if he couldn't get rid of her fast enough. She figured she had as much chance of solving that little mystery as she did performing on Broadway. Faced with the impossible, she invariably gave up and went on to something else.

The something else she chose now was the task Cain had assigned her, and she tackled it with a certain ambivalence. Her help would enable him to finish faster, which meant he'd be leaving sooner. When he left, her life would return to . . . normal.

Normal meant there would be no more waking to the taste of anticipation. She would no longer have a reason to look forward to coming home in the evening, hoping to see him. And she'd forever lose the chance of experiencing just one more of the heart-pounding kisses that turned her blood to steam and made rational thought impossible.

Frowning down at the paintbrush she'd fished out of the sink, she grabbed a bucket of paint and headed into the back bedroom. She did not like the direction her thoughts insisted on taking, so she'd simply drown them out with the radio.

Ellie didn't mind painting trim. But as soon as she finished the bedroom and started in the living room, she discovered that she liked painting walls with the roller better. For the same amount of effort, she had a much more visible result. She liked seeing the progress she made as the walls changed from dingy yellow to clean off-white.

She was humming along with the familiar tunes the radio played when she heard the back door bang shut. The solid thud of boots could be heard crossing the kitchen. As she looked up from where she was finishing the wall with the fireplace on it, she saw Cain pause in the doorway.

His bare chest glistened with sweat and his hair was mussed from all the times he'd shoved it out of his eyes with his forearm. He looked hot and tired and, to her surprise, when he moved toward her, rather amused.

Following his glance, Ellie looked down at herself. There was one drawback to using a roller instead of a brush. It wasn't quite as neat. Fine little paint spatters covered her forearms, making her look as if she had a case of anemic measles.

The sprinkling of tiny off-white droplets on her face was what Cain found the most interesting. "I sure hope you're not contagious," he said, smearing the dots on her nose with his finger. "Look at you. You're a mess."

She hadn't seen him for hours, not since they'd broken for a quick lunch of bologna sandwiches and lemonade—hardly her best culinary effort, but certainly the quickest at that point.

Not at all certain of how someone desperately in need of a shower could be so incredibly appealing, she wrinkled her nose. "You aren't exactly the epitome of neatness yourself."

"At least I don't look like I'm on the war path." Despite the innocence he tried to manage, mischief played over his face. The paint tray she'd been using sat on a rickety old stool beside her. He dipped his index finger into it, his eyes twinkling with a suppressed smile.

"The streak down your nose is perfect. But you need a little more here." A line of paint was drawn at an angle down her left cheek. "And the same over here." She took a step back as she opened her mouth in protest. The feel of his free hand cupping her chin stilled her and a matching line was added to the other side.

She tried to glare at him, but the serious way he scrutinized his handiwork made that attempt at displeasure pitifully ineffective.

"Are you having fun?" she inquired, crossing her arms over the paint smudges on her top.

"Quiet," he instructed. "I'm creating." He turned her chin first one way, then the other. "You could use a little on your forehead. My Indian ancestors always had white streaks on their forehead."

Grabbing his wrist, she tried not to laugh. His teasing was infectious. "What Indian ancestors?"

"My great-grandfather was a renegade Cherokee." Still holding her face, he drew a mark just above her eyebrows. His touch was feather-light; his expression wonderfully free of its usual guardedness. "Mom always said I took after him. Hold still."

He started to reach for the paint tray again.

"Don't you dare."

"You're daring me?"

A moment ago, she'd seen mischief. Now, she saw a glint in his eyes that didn't bode well for an easy capitulation. Knowing she'd lose this particular challenge, she ignored his question. "You know, I think I am contagious."

Reaching behind her she picked up the small brush she'd been using on the baseboards. One little snap and he could be just as speckled as she.

Cain obviously realized that as he dubiously eyed her weapon.

What Ellie realized was that all the weariness was gone from his features. So, too, was the guardedness that kept him locked up so tight inside. At that moment, she could see childlike pleasure in him. He was enjoying himself immensely and didn't mind letting her know it. That knowledge made her heart feel wonderfully full.

"You wouldn't," he said, his voice flat.

"Wouldn't I?" She raised the brush. "I'm supposed to be on the war path. Remember?"

His hand left her face to grab her wrist, laughter lighting his eyes. Then, slowly, the laughter began to fade. In its place came hesitation as his glance moved from her mouth to the quickened rise and fall of her breasts, lingering there for an agonizing moment before he raised his eyes to hers again.

The air in the room felt as heavy as the atmosphere just before a tornado—heavy, silent, expectant. Cain had yet to release her. Caught in the grip of his stare, Ellie didn't think to break that contact on her own.

He swallowed past the dryness in his throat, calling back some semblance of the smile he knew had vanished. "You really are a mess now," he said, thinking she made a perfectly beautiful brave. "You should go wash up."

"I suppose I should," she heard herself say, wondering if he knew his thumb was moving in little circles over her wrist.

"Ellie."

He hesitated, searching for the words he wanted to say. They weren't easy to find, partly because what he felt at that moment was too complicated to express. But mostly because they would leave him wide open and Cain always protected himself. At least, he always had before now.

That need for protection was still there. But equally as strong was the need to give back just a little of what she'd given him. He needed to let her know what it meant to feel free enough to share laughter, and to know there was someone who cared enough to be upset for you. He wanted her to know how good it was to have a friend, and how good it felt when she smiled at him.

There was more. So much more. But he was afraid that what he was feeling was getting all tangled up with his aching, almost overwhelming need to possess her. Something about that seemed very, very dangerous.

Allowing himself only to touch her cheek, he offered a quiet "Thank you," then announced that he was heading for the shower. He wondered if she'd noticed that his hand had been shaking.

Ellie noticed everything about Cain. She couldn't help it. And the more she worked with him, laughed with him, became exasperated with him, the easier it was for her to see beneath the gruff and sometimes unyielding exterior.

In a way, it seemed to her that his caring and protectiveness were his biggest faults. It was because he'd cared about his family that he'd first run away; and because he'd wanted to protect his mother's name that he'd first gotten into the fights that had earned him the reputation others refused to forget. Cain had obviously learned to mask that caring over the years, and perhaps deadened himself to its accompanying emotions, but he couldn't hide the essence of it from her no matter how hard he tried. A person had to care before he could hurt and, the closer he let her get, the more she sensed some deep and unhealed wound buried inside him.

She was aware of that most when conversation would turn to his mother. Every time it did, he changed the subject.

Her mother, on the other hand, wanted to talk of little else.

Stu and Claire Bennett returned from their vacation right on schedule, which was just how they did everything. They had their meeting nights, their card nights and their movie nights. They had chicken every Sunday, liver every Wednesday, and on Friday afternoons, Ellie's mother baked. This particular Friday, the day following their return, Claire was in the kitchen as usual. Instead of baking, though, she was making meatballs for Jay's birthday party on Sunday—and trying to comprehend how her daughter had again become the focus of so much talk.

"I just really don't understand what's going on," she was saying, tying a pink gingham apron over her muslin housedress. Beneath a crop of gray-streaked auburn curls, her worried brown eyes scanned Ellie's face. "We're gone for a couple of weeks and when we come back, the entire town is buzzing about you and Amanda Whitlow's son. You're not really seeing him, are you?''

Ellie stood at the long, sunlit counter and pinched off a sprig of parsley from one of the terra-cotta herb pots in her mother's window. She tossed the parsley into the large bowl of hamburger and chopped onions, her attention on the meatballs she was forming.

As defensive as she felt now, it was hard to believe that less than an hour ago, she'd been so anxious to visit with her parents, to hear about their trip and to see the souvenirs her mother always brought back from their travels. Her mom had collected spoons with state symbols on their handles for years, and her newest acquisition was usually the first thing she showed Ellie—until today. Ellie had no sooner given them a hug at their front door than she'd sensed her parents' displeasure. A knot had immediately formed in her stomach, the sensation quite the same as it always was when she met with their disapproval.

That knot had doubled when her father, shaking his head at her as he released her from his hug, said, ''You talk to her, Claire,'' and headed off to the barbershop for a haircut.

''I guess that depends on what you mean by 'seeing.''' Placing the ball she'd formed into the pan her mother had set between them, she reached back into the bowl. ''I see him every day. I told you I'm helping him paint Amanda's house.''

''I mean as in dating,'' her mother clarified, not looking terribly pleased with Ellie's semantics. ''Have you gone out with him?''

The only place Ellie had ever gone with Cain was to Greely. That trip hardly qualified as a date. Therefore, her quiet ''No'' was at least grounded in truth.

The concern vanished from Claire's pleasantly pretty face, leaving only the more permanent worry lines that fifty-one years had produced. "I was sure you hadn't," she said, sounding relieved anyway. "But after Hanna said she'd seen you running around after him looking like that Daisy Mae character that used to be in the Sunday comics, I didn't know what to think."

Ellie rolled her eyes toward the milk-glass chandelier hanging over her mom's maple kitchen table. "I was wearing an old pair of cutoffs because I didn't want to get paint on my good clothes. And I was hardly running around after him. What I did was meet him at her house so he could fix her air conditioner for her." Sounding a little more terse than she'd intended, she added, "I don't suppose she mentioned that."

"As a matter of fact, she didn't. Once I told her I had the seed packets I promised to bring her from Austin, she got off on a tangent about wild poppies and I didn't think I'd ever get off the phone. You know how she is about her flowers," she added, searching in the cabinet by the stove for her favorite saucepan. "Once she gets started, it can be hours before she runs out of wind." Pots and lids clanked as she reached farther back, emerging a moment later with the pan.

"Anyway," she continued, opening and closing other cabinets as she gathered the ingredients for her "secret" tomato sauce, "the main thing is that the rumors about you and that boy aren't true. Even if he has made a name of sorts for himself, that doesn't change his background, and I knew you had more sense than to get mixed up with someone like that. I told Jo that very thing when she and Hal were over last night."

Placing a quart of her home-canned tomatoes on the counter, she gave her daughter a sympathetic smile, the same kind that had soothed bruised knees and young tears so long ago. "I know the talk bothered you after you and Brent divorced. I can't imagine that you'd deliberately put yourself, or us," she added, because that was a consideration, too, "in that position again. It's like I told Jo, you know how important reputations are and you're not about to let yourself be taken in by someone like that. Helping him fix up the house so he can sell it only means that you're taking pride in where you live. That place has needed work for a long time."

Ellie smiled weakly when she received a pat of commendation on her arm. A moment later, her mother was wondering aloud if she had enough fresh basil or if she'd have to use dried.

Ellie ignored the mumblings. Claire was like a prickly hen when it came to protecting her young. She tolerated no criticism of her children's actions, defended them blindly and absolutely refused to believe that their thoughts were any different from hers. She even provided excuses when necessary, believing her rationale to be nothing less than the truth.

It was very difficult to make someone like that listen to you, so Ellie didn't try. Instead, finishing up the meatballs while her mother debated the amount of food they'd need for Sunday's party, she tried to imagine what had transpired during her aunt and uncle's visit last night. It wasn't difficult.

Her father and her uncle had no doubt sat on the veranda smoking those god-awful cigars Hal seemed to enjoy so much and rehashing whatever transgressions they could recall Cain's having committed. At the same time, her mother and Jo had probably sat at the kitchen table, drinking ice tea while Jo repeated everything that had happened during their absence. Ellie could almost visualize her mother's face as she went from disbelief to indignation before rushing to her daughter's defense.

Ellie knew her mother had no concept of how suffocating her affection could be. Ellie hadn't really realized it herself, until just now. Claire regarded criticism of her child as criticism of herself and it was so important to Claire that others approved of her. Maybe that was where Ellie had acquired her diffidence. She didn't know. And it really didn't matter. She knew only that she was feeling a little protective, too—of Cain.

"He's nothing like everyone seems to think."

Claire sniffed at the sauce she was brewing on the stove. Having dispensed with her own concerns, she'd obviously forgotten what they'd been talking about before her thoughts had turned to the party. "Who isn't?"

"Cain. He may be a little difficult to get to know, but he's very responsible." Knowing her mother would approve only of the quality she'd mentioned, she refrained from adding understanding, fun and sexy.

Ellie didn't have to look up from her spot at the counter to know that the brown eyes so like her own had narrowed.

"I'm glad to hear that. For his sake. The boy didn't have much of an example to go by, so if he's grown up to accept some responsibility, it's a credit to him."

Claire was nothing if not charitable in her conclusions. It was a qualified form of charity, though, extended only so long as the giving didn't take from anyone she cared about. Still, Ellie felt compelled to test that generosity. "I wish you'd say that to the likes of Hanna when they talk about him, then. I don't think people are being very fair."

Her mother's glance was as tolerant as her tone. "Oh, Ellie," she said in that way that set Ellie's teeth on edge. "All you have to do is look at the boy's past and look at him now. He knows he doesn't belong here. He may not be getting into fights the way he used to, but he's not trying to fit in, either. He's keeping to himself over at that house, not making any effort to be friendly to anyone. Jo said the only time he sets foot out of the place is to get what supplies he needs."

Ellie knew that it wouldn't make any difference if Cain did make that effort. He was damned if he did and damned if he didn't. She would have said that to her mother, too, but Claire got in the last word, as usual.

"What he does over there doesn't really matter," she concluded on her way to the porch for another jar of tomatoes. "From what I hear, he'll be gone soon and we won't have to concern ourselves with him anymore. Give that pot a stir, will you, dear?"

When she returned a moment later, she had dismissed the matter of Cain Whitlow entirely and was grinning from ear to ear. "I almost forgot to tell you," she said, looking at Ellie with all of her considerable maternal pride. "Jo's decided to sell the shop. And she wants to sell it to you. Isn't that wonderful?"

Whether it was wonderful or not, it was certainly a surprise. "Why does she want to sell it to me? She can just keep it, and I'll run it for her as I have been."

"Well, that's not what she wants to do," Claire replied reasonably. "She didn't say I couldn't tell you, and I know she wants to talk to you about her plans herself but basically, she's just tired of the place. Hal's planning on retiring in a few years and she doesn't want the bother. You know how hard it is for her some days anyway, especially on the damp ones when her arthritis kicks up.

"We think it's a wonderful opportunity for you," her mother went on, too busy blending another pot of sauce to notice her daughter's lack of enthusiasm. "By owning the business, you'd be making more money. You could even afford to buy a house. You know," she continued, growing more excited with the plans she was making for her offspring, "now that the Whitlow place is getting all cleaned up, you could buy it. Like you've said, it is close to the shop and you like your neighbors over there. With all the work you've put into it, that boy would have to be pretty ungrateful not to give you a good price." Another thought occurred, nailing yet another aspect of Ellie's future in place. "You could even rent out where you're living now, like Mrs. Whitlow did. Your apartment would be just right for Lon and Aida's daughter and her new husband. They're living with his family now, you know, but they want to get closer in so it's easier for her to get to work at the café. With the extra rent money, you could . . ."

Mercifully, the phone rang before her mother had a chance to tell Ellie what she could do with her presently nonexistent rental income. Wiping her hands on her apron, Claire hurried to the phone. Her face was beaming when, a moment later, she announced that the caller was Dan, Ellie's brother.

Ellie knew the exact moment when Dan said he and his family wouldn't be coming for the party. Her mother's smile crumpled. He'd already called Ellie a couple of days ago to tell her that and to request that she prepare their mom for the news. With Dan's wife due to deliver their third child soon and his veterinary practice outside of Wichita demanding most of his time, they wouldn't be able to get away. Ellie had been disappointed herself at not being able to see him and Sue, and especially her two young nephews, but being subjected to her mother's cross-examination had made her forget all about Dan's request. She felt bad for not having softened the news for her mother. Claire practically lived for her grandchildren.

That call was followed within moments by another, this one from a friend who'd heard that they'd gotten home yesterday and was anxious to get the rundown of who all would be at Sunday's party.

As her mother rattled off the names of just about everyone in town, Ellie looked over at her. *Really* looked at her. Claire Bennett was a good person, kind and generous. Her family and her friends were precious to her and she did whatever she could for them. When a friend had a problem, it was always Claire to whom they came for advice. Even if she didn't have the answer, she always had a compassionate ear.

But Ellie never had been able to talk to her. She was not a child, yet in her parents' home, she felt like one. She still maintained an unquestioning silence when she should have been exercising her adult's right to speak. She never had her own voice here. Even if she had, she didn't think anyone would have heard it.

So many times, she'd wanted to—tried to—talk to her mother, but her mother never seemed to listen to what she had to say. Right now, if the moment her mother got off the phone, she were to say that she cared very much for Cain Whitlow, her mother would probably only assure her that she didn't really and tell her that she knew she had more sense than to do something so foolish.

The odd thing was, caring about Cain didn't feel foolish at all. It felt like the most natural thing she'd ever done.

Chapter Ten

It took Ellie longer than it should have to get ready for her Uncle Jay's party Sunday afternoon. Every few minutes, she'd find herself at her window, lifting the edge of the curtain to peek out at Cain—just to make sure he was still there.

No matter how hard she tried to shake it, she couldn't overcome the feeling that he was about to take off. It wasn't unusual for Cain to be silent around her. In some ways, the silences they shared had become as important to her as their conversations. The quiet mood he'd been in this morning was different, though, and it scared her a little because she wasn't quite sure what it meant.

He'd been edgier than usual yesterday and oddly withdrawn this morning. They'd had breakfast together on the little picnic table under the redbud tree in the backyard—something they'd done all week since Cain had nothing to cook with, or on. Cain had said little as he picked at the scrambled eggs and blueberry muffins she'd prepared. Af-

er making a few attempts at conversation and finding his
solemn mood impenetrable, Ellie had left him alone. It
seemed to be what he wanted most.

Having assured herself that Cain hadn't disappeared yet,
she let the curtain fall. At the moment, he'd stopped the
rescreening project he had going in the backyard and was
washing his car. Instead of worrying, she figured she should
be doing something constructive, too, like getting dressed.

Ellie hurried through the last of her preparations, put-
ing on Grandma Bennett's pearl earrings even as she
slipped into her strappy white high heels. A quick glance in
the mirror for a final check didn't reveal the desired result.
Instead, what she saw brought a sigh of disgust to her lips.

She'd taken such pains to give herself a more sophisticated look, but there was apparently no taking the country
out of the girl. Trudy at the mercantile had said that ba-
nana clips were the latest thing, so Ellie had bought a silver
one to hold her hair up and away from her face. The bur-
nished curls cascading down her back were attractive
enough, but the hairdo looked suspiciously like the one
worn by Trudy's twelve-year-old daughter.

Leaving her frown in place, she glanced at the rest of her
image. A row of tiny buttons ran from the scooped neck-
line of her white eyelet sundress, ending at the point of the
basque-style waist. The dress was pretty—what her mother
would call charming—but there wasn't a doubt in Ellie's
mind that Trudy's preteen daughter would have done a bet-
er job of filling out the bodice than she did.

That thought was all it took for Ellie to pull the clip from
her hair. Tossing it onto the dresser, she whipped the brush
through the curls to smooth them, then tossed the brush
down, too. She'd never had any luck trying to look like
anything other than what she was—which was plain old El-
ie Bennett.

* * *

By the time Ellie approached Cain a few minutes later, she wasn't concerned with anything as mundane as her appearance. She was concerned only with the way he was ignoring her. He had to know she was there, because she'd seen the muscles in his bare shoulders tense when she called his name. That was his only acknowledgment, however. Barely breaking his stroke, he continued making foamy circles along the side of his car with an old red rag.

Ellie moved closer, stepping over the hose he'd left running beside his car's front tire, and stopped by a yellow plastic bucket filled with water and soap.

From the corner of his eye, Cain saw the delicate white heels on her feet and tried to put a lid on the irritation he'd been fighting all morning.

There was little that annoyed Cain more than being idle. Just the prospect of not having anything to do made him uneasy and he was faced with that prospect now. The work on the house was almost finished—which left him with little to do other than stretch out the few remaining projects while he waited for the appliances to be delivered midweek. The closer he came to finishing up those projects, the more restless he became. To Cain's way of thinking, hell could be defined as being stuck in Aubrey with nothing to keep himself occupied.

One other matter contributed to his impatience this morning.

It was stupid, childish, unrealistic and petty, but he didn't want Ellie to go to her uncle's party. Not because he had anything against Jay. He didn't even know the man. He didn't want her to go because she would be surrounded by her family, and he didn't want them jerking her around anymore. When she came home from her mother's the other day, there had been less spark in her eyes, less animation in her smile. Her family drained her of the vitality they probably didn't even realize she had, and he hated that she let them do that to her.

More to the point, he hated that she made him care enough to let what her family did to her bother him.

He finally looked up, knowing she'd stand here forever if he didn't.

"You look nice," he said, when what he meant was that she looked sensational. With the sunlight setting fire to her hair and the almost virginal white dress flowing so sweetly over her slender body, she was the most clever combination of innocence and seduction he'd ever seen. The truly amazing part was that she probably had no idea how sexy the combination was.

Ellie's smile faltered. As compliments went, Cain's words were far from expansive. But the heat in his eyes touched her at the most elemental level, speaking his approval much more openly. Beneath his blatant perusal was something raw and hungry, and its force was enough to drive the strength from her voice.

"Are you sure you don't want to come with me?" she asked in what was probably little more than a whisper.

The heat in his glance cooled with his terse "Positive."

When she first asked him, she hadn't thought he'd change his mind. She was actually grateful that he'd turned her down. As much as she disliked the thought of his being excluded, she didn't want to put him in the position of being uncomfortable, either. She hadn't, however, thought it necessary that he be so abrupt.

His refusal stung. Cain could clearly see that as Ellie drew her bottom lip between her teeth and turned her eyes to the river of suds and water flowing from the driveway into the street. Wanting very much to take her into his arms and make her understand that it wasn't her fault he was in such a lousy frame of mind, and knowing how truly unwise touching her would be, he did the next best thing. He tried to make her smile.

Mindless of the water he dripped onto his jeans, he dunked his rag into the soapy water. Without squeezing out the excess, he slapped the sodden cloth onto the fender. "Don't pay any attention to me. I'm just getting ready to start my transformation. The day before is always a little rough. Makes me testy."

Instead of hurt, she now looked puzzled. "What?"

"Tonight's a full moon," he went on, making wide sweeps with the rag. "We always get a little out of sorts when the moon is full."

"What are you talking about?"

With all the innocence he could muster, he turned toward her. "Surely you know I'm a werewolf."

He got the smile he was after. Ellie's look of reproach was completely ruined by her amusement.

"A wolf, yes," she returned, thinking of the searing look he'd given her only moments ago. "A werewolf, no. You're too much of a skeptic to believe in hexes and all that."

He could have argued her point. In some ways, she seemed to have cast a sort of mystical spell over him. When he was upset, all she had to do was smile at him and his agitation seemed to lessen. Ellie wasn't being any more serious now than he'd been moments ago, though, so he dropped the matter completely.

"Do you have the wine?"

She'd had it clasped behind her back. "Right here." She held it up, showing him the bottle she'd wrapped in crinkly blue cellophane and tied with a huge trailing ribbon around the neck. She'd managed to talk Cain into having only one bottle sent by his friend, but he still refused to let her pay him for it. She had the feeling that, in a way, it was as much a gift to her as she intended it to be for her uncle.

"Good." Cain smiled at her then, but there was strain in that smile. "I hope he likes it. Don't you think you'd better get going?"

The party didn't officially start until four o'clock when her uncle was scheduled to arrive, but she'd promised her mom and Aunt Jo that she'd be at the Grange Hall—the only place in town big enough to hold all of Jay's friends—a couple of hours early. Cain knew that because she'd mentioned it to him this morning. But he wasn't being helpful with his suggestion. He was dismissing her.

He was also pulling back into himself, but there was nothing she could do to prevent it at the moment. A car pulled up along the crumbling curb, the honk of its horn jarring in the placid stillness. The birds squawking in the cottonwood even seemed stunned, but only for a moment. Even as both Cain and Ellie jerked toward the sound, their chirping started again.

Ellie scarcely noticed as her heart took an anxious beat. The blue sedan at the curb had a gold star on the door, the words Lassiter county Sheriff forming a circle in the middle. Her Uncle Hal, out of uniform for the occasion, sat with his arm angled out the open window while he casually adjusted his mirrored sunglasses. Through the pattern of sky and leaves reflecting off the car's windshield, Ellie just barely noticed that Aunt Jo was in the front seat with him.

Though it was impossible to know for certain because of those concealing glasses, Ellie was sure her uncle was staring straight at Cain. Cain, she *did* know, was staring right back. He'd drawn himself up and now stood stock-still by the fender of his car. Quite unconsciously, Ellie took a step closer to him, which brought her only an arm's length away.

Ellie saw Hal glance toward the house, seeming for a moment to study it. The siding now gleamed with its fresh coat of white paint, and the shutters and trim were a subtle gray-blue. It scarcely resembled the building that had been there just a short time ago.

"Nice job," she heard her uncle say, but there was no compliment in his tone. "I see you replaced the broken-out porch slats."

There was a definite edge in Cain's voice, along with a tension in his body that, to Ellie, was almost palpable. "You saw that when you were by Tuesday."

Hal's smile was smug. "You noticed I'd been by, huh?"

"As far as I can tell, you haven't missed a day since I got here."

"Observant, aren't you? Listen, Whitlow," he went on, his bland tone managing to goad somehow. "Me and the boys will be by the first part of the week to get the things you're donating. Since it looks like you're about finished here, there's no sense in you waiting around for us to do that. Just leave a key with Ellie and we'll clear it all out for you. Wouldn't want to hold you up." His consideration was anything but sincere. "I know how anxious you must be to get out of here."

Cain said nothing. To his credit, he merely turned his back and reached for the hose to rinse the soap from the fender. It only took Ellie one glance at his profile to see that he was far from being unaffected by the exchange. He was angry, but his anger was contained. Far too well. He was quietly seething inside, yet his actions on the outside betrayed nothing. And that made him look quite dangerous.

Apprehensive, Ellie looked from Cain to her uncle. When several seconds ticked by and nothing happened, she began to feel the numbing calm of realization. She'd had no idea that her uncle had been checking up on Cain; while Cain had obviously been aware of her uncle's surveillance. That had to be part of the reason for his restlessness. Since most of her own actions had been subjected to the scrutiny of others most of her life, she was fully aware of how fidgety—and how resentful—a person could get in those circumstances. She sensed that same resentment in Cain now. He deserved to feel it.

She felt it, too. She loved her uncle, but until that moment, she hadn't realized how subtly he could manipulate.

"Come on, Ellie," she heard her uncle call. "We came by to give you a ride over to the hall. Your aunt thought you might not want to walk that far in dress shoes. Hurry up, now," he added when he saw her hesitate. "We're already running behind."

Ellie didn't move, hoping that Cain would at least look at her. He didn't cast her so much as a glance. The cool fury setting his jaw so rigidly seemed to block everything else from his mind, and that made her more uneasy than ever.

Her voice was quiet, barely a whisper. "Will you be here when I get back?"

He went still, his shoulders seeming to sag slightly. "I don't know," he said, and an instant later, the tension reclaimed him.

She'd stay, she thought, if only he'd ask. But he wouldn't, and she wouldn't be able to stand it if she offered and he refused. She'd never really thought of protecting herself from him before, but this time, for some reason she couldn't begin to explain, that need was there.

Someone counted 104 people in the Grange Hall. By Aubrey's standards, it was hardly an intimate gathering, but it must have seemed that way to the man who had attended the last two presidential inauguration balls and routinely found himself at sit-down dinners for five hundred. Returning to his roots meant a lot to Senator Jay Bennett, even if he didn't get to do it often enough to suit him.

Ever the politician, he relayed those sentiments to the assembly of old friends and family right after Ellie's father offered a happy-birthday toast. He also added that he'd never been surrounded by so many people who meant so much to him, or eaten food as delicious as that spread out on the buffet table. If he could be assured of having Claire's meatballs and Jo's fried chicken every time, he'd turn fifty more often. His sisters-in-law were among the best cooks in the county.

"It's no wonder my Aunt Doris has a crush on him," Jennifer Johnson whispered to Ellie as the senator's comments earned him the applause accompanying him through the crowd of well-wishers. "If I was older... and not married," she added, almost as an afterthought, "I think I'd have a crush on him myself. He'd be a great catch."

Jennifer, wearing peach-colored ruffles that went beautifully with her dark hair but only made her cherubic face look even rounder, picked up her plate of appetizers now that she'd finished clapping. After a moment's contemplation, she decided on a ham and cheese roll from her small selection. "I'll bet half the women in Washington know that, too," she added, before taking a bite.

Ellie had to agree. Her uncle was, indeed, a charmer. He was also very much in demand this afternoon. Other than to give him a brief hug and to say hello when he'd first arrived, she really hadn't talked to him at all. Every time she'd started for him since then, someone else had intercepted.

Jennifer held the ham roll poised for another bite, as her expression grew speculative. "You don't suppose he'll ever get married, do you?"

"I think he's already married," Ellie replied. "To his job."

Jennifer's look of exasperation was joined by a voice of agreement from behind Ellie.

"I'm afraid you're one hundred percent right, dear. The only love in that poor man's life is his work. He deserves so much more." Adele Matlock, one of Jay's staunchest political supporters and Jennifer's mother's best friend, wore a sympathetic smile and the red-white-and-blue-striped dress she usually saved for voter registration days and the Fourth of July. "Do you know that back when he was a young man over in the legislature, he used to spend eighteen to twenty hours a day working for his constituents. Many a morning someone on his staff would find him sleeping on the sofa with files spread out all over the place. Why, I remember one time when that water bill he was trying to get through got hung up on the floor. Let me tell you about that."

Adele droned on. Since she was looking at Jennifer, who was looking back at her over her ham roll, Ellie used the opportunity to slowly ease herself away.

All over the room, little pockets of people were engaged in conversation, while others popped in and out to see whether or not they found that particular topic interesting. If they did, they stuck around to add their two cents' worth. If the chosen subject bored them, they joined those moving around just to see what all was going on.

Ellie was among those wandering through the crowd. Unlike most of the others, she wasn't interested in who was saying what to whom, so much as she was in simply passing time. More than anything else, she wanted to get back home. Yet, even as she wished she were home, she was very much afraid that when she got there, Cain would be gone.

She knew that it shouldn't matter so much. Cain had promised her nothing, and he certainly had never led her on. He had made it abundantly clear that he didn't want her in the way she'd come to want him. The task of taking care of his mother's possessions had simply been easier with her help. She herself had pointed out that very fact to him, so she was hardly in a position to accuse him of using her. Now that he was almost done with the house, there wasn't even that much for her to help him with.

Ellie cut off her rationalization as she realized what she was overlooking. He was *almost* finished, but not completely. Cain wouldn't go until he'd accomplished all of what he'd set out to do. At least, she didn't think he would.

Holding on to that thought, she graciously acknowledged the compliments about the flower arrangements she and Jo had done for the tables, and fielded the speculation about whether she might be taking over the flower shop for good. Jo had only yesterday said that she wanted to talk with her about it, so any comment other than "I really don't know yet," would have been premature.

To keep from getting cornered again, Ellie kept moving.

She passed Uncle Hal, who was with Ed Nelson and a small group of ranchers discussing the break-ins and thefts that had taken place over the summer. No new incidents had been reported in the past two weeks, and for that everyone was grateful. No one was ready to relax his guard, however, and just before Ellie got out of earshot she heard her uncle caution one of the men to let him handle it if he should find anyone on his property who didn't belong there. The vigilante mentality was not one Hal Bennett would tolerate.

Taking a sip from the same glass of champagne punch she'd been nursing for the past hour, Ellie next skirted a group composed mostly of members of the ladies' auxiliary of the church, Ellie's mother among them. The group across from that one was analyzing the chances of the Oklahoma State football team going to the play-offs this year. The Crawfords and the Blakes had sons on the team, but it was

Ellie's Aunt Jo who currently held the floor. Ellie would have joined them herself, but she doubted she'd be able to concentrate on the discussion. No matter how logical she tried to be about Cain, she couldn't quite shake the uneasiness filling her.

As it was, she could only wander around, trying to look as if she was having a good time, while the minutes ticked off on the clock above the framed pictures of past Grange officers and the increasing din bounced off the pale green walls of the large room. Someone had brought an old Doris Day album, Jay's all-time favorite, and over by the dais a chorus of "Qué Será, Será" had broken out.

"Have you ever heard the expression 'lost in a crowd'? That's how you look."

Turning at the sound of the deep voice, Ellie smiled up at the tall and distinguished-looking gentleman with the prematurely silver hair. It was the general consensus that the three Bennett brothers were a good-looking lot, but Jay, the youngest, was handsome in a very urbane sort of way. Even wearing an open-collared white shirt and chino slacks, he had an air of sophistication about him that his casual attire couldn't disguise.

Ellie's smile grew brighter. "I was beginning to think I wasn't going to get to talk to you. I barely had a chance to wish you happy-birthday, and the next thing I knew, someone had dragged you off."

"Well, no one's dragging me anywhere right now. I've been told there's a cake to be cut in a few minutes and, much as I hate to, I'll have to leave shortly after that. Especially after all the trouble everyone's gone to for me. That's why I wanted to track you down. To thank you."

The man had to be one of the most considerate people she'd ever met. "We were happy to do it, Uncle Jay. But Mom and Aunt Jo did most of the work. They had the whole thing planned before Mom and Dad left on vacation. All I did was help where they needed me."

"I'm not just talking about the party. Though this is really nice, too," he quickly added, taking in the festivities with his nod. "I mean the trouble you must have gone to for the wine you gave me. That is not an easy vintage to find."

"I know," she drawled, pleased because he was. "A friend tracked it down for me. He found it in Florida."

"He?" Jay crossed his arms as he studied his niece. A faint smile tugged at his mouth. "Do I detect the sound of a new man in your life?"

Ellie took another sip of her punch. It was warm and flat, but the question had given her pause. She needed to do something while she thought of an answer. "There is someone I care about, but he isn't in my life so much as just passing through it. He'll be leaving soon."

The smile on her face wasn't reflected in her eyes. There, one could see much more than she was saying. What she'd said was the absolute truth, and the truth, just as they said it did, hurt. A lot.

Jay's glance swept the room for a likely candidate. "Is he here?"

Ellie shook her head.

"In that case, do I at least get to know who this young man is?"

Her immediate reaction was to say no. She didn't want to see the disapproval. Not from her Uncle Jay. Though he hadn't actually lived in Aubrey for years, he had to know of the Whitlow family, and she could almost guarantee his reaction when he heard the name. Yet silence somehow seemed terribly disloyal to the friendship she and Cain had come to share.

Tipping her head back, she met her uncle's eyes. "His name's Cain. Cain Whitlow."

For a moment, her uncle said nothing, his only response a quiet and controlled intake of breath as he composed his features in a mask of polite concern. She was almost certain he was going to say something about Cain's lousy reputation, or how a Bennett really should be careful with her associations. Instead, he merely asked, "How is the boy? I heard he'd left some years back."

His interest, strangely, seemed quite real. Ellie, wanting more than anything to talk about Cain with someone who wouldn't speak against him, immediately latched on to that interest. "He isn't a boy, Uncle Jay. He's thirty years old. The same age you were when you were running for a seat in the House."

The comparison brought a thin smile. "Yes. Thirty is hardly a youth."

"He came back to take care of his mother's house. I've been helping him. She passed away a couple of months ago," she went on, her voice gentling with the explanation. "I don't know if you remember Amanda or not...."

Ellie wasn't at all certain why her Uncle Jay's eyes had gone so cool at that moment, but her Uncle Hal didn't give her a chance to speculate. He'd followed Jay over a few moments ago, stopping to speak to the people behind Jay. At least, she'd thought he was talking to them. He'd turned around when she mentioned Cain, and now, clapping his younger brother on the shoulder, he cut in with a boisterous "There you are!" and started to lead him off.

Jay didn't want to go just then. "I'll catch you in a few minutes, Hal," he said, letting his brother's hand slide away. "Ellie was just telling me what she's been doing."

"And what's that?" Hal inquired, sounding interested but looking oddly threatening as he deliberately held Ellie's glance. "What have you been doing, Ellie?"

Not at all sure why her uncle had asked the question that way, she responded nonetheless. "Helping Cain fix up his mother's house so he can sell it. You know—"

Hal cut her off. "Well. There you have it. Come on, Jay. Ed and some of the boys—"

"I said, in a minute. I don't get a chance to see Ellie very often."

Jay refused to budge, his glare fixed squarely on his brother. Hal didn't move either, except for his jaw. It was working so furiously that Ellie thought his gold caps would surely shatter.

The odd confrontation was over within seconds. Hal turned back to his group, which was only a few feet away. Jay took Ellie's arm and nudged her closer to the wall.

"Uncle Jay?" she began, having no idea what to make of the little scene she'd just witnessed.

"He's just used to having his way," Jay said, seeming to dismiss his brother's behavior with nothing more than mild annoyance. "He always has been, in case you haven't noticed. Comes with having too much power."

He'd meant that last remark to make her smile, so she did, and a moment later his annoyance had disappeared.

"You said earlier that you didn't know if I remembered Amanda Whitlow. I definitely do," he assured, a decidedly closed look coming over his face as he glanced in Hal's direction. "So why don't you tell me all about what you and her son are doing to fix up that old place."

There was probably some significance in the pointed glance Jay had tossed in Hal's direction, but Ellie didn't bother to figure out what it might be. Of all the people in the family, Uncle Jay had always taken the time to listen to her. Right now, she could have hugged him for that.

A few minutes—and several interruptions—later, she did.

"Thanks, Uncle Jay," she whispered, wrapping her arms around him more fiercely than a discussion of paint and spackle and discovered birds' nests probably deserved. It had been far too public to discuss much of anything else, but oddly, that had been enough for her.

Jay's embrace was just as tight. "Anytime."

"I wish you were around more often."

He set her back, his hands still on her shoulders. Jay always listened, and sometimes he heard far more than was being said. "The family's giving you a bad time about him. Right?"

With Cain's reputation, he had to know they were. Ellie nodded anyway.

His next words were quieter, a little more intense. "They're good people. And every last one of them means well. Family is important, Ellie, and your family deserves your loyalty. You give them that. Just don't let them have your soul."

She'd thought he might give her advice as to how to handle her family where Cain was concerned. Instead, he was talking about loyalty and her soul. Not sure she grasped his meaning, she would have asked what he meant, but her father had already grabbed Jay's arm, announcing to him that it was time to blow out the candles on his cake. When she stepped back, it was to see that Uncle Hal had been behind them the whole time—obviously listening to every word they'd said.

Something very strange was going on. What had that little showdown between Jay and Hal been about a while ago? Ellie wondered. And why had Jay's brother been so blatantly eavesdropping on him? Or was it Ellie that he'd been trying to overhear?

The traditional song was sung, and generous squares of marble cake, Jay's favorite, were passed to all the guests.

Certain she was being unduly paranoid, Ellie still couldn't help but think that Jay seemed much less gregarious as the festivities in his honor wound down—and that Uncle Hal seemed visibly relieved when Jay departed a little while later. As soon as she was able to graciously do so, Ellie left, too, and during the five-block walk to her apartment she tried to make some sense of her uncle's strange behavior.

That attempt was futile. Every step she took brought her closer to home, and anxiety methodically replaced confusion. By the time she turned the corner bringing her in sight of Amanda's house, the only thoughts occupying her mind were of Cain and the relief she felt when she saw his car parked in the drive.

That relief was premature. The car had just started up.

Cottonwood pods snapped beneath her feet as she hurried over the cracks in the sidewalk. A moment later she slowed to hesitantly approach the open window on the driver's side. It was nearly dusk, and the thin light filtering through the trees made it difficult for her to tell if Cain's expression was as bleak as it appeared, or if it was only the shadows making it look that way.

"Are you coming or going?" she asked, making her tone lighter than she felt like being.

"Going. I didn't think you'd be back so soon."

"Things don't run too late on Sundays around here."

"Things don't run too late on *any* night around here."

There was no mistaking the edge in his voice. Whatever had been eating at him when she left, apparently still was.

"My uncle liked the wine. He didn't open it," she quickly clarified, not even aware that her arms were crossed around her middle to soothe the knot of tension forming there. "But he did say he appreciated the—"

"I'm glad he liked it, Ellie. Look, I've got to go for a while. I'll talk to you later."

"Where are you going?" She hadn't meant to sound so frantic.

Cain didn't notice. "To the lake," he returned, a destination just now occurring to him.

Actually, it didn't matter where he went, as long as it was away from Aubrey. He knew only that if he didn't escape the confines of the town for a while, something was going to snap. All day long, he'd lectured himself about being stronger than this place, about how he'd not let it get to him by keeping himself occupied. So he'd mended the screens and washed his car and vacuumed it out and polished the wheels. Then he'd changed the furnace filters in the house and washed all the windows and taken a shower and paced. He'd read the paper and fixed a sandwich and pulled a tack out of the heel of his boot. Five minutes ago he'd tried to call the plant in Florida to see how the tests were coming along, then remembered it was Sunday evening and nobody would be there.

"Can I come with you?"

Music could still be heard coming from the Grange Hall five blocks away. There were always a few diehards. But most of the people were heading for their homes now. Those close enough walked, but the majority drove because their farms were out a ways. A few of those cars were heading down the street Ellie lived on, their occupants waving as they passed, or when they realized it was Cain she was talking to, staring as they went by.

If Ellie was seen leaving with him, she was bound to be the subject of every supper table discussion in the county tomorrow night.

It didn't matter to Ellie. The way she figured it, if the gossips were talking about her they were leaving someone else alone. "Please?" she added, when it seemed that his silence would lead to his refusal. "I'd like to get out of here for a while, too."

"I don't think that would be a very good idea." Beneath the sleeveless black T-shirt he wore, his broad chest rose with his deeply drawn breath. "Part of what I want to get away from right now is you."

It took all the courage she had not to look away from those fathomless gray eyes. Had she looked away, she wouldn't have seen the need there. "Why?" she asked, her throat tightening around the word.

Defeat registered over the need. Pulling his glance from her, he looked out at the street as another car slowly drove by. Being a betting man, he'd have given even stakes that the road hadn't seen this much traffic in the past two years.

It was clear enough that this was not the best place to talk. Leaning away from her, he reached across the seat and opened the passenger door. "Come on," he muttered when he straightened. "Let's get out of here."

Chapter Eleven

Ellie had barely closed the car door when Cain started backing out of the drive. Before she latched her seat belt, they were at the far end of the block. Two minutes later, they'd turned north and were on their way out of town. She had no idea who saw them, nor did she care. She was too busy feeling certain that the vague sense of dread she'd been experiencing all day had been leading right up to this.

The knot in her stomach had doubled to the size of a small fist. Cain's eyes were focused straight ahead as he drove out the back road that led to the hills and Cherokee Lake. The set of his jaw was as tight as his grip on the wheel, and in the brief seconds Ellie had the courage to watch him, he didn't so much as blink. He looked as tense as a cornered rattler, just waiting to be poked at.

Ellie was neither stupid enough to antagonize a rattler, nor brave enough to try to soothe one.

What she would have done, had it been possible, was push the clock back five minutes so Cain could have left without her. He was making her quite aware that she was intruding on his space, and being the private person that he was, he no doubt resented that intrusion very much.

Clutching her hands in her lap, she wished he'd say something—anything—to break the ominous quiet. Already feeling that she'd infringed enough, she didn't want to encroach upon his silence, too. She knew now that she shouldn't have asked to come along. But her need to be with him had blinded her to what Cain was trying to do, to what he had actually been doing for the past two days. As another minute dragged by, the reason for his gradual withdrawal from her became that much clearer.

Part of what I want to get away from right now is you.

Those words had hurt when he'd said them. They hurt even more when she realized he'd said them because she'd given him no choice.

It was no accident that he'd become so distant around her, or that he'd found her help less and less necessary. His withdrawal was deliberate. Cain would be leaving soon, though not until he'd done everything possible with the house to ensure that he wouldn't have to return. She was one of those details needing to be dealt with, a loose end to be tied up before he left. When he did leave, he didn't want to think about her anymore. He was making a concerted attempt to sever their relationship, but to do it without facing what it was—or what it wasn't. He knew how much she cared about him. He had to, because she'd certainly made little effort to hide it. And because he knew she cared, he'd tried to let her down as easily as he could.

At the moment, however, he seemed to be merely tolerating her presence.

"You should have driven off without me," she said, and when Cain didn't disagree she felt the knot in her stomach move into her chest.

Half a mile of flat, gold wheat fields passed before she tried again. Off in the distance, the silhouette of a barn with its silo could be seen. The lights were coming on in a farmhouse next to it. There wouldn't be another house for miles. "Let me out, Cain."

The muscle in his jaw jerked as his eyes swung toward her. "Why?"

"We just passed the Crawford place. I can get a ride back to town from there."

The needle on the speedometer didn't so much as waver. "I thought you wanted to get away from town for a while."

"And you wanted to get away from me, so if you'll just let me out—"

The expletive Cain cut her off with was short and distinct. The defensiveness in her tone made it clear to him that she'd completely misinterpreted his reasoning. Dealing with his own frustrations made it that much more frustrating to cope with hers. "You have absolutely no idea why I feel the need to do that, either."

"I think I do."

"I very much doubt that, Miss Bennett."

"Then maybe you should explain it to me."

An explanation was actually the last thing in the world she wanted. It was humiliating enough to have him know that she'd become more deeply involved in their relationship than he had. She'd have to be a masochist to want to hear him tell her that. Yet the way he'd bitten out her name had been so goading that she'd felt compelled to meet that damnable arrogance of his.

There was weariness in his response, but the oppressive weight of all the old resentments haunting him obscured it. "You wouldn't understand."

"Because I'm a Bennett?"

His glance was hard.

"Or because you don't *want* me to understand," she continued before he could deny either. "You know, Cain, it's entirely possible that I understand a lot more about you than you think."

He gave a cynical snort. "I hardly have any deep dark secrets. I'm sure that by now you've been told about every sin I ever committed."

"So what if I have?" she returned, not bothering to point out that he'd mentioned a few of them himself.

"Then you should know that I can't be trusted."

"That's ridiculous."

"Your uncle doesn't seem to think so."

So that was it. At least part of his simmering anger stemmed from the way her Uncle Hal had been keeping an eye on him. Even now, after thirteen years, it was assumed that Cain might cause trouble. Ellie could have told him that that was just the way Hal Bennett was; that his basic philosophy was that people don't change—and there was no changing Hal Bennett. She couldn't defend her uncle now, not when she knew he was so wrong about the man beside her.

She said nothing of that to Cain. Her uncle wasn't really the issue. Cain's reputation was. He'd made that very clear with his remark about his sins.

Whether he knew it or not, he'd also made it clear that what she thought of him mattered to him.

"You seem to think your past should make a difference to me. Well, it does," she admitted and saw him stiffen. "It matters a great deal, because you keep letting it get in the way." She turned in her seat so she could see him better. For once she was going to say exactly what was on her mind. That was, after all, something Cain had more or less encouraged her to do. "You once accused me of using you to get back at my family. I could make the same accusation. But neither one of us has played those kinds of games and I'm not going to insult either one of us with such pettiness. If you're upset with my uncle, be angry with *him*, not me. I accept who you are, Cain. What you are. But neither I nor anyone else will stand a chance until you accept yourself."

Ellie had no idea what Cain was thinking. He said nothing. He didn't even so much as glance at her to give her a clue. All she could see in the waning light was the side of his face as he concentrated on the twists and turns in the road as it left the flatland and climbed into the hills. She could tell nothing from his profile.

His brooding silence continued as, a few miles later, they came upon the entrance to the lake park, and he downshifted to swerve onto the dirt road. A rooster tail of brown dust rose behind them as he drove past the empty picnic tables and abandoned barbecue pits.

They drove beyond the more public areas. The huge, meandering lake darted in and out of view when the heavy stands of pine thinned to allow it. The dock had closed at dusk, so there were no boats on the water, and in the pale evening light, the trees reflected off the surface in wavery gray patterns. The deserted road carried them farther into the park.

Cain finally pulled off the road by a small clearing and got out. Ellie, not wanting to just sit there listening to her heart pounding in her ears, followed.

Except for the crickets, the place was deserted. Cain started down a path that led through the trees to the water's edge, then turned to see Ellie hesitating behind him. "Come on," he said and held out his hand.

Ellie took it. Feeling his fingers close around hers, she was more relieved than she'd ever have thought possible. For the past several minutes, she'd all but held her breath waiting for him to respond to what she'd said. He could easily have treated her opinion of him as another insult to his integrity. She hadn't meant to insult him or even to criticize. She'd only wanted him to know that she wasn't going to let him use his past as an excuse to keep her away.

She didn't know if he would consider that or not. She knew only that he wasn't angry with her for what she'd said. Indeed, he seemed to have forgotten all about their conversation in the car.

"What's the matter?" he asked, when she hesitated again.

"My shoes." Still holding his hand, she leaned against him, pulling off first one high-heeled sandal then the other. Dangling them by their straps she held them up. "I can't walk down there in these."

A swift frown darkened his already shadowed features. "It's easy enough to see the path, but it's getting too dark to really see what's on it. There might be glass along here."

There were certainly twigs, pebbles and holes, which were what Ellie hadn't wanted to catch her heels on. "We could go back around and drive closer to the water," she suggested, though except for the glass, she wouldn't have minded going barefoot. She liked the feel of the warm dust beneath her feet.

"Or I could carry you."

He must have made up his mind to do just that even as he said it. In one smooth motion he bent to tuck one arm under he knees, the other wrapping around her back. She'd barely reached her own arms around him to compensate for the loss of balance when he started forward.

"It's not that far," he told her when he saw the startled way she looked up at him. The sound of the gentle lap of water along the shore backed up his assessment.

Already aware of the feel of his hard chest, Ellie found her senses shamefully alert when she inhaled. The clean scent of his soap mingled with the warm night air, the combination seducing her with each breath. With her arms around his neck, she could feel the powerful muscles of his shoulders under his black T-shirt. Since the shirt's sleeves had been cut out, she could feel the heat of his bare skin where the white eyelet fabric of her bodice ended under her arm. She thought it odd to notice such little things when there were others she should have been more concerned about. Somehow, when he lifted her, his hand had gotten under the skirt of her dress and his arm was on her bare thigh.

She glanced toward the path. "Are we going somewhere in particular?"

"Not really. I just remembered that there used to be a bunch of rocks somewhere along here where you could sit and watch the moon come up. I'm not even sure this is the place."

"Did you used to come out here a lot?"

"All the time in the summer."

It seemed odd to be having such an innocuous conversation while being carried in his arms, but if Cain could ignore the intimacy of their situation, so could she. Or at least, she could try.

"Me, too. We used to rent paddleboats," she told him, tightening her grip on her shoes so she wouldn't drop them. "The boys would race the girls over to Hole-in-the-Fence." Hole-in-the-Fence was just that—a spot on the opposite side of the lake where someone had punched a hole in the fence marking the huge park's boundaries. The kids would crawl through there because access was closer than driving around to the entrance. "The losers had to paddle the winners back. What would you do when you came out here?"

"Sit on a rock above Hole-in-the-Fence and watch the kids on the paddleboats." Ducking under a low branch, he casually dismissed that subject and brought up another. "What else would you do?"

Cain had recently discovered that the best way to get his mind off of something he didn't want to think about was to have Ellie talk to him about herself. It wasn't what she said, though he always listened to every word, so much as the sound of her voice that he found so soothing. Its gentleness calmed him, just as did the woman herself—some of the time.

Blocking all but his most immediate thoughts, he allowed himself to concentrate only on the dulcet tones of Ellie's voice and the quiet serenity of his surroundings while he willed the agitation to seep out of his bones. He would think only of the moment. Not of the past and not of tomorrow. Only of now. It was the way he'd learned to survive.

Ellie had just finished telling him how her mom would make her brother take her fishing with him, and the arguments she and her brother had gotten into over that, when Cain stopped to frown at the shore. They'd just broken through the trees. A grassy field off to the left was surrounded by a copse of saplings, and the lake was a few yards straight ahead. But there were no rocks. "This isn't the place."

He didn't sound disappointed, but he did look as if he were considering something as he kept moving toward the water's edge. Then, in the blue twilight, she saw the corner of his mouth twitch in a suppressed smile.

She knew that smile. It was the same one she'd seen just before he streaked paint down her nose. "You wouldn't."

"Wouldn't what?" he returned innocently.

"Cain Whitlow. If you drop me in the lake..."

The dark slash of his eyebrow rose in anticipation of her ultimatum.

Unable to come up with a threat he'd find intimidating, she hedged. "Put me down."

"Here?"

"Yes."

She felt the muscles in his shoulders flex then relax with his shrug. "Okay. If that's what you want."

His capitulation was far too quick, which immediately warned Ellie that being put down just then was not what she wanted at all. Glancing over Cain's shoulder as he turned, she saw that she'd be stepping right into the water.

"No, you don't," she said on a laugh and clung to him that much harder.

"I thought you wanted me to put you down."

"I changed my mind."

"Why?"

"Think about it," she muttered, her eyes reflecting the amusement in his.

"Don't you trust me?"

That lazy half smile still clung to his lips, but there was an import to the question that went beyond the moment's playfulness. "Of course I do," she returned, and kept the *but* to herself.

He bent then and set her down—on a low tree stump at the water's edge that she hadn't seen. He didn't release her completely. His hands were still at her waist. "You're not exactly dressed for a swim," he said, his glance moving down the row of tiny buttons on her dress. "Unless you're up for skinny-dipping. Ever done that before?"

She shook her head. Suddenly, she couldn't trust her voice. She knew that Cain was teasing her. But the thought had a certain forbidden appeal.

"Somehow," he said with a grin, "I think I knew that."

"Did you?"

He wasn't quite sure how she meant the question. "Did I what?"

"Go skinny-dipping?"

"What do you think?"

It was difficult for her to think at all, as she felt his thumbs drawing slow little circles against the fabric below her waist. Still, gamely, she met his teasing. "That you probably did," she told him, the thought making her pulse beat oddly out of sync.

"I shouldn't have brought you here."

The sudden seriousness of the statement threw her. Before she could even wonder what had prompted it, Cain had tightened his grip on her waist and lifted her from the stump. A moment later, he'd set her on the dry ground. Together they went toward the grass growing up to the copse of trees. When Cain reached one of the tall, shadowy pines, he sat down and leaned against it, his knees propped up and his arms resting on them. They could watch the moon come up from here, he told her. Then they'd head back to town.

Ellie, the white skirt of her dress bunching around her, knelt beside him and looked out at the sliver of moon visible above the treetops. As Cain had mentioned this afternoon, the moon would be full.

"I won't ever see you again after you leave, will I?"

There was no question in Ellie's tone. There were certain things in life a person could count on, like the inexorable rise of the moon. That certainty was what Ellie felt now. It made her feel lonely to know that this man, who'd touched her so deeply, would soon be lost to her.

She could feel Cain watching her as he decided how to answer. But he didn't answer her with words. Instead, he reached over, slipping his fingers around the side of her neck and upward through her hair to draw her toward him. For the space of a heartbeat, he looked straight into her eyes, then closed his mouth over hers.

There was such aching tenderness in his kiss that Ellie felt a swelling of emotion in her chest. He seemed to absorb her, and yet to fill her, too. It wasn't desire she tasted on his lips, though buried somewhere among all the other feelings, desire was there. What moved between them was far more complicated. It was sorrow and hurt, and thanks and need, and the bittersweet recognition of what could never be. The more aware Ellie became of each individual emotion, the more desperately she felt the need for Cain's strength.

His hand tightened in her hair and his mouth became more demanding. She encouraged that demand, curving her arms around his neck to draw him closer. She'd been on her knees. Now he pressed her back, his weight bearing her down into the soft dry pine needles. He was over her, then upon her, and the kisses he traced down the curve of her throat nearly turned her blood to steam.

"Oh, Ellie," she heard him whisper in the stillness surrounding them. "This is why I wanted to get away from you." He raised his head, the pale light revealing his beautifully tortured expression as he smoothed her hair back from her face. "But now that you're here, I don't know if I can let you go."

"I don't want you to let me go."

She saw the slow shake of his head, as if what she'd said was beyond his comprehension. He touched his fingertips to her cheek. "You shouldn't be so honest. It doesn't leave you with any defenses."

She wanted none where he was concerned. She knew that was probably very foolish, but the simple fact was that she loved him. That thought came as no surprise to her. It was merely the truth that made what she did feel so very right.

Stroking the hair at his temple, she raised up to touch her lips first to one corner of his mouth and then the other. "Get me out of this," she whispered and moved his hand to the row of maddeningly tiny buttons on her dress.

A certain tightness entered his voice. "You have no idea how badly I want to do that," he told her, easing back to see her hand holding his between her breasts. "But we're not exactly in the privacy of your bedroom."

His concern was for her. Not for himself. And she loved him the more for it. "No one's here, Cain. It's just us." They were hidden from everything but the water, and there wasn't a boat anywhere to be seen. They were completely, utterly, alone.

Cain knew that. But he wanted Ellie to be sure that this was what she wanted. His groan rumbled deep within his chest as his fingers slipped from beneath hers to close over her breast. A sigh whispered from her lips and he lowered his head to capture it.

The kiss deepened, pulling her in by slow, debilitating degrees. The smooth feel of his tongue teasing hers tugged at something deep inside, the caress of his hand at her breast intensifying the hot, liquid sensation. She arched to him, needing more, wanting to give more. Finding the edge of his shirt, she pulled it from his jeans. The skin of his back felt hot, the muscles beneath it, coiled and hard. He tensed at her touch, his breathing becoming heavier as his hips moved against her in a slow, provocative rhythm. Matching those suggestive motions, she urged his tongue even deeper into her mouth and curled one leg around his. The fabric of his jeans felt deliciously abrasive against her skin.

Her skirt had ridden up. She felt Cain push it up farther still, his hand sliding along the back of her thigh to align them more intimately. Both of her legs were around him now, his jeans and the thin nylon of her panties a tantalizing barrier to the explicit thrust of his hips. She shifted against him, thrilling to the leashed power tightening his body and marveling at the intensity of what he caused her to feel. She loved him. Honestly and without reservation. There was a kind of freedom in caring about someone that way.

"Easy, Ellie," she heard him whisper, his tongue tasting the soft skin below her ear. He drew back a little, his breathing ragged against her throat. He worked open the first few buttons of her bodice, his lips grazing the soft swell of her breast. "Easy," he repeated, his thumb rolling over her nipple as he nuzzled the soft fabric aside.

His words were for himself as much as for her. He wanted to slow them down, to prolong the pleasure they could give each other. But as she let out a shuddering breath and he saw the unguarded desire in her delicate features, he promptly forgot all about restraint. He had wanted to take his time with her, but that just wasn't possible. He'd wanted her for too long, and the utter abandon of her caresses had him precariously close to the edge.

He had no patience for the rest of the buttons. Slipping his hand beneath her dress, he drew her panties down her legs. Then, his eyes locked on hers, he slid his belt from its buckle.

The raw passion in Cain's expression was as potent to Ellie as the hunger she tasted a moment later in his demanding kiss. There was a sense of urgency in the way his mouth moved over hers. Caught in the grip of that same insistence, she answered with her own need. Clothes were quickly pushed down and aside, the desire to touch almost overwhelming in its intensity. Within seconds, flesh pressed heated flesh, but that contact wasn't enough for either of them. He pulled her legs back around his, his hand curving under her hips to fit her to him. At the strangled sound of her name, she arched upward, compelled to get as close to him as she could. She was ready for him, but when he entered her, it was all she could to do breathe.

The faint moan Ellie heard could have been hers or Cain's. She didn't know. Nor did it matter. All that did was that he was inside her, part of her, and that knowledge filled her heart to overflowing. Her body tensed, trembling in the grip of sensations that threatened to shatter her consciousness. Then guided by his strong, fluid strokes, Ellie swerved off course when she felt Cain shudder against her. There in that electrifying and suspended state, she felt as if she could have touched the moon.

Long minutes passed as their breathing quieted and their hearts began to beat at a steadier pace. Except for when they rolled onto their sides, Cain hadn't moved. He'd never felt quite as at peace as he did just then, lying there holding Ellie. She was curled against him, her head resting on his chest. She hadn't said anything, but for the past few moments, she'd been running her hand slowly up and down his side.

He smiled at the lazy pleasure he felt at her touch, and tried to ignore the itch of pine needles where his shirt had ridden up. It occurred to him, vaguely, that he should have pulled it down when he'd readjusted his jeans. He couldn't quite believe he'd taken her that way.

A frown touched his brow, replacing the contentment. He hadn't *taken her*. They had *shared* something. But he didn't care to take the thought any further than that. Right now he just wanted to feel the peace.

He brushed his lips against the top of her head. "Are you all right?"

"I'm fine."

She sounded distant, distracted. Whatever else she was thinking, he didn't want her to regret what they had done. "I hadn't meant for it to happen this way. Please believe that."

Raising her head, she propped her chin on her hand. She tried to smile, but she couldn't quite carry off that bit of sophisticated nonchalance. "Neither one of us 'meant' for it to happen. I think we'd have been a little more careful about it if we had."

Cain went perfectly still. He already knew the answer, but he had to ask. "You're not on anything?"

"I haven't had the need," she said in a small, shaky voice.

The only other man she'd ever slept with had been her husband, and it was almost two years since she'd been with him. The birth control pills she'd stopped taking even before they separated had been thrown out long ago. Cain had come into her life so quickly that she'd scarcely had the opportunity to consider such things as pills and precautions.

And that, she now had the opportunity to remind herself, was exactly when things could go wrong. Hindsight was always so damnably accurate.

"Is this a bad time of the month for you?"

"I suppose it could be worse," she said, hoping she didn't sound as panicky as she was beginning to feel.

Shifting to balance himself, Cain sat up, drawing her with him. The moon had risen above the treetops now, bathing everything with a surrealistic glow. In that pale light, she saw his hardened features grow thoughtful. His brow pinched in contemplation, he glanced toward her stomach and laid his palm over it. A strangely soft expression crept over his face, only to vanish as quickly as it had appeared.

He stood then, the dull clunk of his belt buckle as he refastened it the only sound in the otherwise quiet night. A moment later, he reached down to help her up and caught her to his chest.

"We'll just have to be more careful from now on," he told her and closed his mouth over hers. Before Ellie could even begin to wonder what thoughts had prompted his actions of moments ago, she was reeling beneath his gentle assault.

"Let's go home," he whispered. He took her hand, moving it between them until it flattened against his zipper. "I want you already, Ellie, and this time, I want you in my bed."

The house was dark when Cain let them in the back door a little more than half an hour later. He didn't bother with the lights. Holding Ellie's hand, he led her down the stairs and brought her to stand beside his bed. The moon had followed them, shining now through his window, but he closed it out, turning on the small lamp beside his bed so he could really see her. She smiled almost shyly as he flipped the covers back, then became beautifully somber when he reached for her.

He kissed her slowly, deeply—this time learning all the surfaces hidden from him as thoroughly as he would know all of her secrets before this night was over. He wouldn't rush. She wouldn't rush him. Her smile told him she trusted him to do whatever he cared to, and the anticipation in her eyes after he'd made himself undo every last button on her dress nearly made him groan out loud.

The dress finally fell away along with the filmy little underthings she wore. To him, she was exquisite. Small, perfect and infinitely soft against his harder, rougher body. She tasted like honey, smelled like wildflowers and was as eager to feel his hands on her as she was to return those debilitatingly slow caresses.

This time, when they came together, it was with the tenderness their first union had lacked. But where the frenzied desire was missing, the intimacy of gentle exploration created its own torturing heat, melding them into a whole that left Cain more shaken than he'd ever been.

Long after Ellie had fallen asleep in his arms, he lay awake. He was tired, sated, yet he had no desire to pull away from her and go to sleep himself. What had happened tonight was new to him. All he'd ever had with a woman before was sex. He'd never operated under any illusions where that was concerned. But what he and Ellie had done had left him with much more than the physical satisfaction of release. He felt fulfilled rather than empty; part of a whole, rather than a singular being who had no place to belong. At that moment, he did belong—with Ellie, to her. And she, to him.

Maybe, he thought, brushing his lips to her forehead, what they'd done was make love.

The word hung suspended in his mind for an instant, then was banished. Love was too foreign to him to consider, and the sense of belonging, too fragile to last. All he wanted to do right now was savor the incredible peace he felt. He was sure it couldn't last for long.

Chapter Twelve

More. All of her life, Ellie had wanted more. She didn't think it was a selfish thing. She simply acknowledged a lack. The emptiness had existed inside her for so long that, for a while, she had become accustomed to it, had accepted it as the way things were meant to be for her. Until Cain. He had made her see that void for what it was—a part of herself that wasn't yet complete. At first, she'd thought him unfair for making her face that. Now, she realized that she'd had to recognize the need before it could be filled—and he filled it perfectly. With him, she felt complete. He was the more she'd been wanting.

He wanted her, too.

Temporarily.

Ellie stood in her kitchen, unloading a sack of groceries after work just as she'd done every Monday for the past year. Adding two bananas and an apple to the basket on her counter, she decided it probably wasn't very wise to probe the depths of what she felt for Cain. But it was so new, so different from anything she'd ever felt before, and it deserved—no, demanded—a little exploration.

This morning she'd awakened in his arms feeling wholly alive and filled with an eager anticipation. The remembered feel of his kiss as he'd teasingly pushed her out the back door had stayed with her all day, enlivening her smile and no doubt making everyone who saw her wonder what she was up to. It was a wonderful feeling—if one discounted the myriad insecurities that accompanied it. Unfortunately, it only stayed wonderful if one could also ignore practicality and logic. And logic told her that she was in way over her head.

She shoved the milk into the fridge, folded the sack and went to change into a pair of jeans before going down to see if Cain wanted supper. He didn't love her. She knew that. Oh, he cared about her, and he certainly desired her, but he didn't love her. Knowing him as she did, she feared he'd never let himself care that much.

The high-pitched call of a child's voice put a welcomed end to Ellie's disquieting thoughts. "Ellie! Where are you?" came the impatient demand from the other side of her open screen door. "It's me."

Ellie knew who it was even before she rounded the corner. The little girl who lived over on the next block never knocked. She simply hollered. Smiling as she tucked in her T-shirt, Ellie asked anyway. "Who's 'me'? I don't know anyone named 'me.'"

A frown flitted over the freckles on six-year-old Cindy Baker's nose. "*Me*, Ellie," she stressed, poking her finger at the pink balloons on her shirt. "Mommy wants to know if she can borrow an onion."

A moment later, onion in hand, the little girl was racing down the steps toward her bicycle, blond pigtails flying.

After dropping the onion into the bike's basket, she made a quick swipe at the kickstand and started to push the bike forward. It wouldn't budge.

"What's the matter?" Ellie called, still watching from her doorway.

"I don't know. It's just stuck."

"Is the pedal caught on the kickstand?"

The little girl looked, then turned back to Ellie. "Nope."

"Is there something caught in the spokes?"

Cindy checked both wheels. Shaking her head, she looked back up. "Nope."

That was the sum total of Ellie's knowledge about troubleshooting a bicycle. Running lightly down the stairs, she reached Cindy's side and joined her in scowling at the handlebars.

Cindy mimicked Ellie's position by putting her hands on her hips. "Dumb bike," Cindy mumbled.

Ellie sat back on her haunches and jiggled the pedal. Nothing. "I don't think it's the bike's fault, honey."

With all the wisdom of her six years, Cindy let out a gusty sigh. "Guess I gotta walk, huh?" she decided, and leaned on Ellie's shoulder with her elbow, which sported an adhesive strip like the one Ellie had applied a couple of days ago when the girl had ridden her bike off the front curb.

"Problems?"

At the deep sound of the inquiry, both ladies turned around. Ellie stood up straight. She had no idea how long Cain had been standing in his doorway. It was hard to tell from the curious way he was watching her.

It was also hard to imagine why she couldn't seem to stop staring back. It made no sense. She'd seen him dozens of times before, dressed much as he was now in a pair of worn jeans and a half-buttoned black cotton shirt. She'd even seen him beautifully, magnificently naked. But she couldn't recall her heart ever pounding so erratically as it did now.

The memories of last night had come flooding back, making her quiet "Hi" much huskier than she'd intended.

"Hi, yourself," he returned, holding her gaze as he stepped out the door.

It seemed that her heart beat twice for every thud of his boots on the drive. She hadn't seen him since this morning, and though she'd deliberately curbed her anxiousness to see him again, part of her had been a little wary of the moment, too. His moods could be so mercurial.

She needn't have worried. When he stopped beside her, he was so close she could feel the heat from his body. For the briefest instant, she felt his hand at the small of her back, the touch the only intimacy he would allow out here in full view of Hanna, who was peeking at them through her side window curtains, and the little girl, whose big blue eyes had just widened considerably.

"What were you two yelling about out here?"

Cindy remained mute—and backed closer to her bike.

"This is Cindy," Ellie offered, not particularly surprised at the child's reticence. Cain was a big man, and to someone in the three-foot-high category, he probably did look rather intimidating. Especially with his dark coloring. *Most* especially when he wore black. "Something's the matter with her bicycle."

Pulling at the knees of his jeans, he lowered himself on his haunches.

He looked to Cindy, his expression and tone the same as he'd use to address an adult. "Any idea what's wrong with it?"

Cindy took another step back, clearly considering whether or not she should speak to this man. Strangers were a rarity in the life of children who grew up knowing just about everyone in town.

"It's okay, honey," Ellie told the child, running one of her long pigtails through her hand. "Cain is my friend."

The endorsement was apparently enough for Cindy to break her silence. She swallowed, then said quietly, "It won't go."

"It won't go, huh? Well, that certainly narrows it down." Turning his frown to the plate covering the gears, he stared at it for a second, then stood up and walked into the house. A moment later, he was back with a pair of pliers and a screwdriver. "Let's see what we've got here."

"What are you gonna do to it?" Cindy wanted to know, her child's curiosity making her move closer.

The gear cover clattered when he laid it on the cracked pavement of the driveway. "I'm going to try to fix it."

"Can you do that?"

"I don't know yet. I have to see what the problem is first."

"I already told you. It won't go."

It looked as if Cain had started to say something, then decided against it. Within seconds, he'd made his diagnosis. Cindy was clearly waiting to hear it.

"See this right here?" he told her. "That's called a tooth. It fits into this—" he pointed to a space in the chain "—and when you pedal, the tooth pulls the chain forward and makes your bike go. The chain was caught here and that jammed the whole works."

Cindy, now hunched down next to Cain, looked absolutely fascinated. So was Ellie. Not with what he was saying, but with what he was doing. He hadn't hesitated to help this child, and his patience as he explained to Cindy that this tooth wasn't like the one she'd lost last week was extraordinary. He seemed a little confused at how literal she was, however, especially when she told him in all seriousness that she hadn't put the jam in the works. Maybe her brother had.

"Maybe," he said, clearly uncertain that they were actually communicating. Screws were replaced and bolts tightened. A moment later, he was stepping back. "There you go."

Pigtails bouncing, Cindy climbed up and was off, her high-pitched "Thanks, mister!" following her out of the drive.

"That was nice of you."

Cain had been staring after Cindy. Hearing Ellie, he turned with a shrug. "Are they all like that?"

"Who?"

"Little kids. Are they all that..."

"Curious?" she offered, when he couldn't seem to find the word he was looking for. "Literal? Demanding? Energetic? Loud?"

"Yeah."

Smiling, she said, "Some of them are." Then she frowned. "Haven't you ever been around children?"

"Not really. Not ever," he amended, thinking about it. "I mean, I see them in airports and on the street, but I've never paid any attention to them before. They're...interesting."

"You make them sound like a strange form of plant life."

To him, they were. And he had absolutely no idea why he was standing there wondering what a child of his and Ellie's creation would look like.

"I want to show you something," he said, needing very much to get his thoughts back into more familiar territory. Taking her by the arm, he propelled her toward the back door. "The appliances were delivered this morning. I've already got the stove in and leveled, and I've just about got the new hot water heater hooked up."

He sounded so pleased that Ellie felt awful for not being as excited as he was. "Then you're just about finished with the house?"

"One more day ought to do it. I told Carlo I'd be back in Florida by the weekend."

Cain hadn't heard the strain in her voice. She'd hidden it beneath her smile, encouraging the anticipation she could see in his expression. It seemed that just the thought of getting out of Aubrey had already lightened his spirit. It was good to see him smiling. And it hurt so much to know that soon he would be gone.

What hurt more was that, once he left, he had no intention of ever coming back. He'd never made that clearer than he had last night.

The water heater was downstairs. After Cain showed Ellie the new stove, she followed him down to see it. As they stood in the open basement, empty now except for Cain's bed at the far end and the water heater by the oil furnace, Cain told her about the new copper fittings he'd had to drive back to Greely to get.

Ellie nodded in the appropriate places, but she didn't really hear much of what he said. She was too busy remembering the sadness in his eyes when she'd asked if she'd ever see him again, and feeling the same ache that had centered in her chest when his kiss had told her she wouldn't.

"I'm going to go up and fix dinner now," she told him when he'd been silent for a few moments. "Hamburgers all right?"

"Sure. Hamburgers are—hey! What's wrong?"

She couldn't believe it. She'd been doing just fine, and then all of a sudden her eyes had started to burn and her throat got that funny tight feeling in it that told her she was about to cry. It had been ages since she'd cried. A streak of pure pride made her determined to keep from doing so now.

She turned away, taking a quick swipe at her eyes as she gave a little laugh. "Nothing's wrong." The comment was tossed off as if his question were ridiculous. "I'm just going to fix dinner."

"Ellie."

The soles of her tennis shoes made little squeaks on the cement floor as she crossed the basement and headed for the stairs. "Half an hour. Okay?"

"Ellie," he repeated flatly. "Neither one of us is starving. Will you at least tell me why you're in such a hurry to get out of here?"

"Because I don't want to make a fool of myself."

Behind her, she could hear his approach. "How would you make a fool of yourself?"

"By telling you that I don't want you to go."

The feel of his hand on her shoulder was gentle, his expression when he turned her around, was not. "Don't do this, Ellie. Please. You know I can't stay here. My life is a million miles away from this place."

"I'm not asking you to stay," she told him, pride drying her unshed tears. "I'm only saying that I don't want you to go. There's a difference."

Cain must have understood the distinction. Slipping his hand around the back of her head, he drew her against him and pressed his lips to her forehead. Needing the closeness he offered, she curved her arms around his waist.

The gentle scent of fresh air and wildflowers clung to her hair. Breathing it in, Cain rested his cheek against her head, holding her much as she was holding him. He'd had the feeling this would happen sooner or later. Something was happening between him and Ellie, and he wasn't at all sure that he could handle it. He was willing to acknowledge that there was some kind of bond holding them together. But he didn't want that bond to exist. Most especially, he didn't want it to be as strong as it had become. It threatened him somehow, and when a man felt threatened he had two choices: he could either fight back or run.

A third alternative, he supposed, would be to sit back and let fate take its course. But since fate had dealt him some truly lousy hands in his time, he decided he'd rather not chance that one.

He felt her stir against him and he loosened his hold. A tentative smile touched her lips as she raised her hand to his cheek. The suspicious brightness had left her eyes, but the thought that he had brought her to tears was not a comfortable one. He didn't want to hurt her, but he feared very much that he would. She was hearth and home and family. She could bloom in that setting with a man who could return the love she needed. He'd lived alone for so long he had no idea what a proper home life even was. He wasn't sure he'd like it even if he did know. Besides, he thought, facing questions he'd never considered before, what kind of husband or father would he make anyway? Lord knew he knew nothing about being either.

"I wish it could be different," he said, because he knew she needed to hear that. "You belong here, Ellie. I don't. You have your family and your friends, and from what you were saying the other day, you might even have your own business pretty soon."

Ellie slowly lowered her hand from his cheek, holding his glance even as she did. He hadn't meant to sound patronizing, but knowing Ellie, she'd taken his words that way.

She was getting irritated, much as she had the first time he'd made the mistake of telling her what she did or didn't want.

Within seconds she was out of his arms completely. "I probably will wind up with the shop. Aunt Jo stopped by today to talk about it some more. It's certainly what *she* wants. Just do me a favor and don't offer to sell me this house. My mother already thinks it would be perfect if I bought it.''

The flash of defiance in her eyes warned him. Cain was nothing if not astute. ''No problem,'' he said in a voice as smooth as butter. ''I wouldn't sell it to you if you got down on your knees and begged for it.''

Her agitation was downgraded to confusion. Defused by his calmly delivered statement, she could only say, ''You wouldn't?''

''No. But I would give it to you. Which reminds me,'' he hurried on, leaving her with her mouth open. ''There's something I *have* been meaning to give you. Hang on a minute.''

He'd give her the house?

Ellie could do nothing but stare at Cain's broad back as he walked over to his bed, pushed his leather travel bag aside and reached under it.

He would give her the house, she mentally repeated, only this time there was no question. It was the flat statement of certainty. The man, she was discovering, could be generous to a fault. But she didn't want his house unless he was in it. And that wasn't what he offered.

What he *was* offering brought a frown of confusion to her brow. Crossing back to her, Cain carried a leather box—the same one that had held the letters he'd been reading the evening she tried to ease his grief.

''Come on,'' he said, tucking the box under one arm and placing his other arm over her shoulder. He dropped a tiny kiss on the corner of her mouth. He started to say something, then seemed to change his mind and moved back for another kiss, this time a deep and thorough one that left her a little weak in the knees. ''I've been waiting to do that all day.''

She had been waiting all day for it, too, but she didn't have a chance to tell Cain that. He nudged her up the steps and out the door. It wasn't necessary to mess with the barbecue grill, he told her. Fried hamburgers were fine with him. He'd even make them while she sliced up the tomatoes, he said, then proceeded to do just that while he told her, in great detail, about a driver named Rudy who made the hottest hamburgers in the world. Rudy was from Argentina and Cain suspected that at least half of the meat mixture he used consisted of ground chilies. But if you piled enough other stuff on the burgers, he went on to explain, they were wonderful.

It wasn't unusual for Cain to relay bits and pieces of his life on the circuit while they worked together. Ellie had certainly encouraged him often enough, and normally she would have prodded for more. At the moment, however, she found what he was doing too surprising to concentrate on much else. He was procrastinating. Quite deliberately.

It was obvious that whatever it was Cain wanted to give to her had something to do with the box. It seemed just as apparent by the way he avoided mention of it, that he intended to delay relinquishing possession. He seemed perfectly content to let the matter rest, literally, on the stereo while Ellie's curiosity ate at her and they ate dinner. To her credit, not once during the meal did she bring up the subject, though her curiosity was hardly subtle as her eyes kept straying toward the stereo.

The third time Cain caught her glancing in that direction, he began to feel a little uneasy. Had he not been so relieved by the excuse the gift offered, he might even have felt guilty for letting her suspense build. It was entirely possible that she would be disappointed. All he wanted to give her was the cameo. She might not even see the resemblance in it that he did, which was the only thing that had made the piece of jewelry matter to him. But her mind was taken off his departure, and for that he was grateful. He didn't want to think about it himself at the moment. He knew that his memories of her would make forgetting that much more difficult, but he still intended to put Aubrey out of his mind forever once he was gone. He just wasn't quite ready to deprive himself of the peace he felt with her. Oddly, it hadn't vanished as quickly as he'd thought it would.

After clearing away the dishes, Ellie began to suspect that Cain wasn't procrastinating any longer, but that he'd actually forgotten about what had been taunting her for the past half hour. He was getting ready to turn on the television news. "All right, Cain." She tossed aside her dish towel, and waved in the general direction of the stereo. "Would you please tell me why you brought that thing up here?"

His almost apologetic grin was completely disarming as he abandoned the television in favor of the leather box. "Actually, I brought it up for a couple of reasons. I want it out of the way when they haul the bed and dresser out of the basement so it doesn't get taken by accident. I thought I'd leave it up here, if you don't mind. And I wanted to give you this."

Opening the box he'd set on the table, he moved aside some of the old letters and drew out a small blue velvet bag. A gold string gathered the neck. Loosening it, he shook a small pin out into his palm and held it out to her. "I don't know how valuable it is, but it was Mom's. She kept it in here, so I think it must have meant something to her."

Ellie hesitated for a moment, then took the brooch. It was a cameo, its background the soft gray-blue of Wedgwood china and the exquisitely carved feminine profile, a delicate ivory. Edged with gold filigree, it was a truly lovely piece. "You want me to have it?"

She'd thought he'd say he wanted her to keep it because she'd been his mother's friend. She'd have accepted it gratefully in that circumstance. But his words weren't of Amanda.

"I thought about keeping it myself." And taking it out when I want you so much that I ache, he thought, recalling nights when he'd done just that. But he didn't want reminders of her. Clean breaks healed faster. "It reminds me of you."

Her eyes darted to his. In those smoky-gray depths she saw the look of someone who wasn't quite sure how his gift would be received. He wanted her to appreciate it, but he'd never let her know if her reaction disappointed him. There were some places in that wall of his that were so much thicker than others.

"I don't know if you can see it," she heard him say when her glance was drawn back to the pin, "but that's your profile."

For a moment, she stared in fascination at the object she held. Then, as she realized what he was saying to her, she also became aware that she really couldn't see much of anything at all. Her vision was becoming blurred. "Thank you," she whispered, wondering if he really thought her beautiful, because the profile truly was. There was a nobility about it, a kind of grace she certainly couldn't have had. Yet, if he saw her that way...

"Ellie?"

The gentle question in his voice beckoned her. Willing the ache in her throat to go away, the stinging at her eyelids to cease, she kept her head lowered. All she needed was a couple of seconds and she wouldn't have to embarrass herself by letting him see the tears. She wasn't unhappy. She'd simply been moved by his gesture and by the compliment. It wasn't like her to let her emotions run so close to the surface. She'd always been on such an even keel, until she met him.

Cain didn't give her those seconds. Taking her face between his hands, he tipped her head back. Her vulnerability was haunting, her struggle to cover it more than he could bear.

"Oh, God, Ellie," he groaned. "I didn't think it would make you cry. Please." With the brush of his lips, he caught the tiny tear glistening at the corner of her eye. He moved to the other, kissing her eyelid as if to keep the tears behind it. "I don't ever want you to cry."

Then love me, her heart begged, but her voice was silent as his kiss claimed her. Folding the cameo into her palm, she leaned into him, knowing that what she wanted would take time, and that time was the one thing she didn't have. To love Cain was to chase moonbeams. Futile. Hopeless. Yet, the beauty of it beckoned relentlessly. It was beyond reason to expect him to simply drop all the barriers he'd spent years erecting and let her into his life. Not in a matter of mere days or weeks.

She felt the infinite gentleness in his kiss, and knew she had come as close as anyone ever had to touching him. For her, he'd let down just enough of his guard to let her see that he was capable of caring and caring deeply. That capacity was in the gentleness of his lips as they moved from her mouth to her temple and down the curve of her neck—and in the way he whispered her name against her mouth just before his hold on her turned a little more possessive.

In the next few moments it became impossible for Ellie to remember why Cain had tried to soothe her. Where his touch had been gentle, it was now coaxing in an entirely different way. His hand slipped down her back, curving over her bottom to pull her against him. Even as a kittenish moan gathered in her throat, his tongue moved over hers, encouraging the tiny sound.

Rational thought fled. In the back of her mind, Ellie knew that what she was letting happen was utter madness. She should be taking a lesson from Cain and building defenses, not letting go of whatever protective instincts she had—which so far had proved abysmally lacking where he was concerned. Consequences didn't matter right now. For once she was going to take what she wanted and hang on to it for as long as she could. She loved Cain. No one could take that from her. And right now, he wanted her.

A faint breeze fluttered the curtains of the open window. It was sunset, and the sky outside was on fire with the brilliant orange and pink of the dying sun. That blush-tinted light fell through the window to her bed. Cain led her there, his face taut with need as he slipped her shirt over her head and nudged her back on the mattress to pull away her jeans.

Everywhere his hands skimmed, his lips followed. He stripped away her filmy undergarments, his touch almost reverent, his whispered words of need like a benediction. He made her feel beautiful, and then he made her feel only sensation. His fingers feathered over her, his mouth and tongue teasing her breasts. Then he wreaked absolute havoc on her already sensitized nerves by trailing moist kisses to the hollows of her hipbones and below. And when his caresses had taken her to the point where she thought she might die of wanting, he led her gently back down to start the ascent all over again.

It was the most exquisite kind of torture and the most frustrating. Ellie could bear it no longer. Grasping his hands, she pressed a kiss into each callused palm, then began a sensual exploration of her own by pushing him onto his back. His clothes had joined hers long ago, and every time she looked at him, she was struck anew by the sheer magnificence of his masculine body. Hard, taut, lean, he was at once formidable and beautiful. And the light of desire in his eyes was only for her.

"Tell me what you want," she whispered, running her hands down his flanks. "Tell me what to do."

She felt his stomach tense beneath her lips and heard his quick intake of breath. A moment later, he grasped her upper arms and dragged her up his body.

"I want you," he told her fiercely. "And I don't need to tell you what to do. You're already driving me out of my mind."

He brought her head down to meet his, his mouth hungry on hers. Beneath her she felt his muscles tighten as he wrapped his leg around hers to pull them apart. Her breathing accelerated. His quickened in turn. Aligning her more intimately, he cupped her bottom and guided himself inside her.

Sensations piled on top of one another. The feel of his palms pressing her flesh, the fullness of him that turned everything inside her to liquid, the vibration of his mouth against her neck as he told her quite explicitly how good she felt to him. All those feelings combined with an aching need to hold him as tightly as she could. As he began a steady rhythm of slow, fluid strokes, she felt that need increase. He was making the world spin completely out of control.

The glow of the sun faded to the cooler grays of evening. Ellie lay beside Cain, the sheet thrown over them and her hand in his as he held it up to the light of the lamp beside the bed. He was looking at the inside of her forearm. "I noticed these before," he said, referring to the three faint white lines running from just below her wrist to a few inches above the bend in her arm. "What are they?"

"Cat scratches."

"Nice pet."

She smiled, liking the way she'd messed up his hair. There was almost a little-boy charm about the way it fell over his forehead.

That thought broadened her smile even more. "It was a stray. I tried to pick him up and I shouldn't have."

"Live and learn." He drew her arm forward, pressing a kiss to the faint scarring. "When did it happen?"

Nestling her head against his shoulder as he lowered her hand, Ellie had to consciously quell a sigh of contentment. If she could stay like this forever, she could want nothing more. Lying here with Cain, talking so easily, even if it was about her silly old scars, was as close to truly happy as she was ever likely to come. "A long time ago. When I was eleven. It was my own fault. Mom warned me that just because it came to the back door for food every night, that didn't mean it was tame. I figured if it let me feed it, it should let me pick it up. My brother wasted no time in informing me that my logic was totally out of whack."

"Is that the brother who used to take you fishing?"

She was a little surprised he remembered her telling him about that. "The same. And the only. He's a vet now."

"Sounds as if he knew his animals even when he was a kid. You two get along pretty well?"

"Better now than when we were growing up. He was an awful tease."

As they talked, Cain's fingers had been wandering slowly up and down her arm. For a moment, the motion ceased, then started again. "I have a half sister somewhere."

It wasn't like Cain to just drop a piece of his past out of the blue like that. He was usually so protective of it. "I know," she returned, hoping he would take her response as encouragement.

He sounded oddly hopeful. "Did Mom ever say anything to you about her?"

Amanda had never mentioned the child. Ellie, however, had certainly heard the rumors about it. "No. I'm sorry, Cain. She never did."

"It doesn't matter. I was just wondering. I think about her every once in a while. She'd be around your age by now."

Ellie laid her hand over the strong beat of his heart and pressed a kiss to the warm skin above it. It was all she could think to do. The only family Cain had left was completely unknown to him and would forever remain so. How much worse to know that there was something you wanted and could never have than to simply know you had nothing.

Cain was barely aware of what Ellie had done. His mind had drifted back to the years right after his father left him and his mom. It hadn't been an easy time. He remembered being alone a lot because his mother worked nights. When she was home, she slept, exhausted from pulling her usual double shift at the tavern. But those days were bliss compared to what followed when she got pregnant. His father had been gone for a couple of years when that happened.

As young as he was, Cain had understood even then that his mother had been sleeping with someone. Or several someones, as the other kids had implied with their cracks about her. Some of those remarks had gone beyond implication and the names he'd ultimately heard had no business coming from the mouths of children. He'd been called a few choice names himself. His own parentage was called into question on occasion—usually in the school yard. That was when Cain's fighting had gone from an occasional scrap to bloodletting brawls. He'd been angry and frustrated and, though he hadn't recognized it at the time, very frightened. He'd fought because of anger, but mostly he'd fought because he hadn't understood the turmoil he was going through—especially after his mother had the baby.

She hadn't come home with it like the other kids' moms did when they went to the hospital in Greely to have babies. She'd come home with nothing but the bag she'd left with and a tiny identification band that said Baby Girl Whitlow. She'd given his sister away. After that, Cain, not understanding, had fallen asleep every night fearing that someday she might give him away, too. He must have been twelve or thirteen before he'd stopped thinking about that.

"I never knew who the father was," he said, his voice betraying the old tension that had seeped back into him by degrees. He'd never seen his mother with a man. She'd never brought anyone home.

Ellie wasn't sure why Cain's expression had become so clouded. He never told her the things that hurt him the most. She was sure of that. She knew only that talking about the half sister he'd never seen had taken him very far away from her.

"Don't," she whispered, cradling his face with her hands. She didn't want him to remember whatever it was that hurt him so much. She wanted to erase it all, to make him forget.

And for a while, soothed by Ellie's healing kiss, that was exactly what Cain did. The peace returned—only to be shattered completely the next morning.

Chapter Thirteen

Bernice Pruitt was leaving the flower shop with a vaguely offended air and her purchase of a greeting card as Ellie's Aunt Jo was coming in. From behind the counter, Ellie heard the brief exchange of good-mornings and grinned openly at her aunt. Though Jo was still moving forward into the shop, her frown was following Bernice past the window.

"What's wrong with her this morning?" Shaking her head, the overhead lights picking out the silver in her brown curls as she did, Jo turned toward the counter. "She acts like she had sour prunes for breakfast."

"She's just annoyed with me," Ellie returned, not sounding at all concerned.

"With you?" Her hazel eyes registering genuine shock, Jo reached for the stool in front of the bridal arrangement catalog and eased herself up on it. Slowly crossing her arms on the smooth white countertop, she leaned toward her niece. She gave no indication of being in pain, but the caution in her movements told Ellie that her arthritis was definitely bothering her today. "Whatever for?"

Ellie's smile had already started to fade at her aunt's discomfort. It disappeared completely now. Reluctance took its place.

Pulling out a figurine brochure she'd been meaning to peruse, she thought about waving the matter off as inconsequential. She immediately dismissed that idea. Jo would never go for it. Instead, she traded hesitation for resignation and drew a deep breath. If she didn't tell her aunt, someone else would.

"She saw me in the car with Cain after Uncle Jay's party," she said, flipping through the pages. "She wanted to know where we went. I told her it was none of her business. But in case you're interested—" and from the quick arch of her aunt's eyebrow, Ellie knew she was "—we went to the lake. Cain wanted to get away for a while."

Ellie had tried to make the event sound inconsequential. She almost managed it, too, except for the telltale note of defensiveness that crept into her voice. Bracing herself for the admonition she was sure would come, she abandoned her study of porcelain birds and raised her eyes to meet her aunt's very direct stare.

To Ellie's amazement, what she saw wasn't disapproval. It seemed more like resignation; as if her aunt had been expecting something like this and hadn't quite decided what she wanted to think of it. Ellie didn't know what to make of that unexpected reaction. She didn't necessarily believe Jo's attitude to be as casual as it seemed when she drew the abandoned brochure toward her and began to casually flip through its pages herself.

"Have his plans changed?"

"What do you mean?"

"Has he decided to stay in Aubrey?"

Quite unconsciously, Ellie moved her hand to cover the yellow daisy embroidered at the top of the green, butcher-style apron she wore. Beneath it was the cameo she'd pinned over the top button of her V-necked white blouse. "He's not staying. He wants to go as soon as he finishes up everything with the house."

"What will he do if the place doesn't sell?"

"It will. The real estate office he signed with guaranteed to sell it within ninety days or they'd buy it. He won't get as much for it if that happens, but he doesn't care."

"I see." Paper rustled as Jo turned another page. "Then he'll be leaving soon?"

Jo's voice was amazingly light for the weight of her questions. Not trusting that indifference, Ellie nonetheless appreciated the lack of criticism.

"Tomorrow, probably. After Uncle Hal picks up the things for the lodge auction. Cain doesn't want to leave any loose ends, so he won't go until everything's been done."

To Ellie, he'd actually seemed fanatical about that house. It was almost as if he'd refused to leave anything behind that could be faulted. With all that he'd done to his mother's home, no one could walk by now and shake their head at its shabbiness, or mutter among themselves at its state of disrepair. It looked as good as any in the old section of town.

Maybe that was the message he'd wanted to leave. That his mother had been as good as anybody else.

Looking up from the spot she'd been rubbing off the counter with her finger, Ellie saw her aunt watching her. It was apparent that the woman wanted very much to say something, but wasn't quite sure how she should put it.

The expression "saved by the bell" leaped to Ellie's mind with the ring of the telephone. Since it was within Jo's reach, she answered it. Whatever admonition she'd been about to deliver was preempted by her response to the caller's inquiry as to the availability of peach-colored roses.

While Jo finished the call, Ellie slipped into the small office area in back. Taking off her apron, she hung it over its peg, then fished a couple of dollars from her purse so she could run over to the café and pick up some coffee and doughnuts. Jo had come by to take a break with her, and, Ellie suspected, to show her the papers their lawyer had drawn up for her to purchase the shop. Her mother had told her yesterday that Jo had almost completed the legalities, even though Ellie had yet to commit herself to the deal. Everyone expected her to go along with the plan. Therefore, they assumed she would.

A flutter of anxiety whispered through her. She'd never been very good at asserting herself, but the time had come to do just that. Somehow, she was going to have to tell her aunt politely that she'd have to find someone else to take over her business.

All morning long, Ellie had been doing something she'd never done before—considering what *she* wanted. Ever since she could remember, she'd been caught in the trap of needing to please everyone but herself. It had always been so important to Ellie that the people she cared about be happy with her. Thanks to Cain, she'd begun to see that everyone else's approval wasn't always necessary.

She was tired of other people making decisions for her; of giving up what she wanted because it didn't fit in with someone else's plans, or because someone else didn't think what she wanted was right for her. *She* was the only person who knew what was right for her. If she didn't take responsibility for her life now, she probably never would. That thought was what frightened her the most.

Though she felt about as courageous as the mouse a few people apparently thought her to be, she squared her shoulders and rounded the flower cooler. As soon as she came back from the café she would tell her aunt that while she appreciated the offer to sell her the shop very much, she was going to turn it down. That would be a piece of cake compared to what she had planned when she got home and faced Cain.

All along, he had been giving her little pieces of his trust. For Cain, that was a lot. Now, she could only hope that she could make him see that what they had together was better than what they had apart, and that he could trust her not to hurt him. That, she was sure, was what held him back.

Tonight, she was going to ask him to take her with him.

"Adele needs an oval centerpiece for her card club luncheon on Friday," Jo said as she hung up the phone. "She wants peach and yellow to match the napkins she bought here last week." Ripping off a sheet from the order pad, she pushed it across the counter and smiled up at Ellie. "See if you can—"

"Can what?" Ellie prodded, not at all sure why her aunt was suddenly staring at her chest.

The woman's hazel eyes had narrowed as if she were trying to place something, her frown growing more contemplative by the second. A moment later, recognition turned to puzzlement. "Where did you get that cameo?"

Ellie raised her hand to touch it, the motion unconsciously protective. "Cain gave it to me. Why?"

"Where did he get it?"

"It was his mother's."

"No, it wasn't."

"Aunt Jo." Ellie didn't want to come right out and contradict her aunt especially since the woman was looking a little odd, but she did know where the cameo had come from. She'd seen Cain take it out of a box he'd found in his mother's house. "I know it was Amanda's."

"Amanda may have had it. But, Ellie, that cameo belonged to your Grandma Bennett. Your grandpa had it made for her as a wedding gift. The profile is hers."

Stunned, Ellie stared blankly at her aunt. "Are you sure?"

"Absolutely. It's the cameo she's wearing in the portrait in Hal's and my bedroom. We always wondered what happened to it. It's been missing for years."

For several seconds, Ellie simply stood there, trying to absorb what she had heard. As it slowly began to sink in, her first thought was that it was no wonder Cain had been able to see a resemblance to her in the intricately carved piece. Her father had always told her that she bore a remarkable resemblance to his mother, though Ellie had thought the woman far prettier than she. Since she'd passed away long before Ellie was born, Ellie had never seen her, but she had seen a copy of a tintype of her. Jo had found the original after she and Hal were married and had copies made for all three brothers. It was the portrait she'd referred to only a moment ago.

Now that Ellie thought about it, there *was* a cameo in that picture.

"I'll ask Cain if he knows anything about it tonight," she said, at a complete loss as to how Amanda had come to possess a Bennett family heirloom.

"I think maybe you'd better ask him now. I meant to tell you a few minutes ago. Hal and some of the men from the lodge went over to Amanda's about an hour ago. Ed brought Hal's truck back yesterday and Lester volunteered his, too, so they decided to pick up the donations today instead of tomorrow."

It was all Ellie could do not to run the two blocks home. As it was, she made it in record time, not slowing her pace until she saw her uncle and his friends carting Amanda's furniture down the driveway. The trucks were almost loaded. Cain wasn't anywhere to be seen. At least his car was still there, she realized with relief. It was parked on the street to allow the trucks better access to the garage.

Propelled by a sense of immediacy, she started up the drive to the back door. A quick "Hi" was offered as she passed Ed and Lester by the red truck and Uncle Hal by his brown one, but she didn't wait to receive their greetings. Her only thought was of Cain and that, within hours, he might be gone.

"Hey! Hold on there." Hal's arm snaked out, grabbing her as she passed to slow her down. "What are you doing home so early?"

"I need to talk to Cain."

Behind those damnable mirrored sunglasses, she saw him frown. His discountenance remained as he raised his free hand to wipe the sweat from his brow with his plaid shirt-sleeve.

"What for?" he asked, still holding her in place.

The question rankled. It was none of his business what she wanted to talk to Cain about. Lacking the nerve to tell him that, she simply ignored the question. "Do you know where he is?"

"He's in the house getting his things together. I think you ought to wait out here. You don't need to be alone with him."

Never in her life had Ellie spoken with less than respect to the elder members of her family. But at the moment, faced with the possibility of not having a chance to see Cain alone before he walked out of her life, and totally fed up with having her needs dictated to her, that unquestioned regard vanished like so much dust in the wind.

"Excuse me," she began, in a token attempt at a civility she didn't feel, "but you have no idea what I need, Uncle Hal. Would you please let me go?"

To her relief, her challenge didn't anger him. Instead, he seemed so caught off guard by it that for a moment he simply looked down at her in surprise and disbelief.

"You know, Ellie," he finally said, "you've been going through some changes here lately that we don't quite understand. Frankly, we just don't quite know what to expect from you anymore."

That was fine with her. She didn't want to be predictable old Ellie any longer. "I want to talk to Cain. Please," she repeated, "let me go."

Her insistence was met with grudging compliance. At least, Hal started to comply. He'd barely released her when he tersely demanded, "Where did you get that?"

There was no reason to ask what he was referring to. She knew exactly what had caught his attention. "From Cain," she returned, heading toward the house.

"Where'd he get it?"

"I don't know."

"I'll tell you where he got it." Hal's voice was suddenly tight, and loud enough to be heard quite clearly as she reached the corner of the house. "He probably stole it."

At the accusation Ellie whirled around.

"Don't go looking so shocked," Hal admonished. "It wouldn't be the first time he'd taken something that wasn't his. If he had a grudge against someone, you could damn near bet money they'd wind up with something missing sooner or later. Hell, Ellie, your daddy had to kick him out of school a couple of times, and I sure let him know often enough that his disappearing someday wouldn't break my heart. It would have been just like him to take something that was important to us just for spite."

Hal stood with his hands on his hips, the lines of his weathered face set in grim satisfaction. Behind him Ed, pushing back a red Cardinals' baseball cap on his head, and Lester, scratching his bald head, leaned against Lester's truck to listen. Neither of them noticed that Jo had arrived. She was standing by the cottonwood watching her husband while she caught her breath.

It vaguely occurred to Ellie that her aunt must have locked up the shop and come running after her. That thought was of no consequence compared to the indignation tightening every nerve in her body. It had taken hold so quickly that she had no time to consider how impudent her uncle might think her, or how absolute was her belief in Cain.

"He didn't take it," she stated, refusing to believe that Cain would have lied to her about where the cameo came from. "He found it in some of his mother's things."

"Then he probably gave it to her. Ellie," her uncle went on, sounding weary now, "we've been trying to tell you all along, that Whitlow isn't—"

"Good enough for her? Don't worry," Ellie heard Cain cut in as he stepped out the back door and dropped his travel bag beside it. The screen slammed, the sound like a gunshot in the suddenly still air. "She knows who I am."

It was apparent enough that Cain had heard most of what had been said. What wasn't so clear was how he felt about her attempt to defend him. Though he'd stopped beside her, he hadn't given her so much as a glance. It was almost as if she weren't there.

Her uncle, too, seemed to think she was invisible. "Where'd you get the pin, Whitlow?"

"Ellie already told you. I found it in my mother's things."

"Where did she get it?"

The indignation moving across Cain's features was most evident. So was the steel-edged control he asserted over himself. "I have no idea."

The muscle in Hal's jaw bunched. Not taking his eyes from Cain, he spoke to the men behind him. "Ed, Lester, go ahead and take the furniture over to the storage shed at the hall. But leave the boxes. I want to make sure there isn't anything else here that I should know about."

Ed shuffled forward. Hands in his pockets, the ever-present plug of tobacco ballooning his cheek, he came up to stand elbow to elbow with Hal. "You know," he began, nodding the brim of his baseball cap toward Cain, "it could be that he's the one been helping himself to our tools and such lately. We've been blaming the migrants. Maybe you should have been looking closer to home."

Ed, obviously feeling quite safe with six feet two inches of sheriff standing beside him, glanced pointedly at Cain. But it was Ellie who spoke.

"That's crazy. We've been having break-ins all summer. Cain's only been here for a couple of weeks."

"Ellie, don't." Cain's command was deadly quiet. "They're going to believe whatever they want."

With a sinking feeling, Ellie thought he might be right. To his credit, her uncle wasn't swayed by Ed's knee-jerk suspicion. He dismissed Ed's implication along with Ed himself. But he clearly believed Cain wasn't telling him the truth about the cameo.

"I'll give you one more chance, Whitlow," he said as Ed and Lester prepared to drive off with the first truckload of furniture. "Where did you get the pin?"

As Cain repeated what he'd said before, Ellie realized it was going to take a lot more than the simple truth to convince her uncle. He wanted proof of some kind.

"Show him the box," she said to Cain. "Show him where you found the cameo."

"What good will that do?"

"I don't know," she admitted, conscious of the way her aunt was now watching her. Jo had moved to Hal's side, his surprise at seeing her apparent in the questioning frown he sent in her direction. "I just know you aren't getting anywhere this way."

He looked at her for the first time since he'd recognized her voice and come out to face her uncle and his accusations. She looked a little frightened. As he felt her fingers curling over his forearm, he realized that her fear was for him.

"Where did you put it?" he asked, wanting to allay that fear.

"It's upstairs." Slowly, she withdrew her hand. She hadn't given any thought to touching him. From the slight softening in his eyes, she knew he understood that gesture to be reassurance. From the slight lift of her aunt's eyebrow, she knew that the gesture betrayed a lot more than that. "I'll get it."

Jo was right behind her. "I think we should all go inside. Hanna's practically hanging out her window as it is. Come on, Hal. Cain, you, too."

Hal grabbed her arm and pulled her aside. "Listen, Jo," Ellie heard him say in a voice meant only for his wife, "I'll take care of this. You take Ellie and go back to the shop. This doesn't concern either one of you."

"You have the sensitivity of a rock," she informed her husband, her voice equally low. "It most definitely concerns Ellie. And because she's concerned, I am, too. I don't want to go back to the shop, and I'm quite certain Ellie doesn't want to go, either. Now, are you going to help me up those steps? Or must I ask Cain to do it?"

There was possibly only one person in all of Lassiter County that Hal Bennett thought twice about arguing with. His wife. Seeing her implacable expression, he guided her up the steps behind Ellie and Cain, then held out one of the white wrought-iron chairs for her at Ellie's little round table. A few moments later, Ellie had retrieved the leather box Cain had given her for safekeeping and set it on the table by the bouquet of white mums she'd brought home a few days ago.

"That's what the cameo was in," she said to her uncle.

"That hardly proves that I didn't take it," Cain muttered from where he leaned against her refrigerator ten feet away.

Ellie was afraid her uncle would agree. Instead, he frowned at the box. Flipping it open, his scowl deepened.

"Where was this?"

At the odd question, the veiled dislike that had marked Cain's expression gave way to incomprehension. "What do you mean?"

"I mean just what I said. Where was this in the house?" One after another, Hal picked up the envelopes. He quickly scrutinized each one, as if he were looking for something in particular. "Damn it. I looked everywhere for—" Cutting himself off, he muttered another oath under his breath.

The letters he held were those Cain had written to Amanda. There were a few other papers in the bottom of the box, including the mortgage on the house and a copy of Amanda's marriage license. Cain had looked through everything himself, so he knew what was there. And he couldn't imagine what Hal Bennett would have found interesting about any of it.

"You looked for what?" he said, not about to let Hal's slip of the tongue go without comment.

Hal remained silent. He just kept riffling through the box.

"What are you looking for?" Cain repeated.

"It doesn't matter." Dismissing Cain, Hal looked to Ellie. "Was there anything in here that isn't in here now?"

"Like what?" she asked, clearly at a loss as to what was going on. Cain was now glaring at her uncle in much the same way her uncle had been glaring at him only minutes ago. Accusing, suspicious.

"Like *anything*," her uncle enunciated in that strained tone that said his patience was being sorely tested.

She started to tell him there wasn't, then remembered the little sack the pin had been in. It was of no consequence to her, but as strangely as he was behaving, she'd let him decide its import. "Only the bag the cameo was in. It's right here."

The blue velvet bag lay on the table by her sofa bed, still unmade since she and Cain had left it this morning. Those sweet, peaceful hours in his arms seemed an eternity ago as she dragged her eyes from those rumpled sheets and gathered the bag in the palm of her hand. As she did, she felt something stiff beneath the soft fabric.

"Forget the bag," she heard her uncle say, even as she fished the small folded paper from the bottom of the sack. "It's not important."

For a few seconds, the only sound in the room was the shuffle of paper as Hal continued his search through the box. Then, apparently having had enough of her husband's inexplicable behavior, Jo quietly insisted on knowing what was going on. "What are you doing, Hal? And what on earth are you looking for?"

"Maybe he's looking for this."

Hal started forward, but it was to Jo that Ellie handed the bit of folded paper she'd found caught in the seam of the bag. "To my dearest Amanda, with all my love, Jay," Jo read, then looked at her husband. Regret and realization mingled in her sigh. She set the paper on the table. "I think we know now how Cain's mother got the cameo."

Hal said nothing, his posture growing oddly defensive as he looked from the box and its scattered contents. He pushed his fingers through his hair.

"I don't think this is what he's looking for, though, Ellie." As Jo smoothed the fold lines in the note, she grew pensive. "We didn't *know* Jay had given it to her."

"Uncle Jay?" Ellie asked, wanting to be sure she was making the proper connection. "Uncle Jay was in love with Amanda?" She looked to Cain, whose expression revealed so little. All she could see there was a kind of certainty she couldn't begin to understand. That certainty was in his voice, too, as he looked at the man who had yet to apologize for his accusation.

"It was *you* who went through my mother's bedroom after she died, wasn't it?"

Hal's head jerked toward Cain, a denial poised on his lips. His niece was staring at him, waiting for his answer, as was his wife. "How did you know?"

Cain's voice fairly dripped with sarcasm. "The criminal mind has amazing deductive powers, Sheriff. I believe you started to say you'd looked everywhere for something. Was that box the something you were looking for?"

"I don't have to tell you a damn thing, Whitlow."

"Yes, you do, Hal," Jo said, her failure to side with her husband even more astounding to Ellie than everything she was hearing. "I'd like to know what you were looking for, too."

Hal seemed to find his wife's attitude as implausible as Ellie had. "For God's sake, Jo. We're talking about the family name here. No good can come of raking up any of this."

"The questions have already been raised, Hal. What were you looking for?"

"I thought she might have kept a copy of the adoption papers," he grudgingly returned. His voice fell. "If she had, I didn't want someone coming across them while they were cleaning out the place...in case Jay's name was on them."

Chapter Fourteen

The quiet that filled the room was almost palpable. For several moments, the only sounds to be heard were Hal's measured footsteps as he crossed to the window overlooking the drive. His hand was clamped over the back of his neck, defeat slumping his wide shoulders. Behind him, three pairs of eyes followed his retreat, divergent reaction registering in each.

From where she stood beside the table, Ellie saw her aunt cautiously shift her concern from her husband to the man whose chilling silence dominated the room. Ellie had never known Jo to be easily intimidated, which explained how she'd been able to live with Hal Bennett for so long. But her aunt did seem constrained by Cain's implacable stance.

"Why don't you sit down, Cain," she suggested, taking a tentative step toward conciliation. "You might want to also, Ellie."

Cain shook his head, remaining where he stood in front of the refrigerator with his arms crossed and his eyes fixed firmly on Hal's back. Giving him a worried glance, Ellie slid into the seat across from her aunt so she could watch him. The darkness of his expression didn't bode well for whatever it was they were about to hear.

"I apologize if anything I say offends you," Jo told Cain, clearly determined to avoid any further unfairness. "I just don't know how to explain this without being blunt."

She didn't wait for a response. The moment she saw his brooding stare settle on her, Jo turned to Ellie. "Your Uncle Jay and Amanda Whitlow had an affair while he was county representative over in Greely. This was a long time ago, you understand. At least twenty years." She took a deep breath, then slowly released it. "Actually, it was more than an affair. Jay wanted to marry her."

Ellie's glance flew to Cain. He didn't seem to notice. His swift frown was directed at Jo as he attempted to grasp the significance of what he'd just heard. Jo, in turn, looked at her husband, as if waiting for him to object to what she'd revealed. Or, perhaps, to attempt to stop her from saying more.

His back remained to them all.

It wouldn't have mattered to Ellie if Hal had objected just then. She was at a complete loss as to how her beloved Uncle Jay could have left the only woman he'd apparently ever loved. "Why didn't he marry her?"

"It was a family decision," Jo said, and that immediately left no doubt in Ellie's mind that it had been Uncle Hal who'd come between the two lovers. Hal had always been adamant about upholding the family's reputation and place in the community—and family decisions were invariably his.

Once Jo got started, it didn't take her long to explain what the whole Bennett family had kept quiet for so long. Jay's career was on the fast road up when he began stopping at the tavern outside of Greely where Amanda worked. He would visit there with his constituents, the farmers and construction workers who frequented the place. His potential for success had seemed unlimited then and nothing appeared to stand in his way of winning a seat in the legislature—until he fell in love with Amanda. As the two had been scrupulously discreet, no one had suspected their involvement at all until the day he announced to his brothers his intention to make her his wife.

Stu, Ellie's father, had merely suggested that Jay give the matter more thought, which was his solution for everything. Hal, however, was more active in his attempt to make Jay understand how disastrous such a step would be. A man with political aspirations had to choose his spouse carefully. Marrying a divorced barmaid with a delinquent son would have spelled political suicide.

Jay wasn't going to be dissuaded. But Amanda had seen the wisdom in their parting—after Hal had spoken with her, Ellie surmised, though her aunt judiciously said nothing of that. Amanda had told Jay that she couldn't marry him. She was certain that, eventually, he would resent her for causing him to sacrifice his career and his relationship with his family.

"It was several months after they'd broken up when Jay learned that Amanda was pregnant," Jo went on, her voice quiet with strain. "I don't know what all else happened, but I do know she told him that the child wasn't his. Amanda probably knew that was the only thing she could have said to keep him away."

"Did he believe her?" Ellie asked. "About not being the father?"

"I don't think so. Oh, at first, he was angry and hurt by what she'd said, but I don't think he believed her. When he got her to admit that she'd lied to him, it was too late. She'd already had the baby and given it up. I suspect she felt she had no choice. She wouldn't marry Jay, and she couldn't offer a child a home any better than the one she'd given Cain.''

The words faded. Jo unfolded the note to look at it again. "She'd kept him from his child," she said with weary finality. "Though her decision was the best for all of them, Jay was never able to forgive her for that."

As she sat there, absorbing all that had been said, Ellie could actually feel the hopelessness of the ill-fated affair. No one would ever know all that had transpired between Amanda and Jay. But even without that knowledge, Ellie had the feeling that Cain's mother couldn't have won, no matter which way she'd turned. Knowing Amanda as she had, she realized that the woman's decision to give up her child had been a painful one; more painful even than letting go the man she loved so she wouldn't jeopardize his future. Ellie had always admired Amanda's courage. She just hadn't realized until now how truly courageous she'd been.

With that insight came another, this one explaining the mysterious remark Uncle Jay had made after Ellie talked to him about Cain. *Family is important,* he'd told her, *and your family deserves your loyalty. Just don't let them have your soul.*

Remembering those words now, she realized that he must have been thinking of what he'd traded for his success. He, too, had lost, and her Uncle Hal, she thought, had tried to keep Jay from losing more. Ever vigilant in his determination to guard the family name and to protect all that name had earned, he had tried to keep the secret buried. Though it had all happened so long ago, it would hardly help the senator's career to have the whole sordid affair discovered during an election year.

Ellie was just beginning to appreciate how much noise a skeleton makes when it falls from the closet when she saw the disgust move over Cain's darkly handsome features. A knot of trepidation balled in Ellie's stomach when she saw that her uncle had turned and that the two men were now facing each other. A good fifteen feet separated them. Suddenly, Ellie wondered if it was enough.

She had expected to see apology or, at the very least, a little regret in her uncle's face. Nothing so humble marked his weathered features. His face was set in an expression that dared challenge, and without the glasses that so often hid his eyes, she could see their haughty gleam. No one ever questioned him or his motives, and it was clear that he wasn't about to apologize for anything he'd done. The family name had been at stake. He'd done what he felt he had to do to protect it.

"You have something you want to say, Whitlow?"

A faintly charged element skittered through the room, rooting Ellie to where she'd risen beside her chair. The air suddenly felt heavy, much as it did in the ominous stillness before a storm. It was difficult to tell which man could wreak the most destruction. They were both big and they both had their own brand of righteousness on their side. Cain, however, had the power of quiet rage on his.

He felt that rage sweep through him, stronger than he'd felt it since his youth. His fists were clenched at his sides, his heartbeat thudding stronger with the surge of adrenaline coursing through his veins. How many times had Hal Bennett glared at him the same way he was doing now, openly defying him to take a swing at his smug and arrogant face? From the time he'd been old enough to be repulsed by that expression, Cain could recall how the man had always held himself up as superior. In reality, he was nothing but a damned hypocrite. The whole bunch of them were. If it hadn't been for the Bennetts, his mother wouldn't have suffered nearly as much as she had. Her reputation had been in tatters after she had Jay's child. She'd been pregnant and unmarried, and she'd been called everything from loose to a tramp, yet she'd never breathed a word to anyone about the child's father.

His illegitimate sister had been a Bennett.

Cain might have laughed at the situation's absurdity, if his anger had allowed him any perspective. He was too close to his animosity, though, too incensed by the kind of double standard he'd always faced in this backwater town. For all they had done to his mother, they'd still had the nerve to warn Ellie away from him because a Whitlow was of less than desirable character.

The words he spoke burned with venom. "I haven't got a thing to say that you would hear, Bennett. And I'm not going to waste my breath trying to make you understand what a sorry little man you are. Not in front of your wife."

Clearly affronted at having his masculinity minimized, Hal narrowed his eyes dangerously. "No one speaks to me in that—"

Hal didn't get to finish speaking at all, much less inform Cain as to the proper tone of address. Cain had already given him one last burning glare and slammed out of the house. The screen was nearly jerked off its hinges on his way.

"Cain! Wait!"

He heard Ellie's frantic call, then the sound of the door slamming again. A pleading "Let him go, Ellie" joined the pounding beat of her feet on the stairs.

She called his name once more, adding a beseeching "Please" this time.

Cain didn't turn around. He didn't dare. His unfaltering strides carried him straight to his car. Tossing in the travel bag he'd swept up on his way past the back door of the house, he climbed in after it and started the engine. Ellie was just rounding the back of the car to come up to the driver's window when the screech of his tires overrode her pleas for him to listen to her. A few seconds later, he was halfway down the street.

He wasn't thinking clearly enough for the desperation he'd heard in Ellie's voice to register, and no specific thought had been given to his actions. He'd known only that he had to get out and get away and to do both as quickly as humanly possible. It was either that or change the alignment of Hal Bennett's teeth. Cain wanted to think he'd matured a little in the past thirteen years.

What Cain really wanted to do was not to think at all. Shifting into a lower gear as he rounded the corner onto the main road out of town, he felt the wide tires flatten out to hug the pavement. More pressure on the accelerator and he was lurching forward, screaming down the ditch-lined country road. He couldn't seem to escape the town fast enough.

Ellie stood at the curb in front of Amanda's house, staring down the empty street. The distant bark of Cindy's dog was the only sound other than the gentle rustle of leaves in the breeze. Behind her she heard the telltale squeak of the stairs, indicating that someone was descending. She didn't turn around. She couldn't. She was too numb.

"You had to let him go, Ellie," she heard Aunt Jo say. "He needs to be alone for a while."

Not looking from the quiet street, Ellie hugged her arms around her middle as if to quiet the anxieties inside her. "What if he doesn't come back?"

"I can't say I'd blame him if he didn't. But he did leave some of his things here."

"The box," Ellie said quietly, remembering that it still sat on her table.

"And you."

There was a wealth of understanding in the hazel eyes smiling softly at her. But more than that, there was support.

"He doesn't know I'm his, Aunt Jo. I love him."

"I know." There was no disapproval. Just simple acceptance of a fact. "It was there in the way you always defended him. He definitely brought out your protective streak. I'm beginning to think it's an inherited trait. Jay was like that with Amanda, and Hal is that way with me and everyone else he cares about." She placed her hand on Ellie's arm. "Don't judge him too harshly for that."

For a long time after Hal took Jo back to the shop, Ellie sat at the top of the stoop by her door, rolling her aunt's words over in her mind. Protectiveness, she'd discovered, could bring out a lot of different qualities in people—not all of them admirable.

Though she'd never have thought them to have a thing in common, both Cain and Uncle Hal had been driven by the same need—the need to defend their own. Cain had only been a child when he'd had that responsibility thrust upon him, and his lack of control over the events in his life had made him seek that control through aggression. Her uncle was aggressive, too, in a much more sophisticated way. As an adult he hadn't been up against the same odds as Cain had as a child, yet he'd failed to allow Cain any leeway for his lack of maturity. All the time Cain was growing up, her uncle had faulted him for doing exactly what he was doing himself—trying to keep his family intact and defend its name.

Slowly, Ellie drew herself to her feet. Just this morning, she had decided to ask Cain to take her with him. Whether or not she would have that opportunity remained to be seen. She didn't want to think of what she'd do if she never saw him again. What mattered at that very moment was that with or without Cain, she was leaving Aubrey.

She didn't know where she was going. She'd figure that out in the morning, after she'd told her parents goodbye and assured them that she was still in full possession of her mental faculties. Her destination didn't matter at the moment. She knew only that if she stayed here, she would forever be under her family's scrutiny and always fighting for control of her own life. She loved her family, but their kind of protectiveness was too stifling for her, and, where Uncle Hall was concerned, far too threatening. He could manipulate her without her even being aware of it—just as he had when he'd told her she was only imagining that someone had broken into Amanda's house.

Having made the decision, Ellie immediately put herself to work. Storing furniture wasn't going to be a problem. The sofa bed and the dresser went with the apartment. The only furniture belonging to her was the table and chairs, which she'd bought secondhand when the ice cream parlor next to Lucille's beauty shop had gone out of business. Since she had no particular attachment to them, she figured they might as well stay.

She wasn't exactly overburdened by material goods, so it didn't take Ellie long to collect the few odds and ends she did possess and pack them in the two empty boxes she found in the garage. What took time was the disposition of her two African violets and the overgrown fern that had hung by the window. Hanna was overjoyed to get them, the violets especially, but she simply couldn't understand why Ellie wanted to leave Aubrey.

"Perhaps what you need," her elderly neighbor suggested after delicately clearing her throat, "is a man. I've always thought you and my Len would do well together. Now that he's broken off with that widow lady he was seeing, maybe you two could start keeping company."

As politely as possible, Ellie told Hanna that she didn't think Leonard was the answer for her.

Her next stop was easier. She simply hollered over the fence when she saw Cindy Baker in her backyard and handed her the bird feeder and birdseed so the child could take over that task. Cindy was nuts about sparrows, and Ellie was sure the feathered creatures wouldn't mind traveling another hundred yards or so for their dinner.

All in all, the afternoon went rather quickly, and Ellie didn't look at her watch more than a hundred times. She was sitting on the edge of the sofa bed telling herself to stop listening for Cain's car when she glanced at her watch for the 101st. He'd been gone for five hours and eight minutes, and every second that passed seemed to lessen the chance that he might return.

With a shaky sigh she glanced toward her stereo. It had been days since she'd felt the need to escape into her dance. Actually, she hadn't wanted to escape. With Cain she'd felt alive and whole and content just to *be*. Now, she didn't know what she felt, other than scared to death that night would fall and Cain wouldn't have returned. Just because he'd left the leather box there didn't mean anything. He hadn't known about it before he arrived, so it might very well be that it was no loss to him to leave it behind.

It was also entirely possible that he felt the same way about what had happened between them.

Pulling one of her favorite albums from the box she'd packed them in, she placed it on the stereo. She didn't feel at all like dancing, but she needed the music and the escape

it offered. If she could just sit still and listen, maybe the
music might reach inside her and take away the sense of re-
jection that was beginning to hurt so much.

The melody she chose was soft and tranquil, a piece that
could soothe if the mind could be cleared of what troubled
it. She tried to think of nothing, only of the music and how
it surrounded her, beckoning her to become part of it.

For a long time she sat cross-legged on the floor, her arms
hugging her middle as she listened. Her head was bent, her
thick auburn hair falling like a gleaming veil about her face,
hiding her, protecting her.

That was how Cain saw her when he stopped by the open
window next to her door.

He'd gotten as far at Texarkana before he slowed down
enough to start thinking again. One hundred and fifty miles
had lain between him and Aubrey, and he'd thought for sure
that he was rid of that town for good. But every mile had
also taken him that much farther from Ellie, and he hadn't
been able to keep on going.

Drawing his hand through his hair, he fervently prayed
that he'd done the right thing in coming back.

What he'd heard here earlier today had shaken him far
more than he'd have thought possible. This town had held
enough bad memories for him as it was, and his reasons for
disliking it had only increased when he was faced with Hal
Bennett's hypocrisy. There had been a time in Cain's life
when he would have turned his back on any reminder of that
kind of pain or hurt. But too much had passed between him
and Ellie for him to turn his back on her. What was possibly even more important was that she had stood by him,
believed in him when no one else had. That had proved a lot
to him. Whether or not it proved what he hoped it did, remained to be seen.

He called her name when the music faded out, his quiet "Ellie?" sounding a little gruffer than he'd intended. From where he stood, he saw her head jerk up. An instant later, she was on her feet and bolting for the door.

Ellie's heart was beating in her throat as she pushed on the screen to let Cain in. He was back, but there was no telling from his guarded expression what that meant. She didn't try to figure it out. At the moment, her concern wasn't for herself. It was for him.

She took another step forward, wanting to reach for him but not sure if her touch would be welcome. "Are you all right?"

"Yeah," he muttered, his biceps straining against the band of his blue T-shirt sleeve as he combed his fingers through his hair. From the way the dark strands fell back over his forehead, it appeared that the gesture had been repeated often lately. "What about you?"

"I'm okay. Now," she added, wondering if he knew how hard it was to meet his eyes when it was impossible to know what thoughts kept them so unreadable. Fiddling with the cameo she'd yet to take off, she offered him the faintest of smiles. "I was afraid you wouldn't come back."

Her complete lack of pretense still amazed him. It also lessened a little of the apprehension he felt. Not feeling wholly certain as to how to go about what he wanted— needed—to do, he took his encouragement where he could find it. If she'd been afraid that he wouldn't come back, that had to mean that she felt something fairly definite for him.

"I need to ask you something, Ellie." He moved past her into the room. "Actually, I need to ask you a couple of things."

For a moment, it appeared that he might begin to pace. The disassembled state of the room stopped him before he could even start. With a swift frown of puzzlement, his glance darted from the boxes stacked by her TV and stereo to the open, packed suitcases next to them. After a cursory glance toward the bare kitchen counters, his frown settled on her.

"What's going on?"

"I'm leaving."

"When?"

Whenever you want, was what she wanted to say. "In the morning, I think."

"You think?"

"I'm not sure where I'm going yet."

That comment magnified his frown considerably. "What do you mean, you don't know where you're going? You must have some idea."

When she gave her head a slow shake to indicate that she didn't, she saw his scowl fade. Hesitating, his eyes lingered on her face. "No idea?" he repeated.

Their eyes met and held. "None."

"Would you like an option?"

Afraid to move, afraid to hope, she scarcely dared to breathe. "Please."

"Will you answer something for me first?"

She nodded, still held by the intensity of his gaze.

"Do you think you could ever love me?"

"Oh, Cain," she said, her voice gently hushed. "I already do."

Something quite primitive flashed in his eyes as he reached out to push the hair back from her face. "I was afraid that I was only imagining you cared because I care so much about you. I love you, too, you know." His thumb caressed her lower lip, his eyes growing dark. It wasn't desire clouding his gaze. It was uncertainty. "I want so much for us, Ellie. I want what I never had. All of it. I want us to be family. But I just don't know."

The hesitation was back, along with an anxiety she didn't understand at all. At least she didn't understand it until he took a deep breath and quietly asked the question that was disturbing him so.

"Do you think I could be a good father? Eventually, I mean." He pulled her to him then, holding her so fiercely she thought she might break in two. "I love you. I want you in my life for forever. And I want us to have kids. But that part has me a little..."

"Nervous?" she offered, smiling against his shirt as she held on to him.

"I guess that's what it is."

"Don't be. You're going to make a terrific father." He had great natural instincts.

"Oh, God, I hope so. But could we practice for a year or two before we have a baby?" He pushed her away by the shoulders to see how she was taking all of this. Apparently he was encouraged by what he saw. "If you'll marry me, that is."

Standing on tiptoe, she kissed the dimple in his chin. "I wouldn't have it any other way," she assured him, then gave him a teasing grin. "Want to run across the county line?"

He was sure that the smile in his eyes ruined the apology he tried to put in his voice. "Only if you don't mind honeymooning in Monte Carlo." Every time he'd told her about some of the places he'd been, her longing to see those distant countries had been so apparent. Now, he took great pleasure in knowing he could satisfy that yearning for her. As much as he would enjoy that giving, he had the feeling that he'd be getting even more in return. Ellie would make him see all that he'd missed before. He had the feeling that he had no idea how much that really was.

"I've got to be there next week for a meeting. That's why I...we," he corrected, liking the sound of the word, "need to be in Florida by Saturday."

Her smile was so filled with delight that it nearly stole his breath.

"I think I can stand the hardship," she whispered against his lips, and within moments Cain was filled with the sweetness of Ellie's kiss. She seemed to need him as much as he needed her. It was more than physical need, though that was definitely a part of what they felt for each other. They shared a bond of acceptance and understanding that had withstood even his most concerted attempts to deny it. That bond was what had drawn him back.

He had thought that once he left Aubrey, he would leave all of its memories behind. It wasn't going to work out quite that way. When Cain left this time, he'd be taking his best memories with him.

*　*　*　*　*

Silhouette Intimate Moments®

It's time ... for Nora Roberts

There's no time like the present to have an experience that's out of this world. When Caleb Hornblower "drops in" on Liberty Stone there's nothing casual about the results!

This month, look for Silhouette Intimate Moments #313

TIME WAS

And there's something in the future for you, too! Coming next month, Jacob Hornblower is determined to stop his brother from making the mistake of his life—but his timing's off, and he encounters Sunny Stone instead. Can this mismatched couple learn to share their tomorrows? You won't want to miss Silhouette Intimate Moments #317

TIMES CHANGE

Hurry and get your copy ... while there's still time!

You'll flip . . . your pages won't!
Read paperbacks *hands-free* with

Book Mate · I

The perfect "mate" for all your romance paperbacks

Traveling • Vacationing • At Work • In Bed • Studying • Cooking • Eating

Perfect size for all standard paperbacks, this wonderful invention makes reading a pure pleasure! Ingenious design holds paperback books OPEN and FLAT so even wind can't ruffle pages— leaves your hands free to do other things. Reinforced, wipe-clean vinyl-covered holder flexes to let you turn pages without undoing the strap . . . supports paperbacks so well, they have the strength of hardcovers!

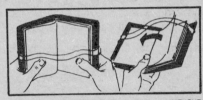

Pages turn WITHOUT opening the strap.

SEE-THROUGH STRAP

Reinforced back stays flat.

Built in bookmark

BOOK MARK

BACK COVER HOLDING STRIP

10˝ x 7¼˝, opened.
Snaps closed for easy carrying, too

SILHOUETTE DESIRE™
presents
AUNT EUGENIA'S TREASURES
by CELESTE HAMILTON

Liz, Cassandra and Maggie are the honored recipients of Aunt Eugenia's heirloom jewels...but Eugenia knows the real prizes are the young women themselves. Read about Aunt Eugenia's quest to find them everlasting love. Each book shines on its own, but together, they're priceless!

Available in December:
THE DIAMOND'S SPARKLE (SD #537)

Altruistic Liz Patterson wants nothing to do with Nathan Hollister, but as the fast-lane PR man tells Liz, love is something he's willing to take *very* slowly.

Available in February:
RUBY FIRE (SD #549)

Impulsive Cassandra Martin returns from her travels... ready to rekindle the flame with the man she never forgot, Daniel O'Grady.

Available in April:
THE HIDDEN PEARL (SD #561)

Cautious Maggie O'Grady comes out of her shell...and glows in the precious warmth of love when brazen Jonah Pendleton moves in next door.

Wonderful, luxurious gifts can be yours with proofs-of-purchase from any specially marked "Indulge A Little" Harlequin or Silhouette book with the Offer Certificate properly completed, plus a check or money order (do not send cash) to cover postage and handling payable to Harlequin/Silhouette "Indulge A Little, Give A Lot" Offer. We will send you the specified gift.

Mail-in-Offer

OFFER CERTIFICATE

Item	A Collector's Doll	B. Soaps in a Basket	C Potpourri Sachet	D Scented Hangers
# of Proofs-of -Purchase	18	12	6	4
Postage & Handling	$3.25	$2.75	$2.25	$2.00
Check One				

Name _____

Address _____ Apt # _____

City _____ State _____ Zip _____

Mail this certificate, designated number of proofs-of-purchase and check or money order for postage and handling to:

INDULGE A LITTLE
P.O. Box 9055
Buffalo, N.Y. 14269-9055